I. Budge

FOR

MARY NAPIER was born at Warlingham in Surrey. She qualified and for some years worked as a Chartered Surveyor before marrying an engineer and having two daughters. In 1965 she took an external honours degree at London University and gained a First Class in History. Since then she has taught part-time at a local Grammar School. She has published three earlier novels under another name.

Also available in Fontana

Blind Chance

MARY NAPIER

Forbidden Places

FONTANA/Collins

First published by William Collins Sons & Co. Ltd 1981
First issued in Fontana Paperbacks 1982

Copyright © Mary Napier 1981

Made and printed in Great Britain by
William Collins Sons & Co. Ltd, Glasgow

1

They had been waiting nearly two weeks, uncomfortably huddled on benches or camped in sand between concrete struts. Three months ago, at the first signs of danger, people had begun to gather at the company manager's house in Haibuk, then he had been arrested as a spy and the company stores set on fire, so they had moved. The flames from the burning store flickered mauve through desert air and gave a sense of ageless patience to the crowds chanting Islamic slogans in the streets. As if they had been there since the time of holy wars, waiting for the cycle to repeat.

The pumping superintendent thought that they should ask the police for a guard, so they went to the police post, only to find the revolutionaries there before them, breaking western china and glass and pouring illicit alcohol down the drain. They tried the company airstrip next, then the oilfields area office, but the mob came there too, so they camped five nights in a highway construction store. At each place they were joined by more frightened, uncomprehending westerners, some angry enough to cause more trouble by shooting the next spitting face they saw; everyone suffered from heat and strain, from unpurified water and the sudden loss of comforts which made life endurable in the Gulf oilfields.

Finally, someone suggested moving to the old parade ground, and they had come here.

It was three miles out of Haibuk, and therefore safe from chance riots: if revolutionaries made the effort to come so far then they intended to kill, and as yet the revolution was at the stage of individual enterprise in the matter of killings. Organized murder would come later. There was also water laid on at the parade ground, and shade under sand-drifted stands while they waited.

Waited, waited, waited. For what, they did not know.

Before the airstrip was taken over, daily situation reports went down to the coast, and before the manager was arrested there had been a telex link with London. One dark night a radio operator had slipped back to the strip and sent a message to say that they were moving to the parade ground; the receiver was smashed now, but they clung to the knowledge that head office knew of their danger.

'They can't just leave us here,' Anne said aloud.

'They'll try to help, people wouldn't work for the company in places like this unless it had a reputation for looking after its own. But just what the hell do you suggest they do, when everything has been taken over by a pack of religious lunatics threatening to blow up pipelines at the first sign of foreign interference?' A technician from one of the outlying fields was lying on sand at her feet, hands linked behind his head, legs bandaged. He had been burned when his installations were set on fire.

'It only needs one aircraft to take us out until things settle down and that lot down in Haibuk would be glad enough to see us go.' Anne stared out over blown sand, thinking that it needed someone with sufficient guts to go and talk to the mullahs while the mob was asleep in the heat of the day. One aircraft off the strip, that was all they wanted.

She sighed; two months ago she had been living in air-conditioned quarters with a thousand pounds tax-free transferred into her bank account each month. Thank God, at least her money was safe in London.

Two months while strikes changed into religious hysteria, sluggish peace into mounting danger and insult; while distant uproar became daily peril in the streets of Haibuk, four hundred miles from the coast, from embassies, governments and bribe-money. Not that it would make much difference if they were nearer civilization. Administration had disintegrated too, together with the old simplicities of greased palms.

'If it only needs one aircraft, then perhaps you'd like to

volunteer as negotiator in Haibuk?' said the technician pointedly.

'A woman?'

He scowled. 'You have a point. Islamic revolutions leave women free to criticize, knowing their bluff can't be called.' He was very young, on a year's contract for the bonus which remote assignments brought, and resentful that he was having to endure rather more than boredom for his money. Since the local gooks were temporarily and happily absent, at the moment he could only vent his anger on his companions.

Anne walked away. She had done her best for him and the other injured, for whining children and fretful, vomiting adults, but their group had lived too closely and squalidly together for too long. Patience evaporated above a hundred degrees Fahrenheit, in the misery of griping bellies and constant threat. Because she had worked in the hospital everyone expected nursing from her as a matter of course, whereas she was a radio diagnostician trained in the use of modern scanners; she knew something about broken bones and could piece together the most fragmentary medical evidence from computer printouts, but understood no more than everyone else about food poisoning and heat exhaustion. The local doctors and nurses at the hospital had joined the revolution, long ago trained by Britons who had left when their contracts expired, lucky devils. The diagnostics department was newly expanded for research into sand-borne disease, and in six weeks her contract would have ended too.

Anne sighed, pushing hair out of her eyes, feeling grit in her clothes, the rasp of sun-dried skin. No good thinking about it, no good thinking of baths or English countryside in a downpour of rain. The English ought to sit on Haibuk parade-ground for a few weeks before they complained about their weather; she pulled herself up sharply. She mustn't start thinking like a foreigner again. One day she would have a place where she belonged and reacting like a foreigner wasn't the way to get it. Nor was sitting at Haibuk, she reflected wrily and smiled to herself, depression lifting.

'It's always a good idea to smile,' observed a man uncomfortably stretched along tiered seats; unless you walked into the desert there was nowhere to be alone. 'What did you manage to think of besides sand?'

'I shall certainly know how to stop myself laughing at the wrong moment in future,' Anne agreed. 'Think of sand and crumbling concrete, then I'll plunge into gloom at once. You're new, aren't you?'

'I came in last night. I've been surveying in the rough and took a while to reach here after my team ran off.' He sat up, rubbing bloodshot eyes.

'What happened when you did reach Haibuk?'

'I was lucky I suppose. I went to Jim Blaikey's house first and found it gutted, so I was cautious. Where is he, d'you know?'

Anne shrugged. 'Arrested. They said they'd put him on trial as a spy or an exploiter, I'm not sure which; perhaps the company will pay to get him out once he's sent to the coast. He may do better than us.'

The other looked at her curiously. She spoke with an edge to her words, even while soft lips and candid eyes belied indifference. 'I doubt it. I wouldn't choose to be a foreign oil-manager in a local jail at the moment.'

'Nor camping in broken-down parade-ground stands. We've three days' food left, four perhaps, before we're forced back to Haibuk and the mob.'

'I think we might try to organize something before then if the company doesn't,' he said lightly. 'I hear there's an airlift of personnel from the coast.'

'We're four hundred miles from the coast and cut off from the strip. You came in last night, it'll seem a little different when you've been here longer.' She could feel despair in her throat; she had been trapped before and knew how it felt, recognized hope evaporating. Those who grew up with help and justice as their birthright could not understand since they expected happy endings as a matter of course.

He stood and stretched, sand rustling from his clothes. He had the kind of unemphatic British accent she still found difficult to place, and looked more like an intellectual than an oilman; underweight and sweated down rather than desert tough, he also possessed the kind of hands she had seen on

8

surgeons; sensitive and excessively scrubbed, absurdly so when the rest of him was so unkempt. 'I'm Stephen Astell,' he said abruptly. 'I understand that all food is shared here, but if your principles aren't too well-polished then I have some reserve rations in my Land-Rover. You might like to join me for breakfast.'

Her spirits rose, he had transport and food; he was also thinking of getting out before they were forced back as beggars to Haibuk. Her principles were not well-polished at all when it came to waiting for prison bars to snap again. She laughed at his formality all the same: camped in a grandstand surrounded by sand and revolution, and he might have been asking her to tea and scones on the best china. Gravely she introduced herself as Anne Storey, and could not resist voicing her thoughts aloud.

'The British rarely eat scones for breakfast,' he replied seriously.

She felt herself flush, it was ridiculous to be so vulnerable to error. 'I was making a general observation only, Mr Astell.'

'Yes, your English is probably better than mine. Where did you learn it?'

She stopped dead, shock flaring. 'In England, where else?'

'I was just asking,' he pointed out amicably. 'Don't tell me if you don't want to, it's none of my business and I detest chatter before breakfast.' He led the way to where his Land-Rover was parked in a dwindling scrap of shade. The sun already struck down as if the earth was its anvil, bodies sweating at the slightest movement, prickly heat rasping after brief relief in the night.

The Land-Rover was piled with the usual expedition gear, a great deal of space taken up by a carrying pack nearly three feet long, carefully suspended against jolts. Anne stared at it while he rummaged amongst supplies. 'You haven't been carrying a thing that size on your back, surely?'

'No, thank God. It's made for carrying—just. Neither far nor often though, and nowhere in these conditions.'

He turned with his hands full of foil packages and Anne felt her stomach contract. They had been living on scraps for days now. All the same . . . 'Don't you think we should save emergency rations in case we have to strike out across the desert?' she asked anxiously.

'The quantity I'm carrying won't make any difference amongst thirty people, so we might as well enjoy ourselves this once.' He stiffened, head cocked. 'Hear anything?'

'I often thought I did when we came here first, but—' She broke off, hearing it too. The unfamiliar beat of piston engines.

Others heard it at the same moment, bedraggled figures scrambling out from under stands, faces turned towards the east. For a long time no one could see anything in white, heat-struck sky, sound growing directly from the dazzle of the sun.

'There,' said Anne suddenly, she could feel herself smile. 'Can you see?'

'I'm not seeing anything too well at the moment. It sounds like something out of an old war film though.' Astell turned his back on the sun, his inflamed eyes were another reason why Anne thought him recently arrived in the Gulf.

'I've never seen anything like it,' said Willie, the pumping manager's son disgustedly. He flew to England every school term and regarded himself as an aircraft expert.

'I have though,' said his father. 'Dakota. DC3 the Yanks call it. I flew more miles than I care to remember in them twenty years ago. I didn't think any had survived into the nineteen-eighties.' David Green was technically competent but normally referred all serious difficulties to higher authority; since Jim Blaikey's arrest he found intolerable the decisions which circumstances forced on him. He scurried anxiously from problem to problem with the quick movements of a mouse: recently Anne had come to imagine a tail sliding over the sand behind him. He stood now, dabbing at his mouth while the Dakota circled, and she immediately saw whiskers growing too. It needed an effort to turn away and see people waving and cheering as they stood in violent, heat-shadowed sunlight.

'It would be better if half of us hid while the pilot makes up his mind,' remarked Astell. 'He's never going to risk taking off from here overloaded.'

'Of course he'll land. Why come here to fly back empty?' Mrs Blaikey stared disapprovingly at him. In spite of years spent on the oilfields she knew little of the uncomfortable facts surrounding life in the Gulf, and had already convinced herself that her husband would be all right in Haibuk jail, her first duty to return to her children in England.

Everyone else immediately agreed that of course the aircraft would land, stood stricken when it flew off in the direction of the airstrip.

Green shuffled anxiously. 'Perhaps we should go there.'

The sun poured down, sweat chafed; as the beat of engines faded only the sound of blowing sand remained.

They looked at each other in desperate disappointment thinking of the strip, its equipment gutted, perimeter huddled with shacks as the slums of Haibuk grew like instant mould along its borders. And of all places, the slums were the most volatile, a mixture of religious frenzy and revolutionary revenge.

They began to quarrel spitefully over whether they should chance going there or not; adversity of the kind they had suffered does not bring out the attractive side of human nature.

'It's coming back,' said Astell suddenly. He alone had been listening rather than arguing. 'Had a look and decided against the strip, I expect. They probably sent a Dakota in case they had to try a rough landing somewhere.'

The old Douglas swept low over the parade-ground, wheels lowered, before circling higher again.

'Markers and wind indicators, you stupid bastards!' yelled a driller, waving his arms. 'Fingers out and give him some help. I was in the RAF not long back,' he confided to Anne as they tore up rags for flares. 'He's either brave or very stupid to try landing here. I'll pace it off, but I'd be surprised if there's twelve hundred feet of concrete. When old Sheikh Ramah reviewed his troops the camels stood on sand and very right too, but if a Dakota runs over the end it's bogged for good.'

No one else showed any doubts. They were all gathering their few possessions or carrying sick children from the shade, as if rescue was a foregone conclusion.

Solid heat struck off concrete when Anne and the driller returned with rags and oil to the cursory pouring of cement which had been adequate for a sheikh reviewing his followers.

11

Anne looked at flaking, uneven humps and thought that, even if the pilot judged everything right, impact alone might somersault the Dakota when its wheels would probably break through such a thin crust.

Astell had already paced the distance. 'Eleven hundred and eighty feet. What do you think?'

The driller whistled. 'I dunno. We didn't have aircraft like that in the RAF.'

'Of course it'll be all right,' said Green irritably. 'I remember Dakotas taking off along the beach in Indonesia.'

'A long beach, presumably.' Astell sounded like a scientist discussing dubious equipment, not at all as if his life would be at stake with the rest, and Anne wondered about him again. 'He may get down if the cement holds, I'm less sure whether he'll ever take off again with the load we'll make.'

'For God's sake,' said the driller. 'Let the bastard make up his own mind. Mark each end of the concrete so he can see it and stand back to watch.'

The Dakota swept overhead, shadow slipping across sand. As it banked away they could see the pilot's face and a faint trail of fumes from one engine.

Since only the driller offered positive advice they did as he said, and stood in the shadow of the stand as the plane flew the length of concrete twice more, its outline smudged by their oil-flare showing wind direction.

'Come on, for Christ's sake,' muttered someone. 'The mullahs will lead a holy war before he makes up his mind.'

'He's making up his mind whether we're worth the risk of killing himself,' said Anne coldly. Astell had gone and she saw him at the back of his Land-Rover, unlashing the pack she had noticed earlier. When she looked back at the sky the Dakota was approaching the marker at the end of the concrete.

He touched down very hard, eddies created by heat making a shallow approach impossible. Twin puffs of smoke from the wheels, an uneven grabbing of brakes as the tail whipped high and the Dakota rolled past the stand at what seemed an enormous speed.

It stopped twenty feet from the last marker.

'Christ, I thought he was going to end up in the cheap seats,' said Green.

'Well, now we know. A Douglas needs eleven hundred and sixty feet to land empty.' The driller ran across sun-blasted grit towards the stationary aircraft.

'If he needed so far to land—' said Anne blankly.

'How the hell is he going to take off again,' Astell finished for her. 'Let's take a look and see exactly where he did land.'

Together they walked the length of the parade-ground, a million sparks of light reflected into their eyes, the horizon dissolved in mirage and haze. It wasn't difficult to see the marks, twin holes punched right through shallow concrete to reveal rock below.

Astell felt torn edges carefully. 'I reckon he's lucky to be alive. Plenty of places to go through and find sand instead of rock.' He paced from the holes to the nearest edge of dune. 'Seventy feet. I don't know enough to say whether it is sufficient if he uses every extra inch.'

Anne shivered. 'I've never cared for flying.'

He stared at her, eyes screwed up against the glare. 'Would you prefer to take your chance driving to the coast?'

It was difficult to think clearly. Sun lanced into brain and sinuses, the weeks of discomfort carried like baggage by weary muscles and griping stomach. It would take days to reach the coast, every mile a misery of tainted food, uncertain fuel supply and watching, hating people. 'No,' she said at last. 'I'd sooner get it over one way or the other. But after today I go on holiday by train.'

He laughed. 'I can't say I'm sorry for your choice. Mike Evans, the company surveyor who was with me, went down the highway to recruit men after our team ran off. He had a hand-set and radioed that he couldn't get back.'

'What happened?'

He shrugged. 'What the hell usually happens in situations like this? Nobody knows. He talked his way through the first block because I watched him from the dunes. His family was at el-Shakir the wrong side of the second: he was either held there or decided to go and look after them and spin a tale to the company after. I certainly don't blame him if he did.'

13

'Why didn't you go too?'

'Because, as you said, my pack is too heavy to carry far and I knew I'd lose the Land-Rover at the first block I came to. If we'd decided to try for the coast it would have had to be cross-country.'

'What is it?' she asked curiously, watching him adjust straps on his back, grunting. Mounted on a steel pack-frame and wrapped in dust-proofing, it was an unwieldy load.

'Surveying equipment and definitely too good to be left for the mullahs, so let's hope no one thinks that it might cost us another six inches of take-off space.'

Anne stared at the pack with sudden dislike. 'I'm thinking it.'

She's just missed being beautiful, he thought. She had all the conventional components of beauty: slim body, good legs, hips and breasts delicately proportioned even in sweat-soaked, grubby clothes. Her eyes were large and grey, once freed from sand her hair would be warmly fair; her mouth softly responsive when she forgot herself and laughed.

Perhaps it was the clear structure of cheek and jaw, the tough confidence of her body which prevented her being a beauty, the way too in which vitality and warmth were hidden by reserve. Once she had been different, he was sure.

He half expected her to make sure that the pilot noticed the weight of his pack, but she did not. As each person scrambled into the Dakota, they were stacked forward against the bulk-head, but when he casually tied his load with the company records Green had brought, no one noticed, preoccupied by fear of the coming take-off. There were no seats in the aircraft, only the bare spars of a machine surviving from another age. The pilot was a survival too, a roustabout from times when flyers thought of ground-control as something occasionally useful in fog. He wore a flying jacket over a bare belly, called himself Joe and offered no surname.

'I'm hired to fly oilmen out of holes like this, at a time when flights are forbidden, strips and aids buggered into nothing,' he said when Green questioned him nervously. 'I come expensive when there's trouble, in between times respectable companies forget they know me. When the shit flies I fly with

14

it, and Haibuk looked like a brothel with the pigs in when I flew over it to the strip. Be on their way here by now.'

'You led them here,' said Mrs Blaikey accusingly. 'Flying over the strip like that instead of landing here directly.'

Joe stared at her, the smell of his jacket unpleasant in the cramped aircraft. 'Do you know what, lady? I didn't fancy landing here if I could help it, and I fancy taking off even less. You walk if you like, but if you stay, then a mob half way between here and Haibuk isn't going to bother you whichever way you look at it. If we don't unstick, then they'll never pick up the pieces. I'm pouring every ounce of power I've got into this takeoff.'

He was asking them all the question and everyone stared back, faces gleaming in the dim fuselage. One by one heads shook in denial, words stacked out of use by fear. Whatever the risk it seemed preferable to accept it together, when the alternatives were the aloneness of great spaces or alien frenzy on the road to Haibuk.

No one left, and Joe slammed the door.

Anne put her head on her knees, hands slippery wet. She felt the aircraft slew into the wind, the shudder of brakes, tailwheel bumping on sand at the end of the parade-ground. Slowly, each engine came to maximum power and was allowed to run out again. Even Joe can't quite bring himself to commit everything to this, she thought. If we wait much longer he'll lose his nerve and certainly there'll only be pieces to pick up.

She moved sharply, she must have been crazy not to get out while the chance offered.

'Steady,' said Astell quietly. 'It only needs one to move and the whole lot will be hammering to get out.'

Too late for anything except to wait for it to be over. Again the engines were brought up together, one seemed rough and she remembered the vapour she had seen when the Dakota circled. 'The concrete gets shorter each time he does that.'

God, yes, he thought, touched by an attempt at lightness when he could see her lips trembling. He put his own head on his knees and held her tightly against him.

Abruptly, the aircraft lurched forward, brakes released at the precise moment when surging power would have mastered

15

them. We're too slow, Anne thought dully, not much faster than a car; vibration in the fuselage was fierce, jarring her spine on steel, but only the beat of engines mattered now. A single hesitation and they would be dead.

She felt the tail lift, speed still absurdly slow when her only experience was of modern jets, and heard a crunch as the wheels retracted before she even realized the Dakota was off the ground. As the wheels slammed home the aircraft settled and hung for the beat of a heart in heat-deadened air, propellers screeching, bolts rattling; then ancient design triumphed once more over gravity and slowly they began to rise.

2

There are few things quite so exhausting as real, gut-shrivelling fear, and uncomfortable though they were, most of the Dakota's passengers slept through the flight. Several were feverish after weeks of rough living, and sank back into apathy once terror dulled.

Anne woke hours later, aware of both comfort and extreme discomfort. She was enormously grateful to be away from Haibuk, as well as for softness at her back and head – she sat up, creakingly stiff, legs numb from lying on the floor; sleep had only been possible for so long because the rest of her had been lying across Stephen Astell.

'You must be in agonies!' she said guiltily. 'You should have woken me hours ago!'

'Soft-hearted Steve,' he agreed, massaging his legs. 'I reckoned I owed you something for not having my other half thrown out.'

She stared at his pack lashed by the door. 'What exactly is it?'

'Survey Systems 2DX, or Twodex for short. Onedex wasn't much good, and Three is still full of bugs, but I couldn't have devised a better field test for this one if I'd tried. I should have hated to leave it in the sand of Haibuk.'

'Would you have left it?'

'No, I don't think so. I'd have chanced the coast in the Land-Rover and probably lost it anyway. I've a great deal of cash and some fairly close dealing staked on Twodex, so I'm relieved it didn't happen.'

It was some kind of mineral scanning equipment she gathered, but his explanations were uninformative and now its weight hadn't killed them, she wasn't much interested. When feeling returned to her legs, she stood and peered through perspex at lights far below. 'Where are we, do you know?'

'Joe isn't too explicit, but we landed at some emergency strip he knows a couple of hours back and won't have to refuel again before the Mediterranean. Then we've all to stay in the aircraft while they hand-pump petrol out of drums. Another heart-attack for any respectable airline.'

'Where are we making for, or is that secret too? I expected we'd fly to the Gulf coast and not west like this.'

'So did I. I rather think that Joe and his Dakota are unwelcome on the coast; he might be the only madman the company could find who was willing to try landing on eleven hundred feet of under-proof concrete, but I bet they don't want their connection with him advertised. Joe says he uses a strip in Italy where no one asks questions and he'll offload us there. My guess is that our fuelling stop will be on one of the Turkish islands; Joe's trade probably includes drugs and a great many routes run through there. His other clients wouldn't welcome a pack of oilmen nosing about their concerns.'

Anne stared around her distastefully, the Dakota smelled of so much that it must be imagination which made her smell drugs now. She owed her life to Joe, she ought not to condemn him on a guess. She couldn't help it though, when they were all kept locked in, surrounded by high-octane fumes while the plane was refuelled in darkness. A brief flick of landing lights as they took off again, then they droned on westward through heavy cloud, rain rattling on the fuselage.

'Rain! It's more than ten months since I saw rain.' Anne tried to glimpse the ground but it was completely dark, the aircraft pitching in turbulence. Was she being absurd when she thought that the engines sounded rough again?

'Lucky you. It was pelting when I left London three weeks ago.'

'I like rain. And the pleasure of not knowing what tomorrow will be like.'

'Why go to Haibuk then?'

She sat down again, ears strained for the uneven beat she was certain she had heard and wondering whether she would ever fly again without remembering missing Haibuk grandstand by the width of a wing. 'For the money. A change. It was a good offer at a time when things weren't working out. Why did you go there?'

He laughed. 'You could say for the money. Eventually, I hope.'

'And to try out Twodex, Mr Astell?'

'Do you think you could manage Stephen under the circumstances? Yes, that too.' He stood and peered out as she had done, hand on duralmin, head slanted, listening.

'Stephen,' she said, and smiled. 'You hear it too?'

He looked down, surprised, then nodded. 'For a while earlier, then it seemed to improve. Now, I'm not sure.'

No one else seemed to have noticed anything, bodies huddled in sleep, a child crying, everyone stupefied by exhaustion. Anne stood again and they both stared out, seeing nothing, sensing something wrong, some desynchronization neither was knowledgeable enough to place.

'Perhaps only we can hear it because we're exactly in line with the engines here,' said Stephen finally. 'I'm going to speak to Joe. It's possible he hasn't noticed anything, God knows when he last had his instruments calibrated.'

She followed him through the bulkhead door to the dim light of the cockpit, it was her life too, after all. Joe was standing, shining a powerful flashlight along the starboard wing.

Stephen said something and as Joe turned to reply there was a dull thud, a spark of fire along the wing. The plane lurched and Joe threw himself back in his seat, yelling a warning as the Dakota dived steeply.

Anne felt herself tossed sideways, metal grinding into her ribs as she partially blacked out, arteries thumping in face, wrists and legs.

When she opened her eyes, there was an enormous noise everywhere. A perspex panel had smashed, wind and engine roar loud enough to vibrate ear-drums. Joe was shouting at his co-pilot, controls screeching each time he handled them.

They were flying more or less level again, but heavily canted to starboard. When Anne pulled herself up and looked out there was no fire but she could see the uneven engine shape creating enormous drag as it sagged from melted mountings.

They were very low. Rain beat out of cavernous cloud, driving through broken perspex and sprung fuselage joints until it collected in streams and slithered over the floor. Nothing to be seen, only savage jolting to tell of contours just out of sight.

'Strap yourself in!' yelled Stephen. He half-pushed, half-dragged her up slippery, sloping floor to a tip-up seat behind the pilots and sat in another himself. The Dakota seemed to operate on a crew of two, and Anne wondered which Air Registration Board Joe bribed his way past each year.

They were certainly going to crash. Vibration, roughness, the protesting squeal of control-cables, all were worsening; Anne could tell from Joe's hands that they were still losing height, searching desperately for somewhere to land while the co-pilot shouted above static on the radio. Horrified, she watched the compass turn slowly and erratically, stop for a second and then start back again.

She had to shake Stephen's arm to attract his attention above the turmoil. 'Should we go back to the rest while there's time?' God, she had always loathed flying, been an original, paid-up member of the If-God-had-wanted-us-to-fly-He'd-have-given-us-wings society; if she survived this she'd vote for the Channel Tunnel in every election until she died.

He shook his head. 'We'll do better strapped in.' If we crash as hard as I think we're going to crash, then it won't make any difference; she could see the thought on his face.

'I've raised Corfu! They say they can hear our engines!' The co-pilot was grinning like a maniac. 'Over to starboard about five kilometres, they think.'

'Five kilometres to starboard!' mimicked Joe savagely. 'Why the hell don't they give us a radar track and talk us down?'

'Engine noises fading,' the co-pilot pressed earphones to his head as if the crackle of voices was the touch of tarmac. 'He says they can hardly hear us any more.'

Joe cursed and began a lurching sweep to starboard, their trailing wing and strained controls making impossible the sharp bank to port they needed. The Dakota crabbed heavily, remaining engine shuddering. 'Radar! Tell the fucking monkey-men to give us a bearing!'

Anne watched the compass start again on its swing, wondering whether Joe realized that his dive to put out the fire had affected it in some way. The cockpit showed no signs of more modern aids so it could be vital.

'No radar! He says they haven't radar!' In greenish cockpit light the co-pilot's face looked ghastly.

'It's an international airport isn't it?' Joe slewed round and shouted at Stephen. 'Under the shelf there . . . a clip of papers . . . find the landing instructions for Corfu.' The aircraft lurched savagely, hung an instant on one wing and skidded several hundred feet lower before he caught it somehow.

Anne closed her eyes, fingers on her face, bones twisting. Nothing to do but wait for the explosion which would be death.

Stephen had the torch, shuffling through paper somehow in the fierce draughts of the cockpit. 'Got it! International airport, landing length one mile, controlled by traffic lights one end where the main road intersects the runway.'

'For Christ's sake! An international airport should have a two mile runway!'

'Well, it hasn't. Mountains either side, one mile runway and traffic lights. Closed in bad weather, visual approach only. Alternates are Athens, Belgrade or Brindisi.' So it was Corfu or nothing. All possible alternates were too far, across sea or mountain.

Anne found herself thinking of the fair-haired, gangling boy who had helped uproot her from her home almost for a joke ten years ago, whom she had not seen again once it was done: what an extraordinary triggering of events had placed her aboard an aircraft about to crash in the Greek mountains. She would probably die within seconds, yet felt no regrets.

How strange. She had to face the ultimate payment before she knew beyond doubt that she would have done the same again. No sense of blame, only acceptance.

Though I'll blame Joe if we crash, she thought, spine cold even while she smiled. Who ever heard of a Dakota still flying in the nineteen eighties, after all?

Stephen Astell saw her smile, and resented it. She could not be such a fool as to be unaware that they must crash soon. He thought of Twodex with mild regret; let his creditors sort it out, the police too if anyone thought of checking government records.

The Dakota's fuselage reverberated with dull, heavy booms as turbulence twisted it. He leaned forward and braced his feet on the floor, if Anne had not smiled he would have offered her such comfort as he could, instead he was paralysed by the dreadful physical fear which drains guts and fills mouths with gall. Perhaps she should comfort him instead. He found himself smiling too, at the absurdity of such thoughts then; without further reflection he reached out and held her hand.

On Corfu airport the duty crew stood in downpour, listening; every light was on, opalescent through rain. Someone was shouting over the radio, warning of mountains.

There was no reply from this mystery aircraft sprung out of nowhere but it wasn't down yet, somewhere in the scud they could hear it still.

'Tell him he is further, Giorgios. Sixty-seventy degrees to the east.'

'He isn't receiving. Listen to him . . . some old heap which should have been junked years ago.'

'He is too far, the mountains—'

'He is turning away! Fire lights, for God's sake!'

'We are closed! We are not an airport for bad weather. He would not—'

'Can you hear him?'

They fell silent, listening 'I think so,' said one, then shrugged, unsure.

They all stared into murk and pretended they had heard something too. They heard nothing.

The vibration was so bad that even fear was almost lost in the desire for it to end. Stephen stared at the wing and realized that what he saw was fire glowing there again. Not flame, but a sullen heat eating into spars, while smoke seeped out through buckled plates.

He shook Joe by the shoulder and stabbed at it with his finger.

Joe nodded, it was too noisy for words, and made a gesture

with his hand; it doesn't matter now. This aircraft was about to fall out of the sky.

A grey mass in mist, there for an instant and then gone again without a moment to chance a crash-landing. The rain was less and in its place fog pressed against perspex, clammy wrappings of it racing past. Without warning, trees hurtled out of murk and Joe banked instinctively. The Dakota responded like a foundered thoroughbred, lifted a vital few feet before falling on rock: no speed, no control, no lift any more.

A terrifying crash echoed through the fuselage, a jolt which squeezed flesh from bones and tore Joe's hands from the controls. An enormous bounce and then another, they were hurtling through the air, metal screeching, unidentifiable objects tearing past, their muscles liquefying, mouths gaping.

The shock threw Anne forward with unbelievable violence, straps cutting into flesh. The thought flashed through her mind that if they broke then her face would be smashed on ranked knobs and levers. Her eyes bulged to fill her face as ground and rocks were all she saw. Carried forward by a momentum which had been insufficient to keep them flying but seemed enormous now, the Dakota stood on its nose, rose up on one wing and hung there for a fraction of a second, Anne found windshield and instrument panel directly below her feet and reared back frantically, clinging to something she could not see, the ground a wall in front of her.

With a crash like a myriad furnace doors closing, the Dakota fell back on its belly.

Anne's senses had almost drained away before the sound of liquid vapourising in white heat roused her to fresh panic; there was smoke everywhere and she tore at her harness, terrified afresh at being trapped, thinking only of flame and how old aircraft used petrol instead of kerosene.

Her hands could not master the trick of the military-style harness. Voices were screaming in the passenger cabin and someone was moaning by her feet. The co-pilot, she thought, and forced herself to concentrate on the simple movements necessary to unsnap her harness. She fell forward on the controls; the Dakota was still tipped forward and it was impossible to tell whether the sounds she heard were fuel pouring on hot metal or rain which might save them all. The smoke was choking, densely white and spectral in near-darkness.

Others were cursing and struggling to free themselves in the cockpit. Only the co-pilot was still, silent now too. Joe swore loudly in her ear. 'Jim?'

'No. He's hurt, badly I think. Have you still got the torch?'

He hadn't, but while searching for it Stephen found an axe clipped with emergency tools and began smashing out fragments of windshield. Icy air blew in, mercifully clearing smoke.

Grunting and slipping in the steeply angled cockpit, between them they hauled the co-pilot clear of levers and instruments; no one said so, but each knew he was dead yet felt unable to abandon him under the threat of fire.

The danger seemed less though, definitely it was rain drumming on the thin-skinned fuselage.

Stephen squeezed through the hole he had made and was immediately drenched. 'Wait!' he shouted, and crawled out of sight. From inside Anne could see only scudding clouds and a suggestion of hillside humped into murk; there was also the sound of wind roaring through trees. She was shivering from shock but it was also at least sixty degrees colder than it had been the previous morning in Haibuk.

Stephen poked his head through the hole. 'No fire, and no chance of one in such rain now everything must have cooled. We'd best stay inside, there's no shelter except the aircraft.'

'No lights? Someone must have heard us hit, surely, and Corfu will have put out an alert.'

'Nothing, nor is anyone likely to find us until dawn. We might be fifty yards from a road and no one know we were here.'

Joe grunted, and turned his attention to the jammed bulkhead door; he was too solidly built for scrambling through holes anyway. 'Find that torch, it's here somewhere,' he said to Anne.

They had laid the co-pilot's body across the instrument panel and while searching she kept touching him. Each time she did so his flesh was colder, no doubt any longer that he was dead.

'It's a bloody shambles back there,' said Joe. 'Haven't you found it yet?'

'No,' as she spoke her fingers closed on it. She flicked the switch and to her astonishment, it worked.

The passenger compartment was indeed a shambles. Everyone had been thrown against the roof since they lacked either seats or seat-belts, and lay in all attitudes of death and agony. The tail of the Dakota had snapped off, everywhere was slippery with rain and blood, the wind freezing cold.

'Christ almighty,' said Joe quietly. 'Not many of them will see the night out.' His face was trembling; after thirty years of shoestring flying he had finally killed a freight of passengers, and was unable to grasp anything else.

Stephen took the torch from him and turned to Anne. 'He'll be better once we get started. Try to see which ones we might be able to do something for, while I shake sense into those on their feet and block out some of the weather.'

She nodded and stooped over the nearest. They must go through the motions of helping the injured but there was almost nothing they could do.

3

Two old men came to look at them soon after dawn.

They stood in the shadow of some trees, talking quietly to each other and throwing up their hands at intervals. They wore sleeveless jackets and baggy trousers, like figures off a tourist postcard, and retreated into the trees when one of the women passengers who had read Greats at Oxford went over to try her classical Greek on them.

'Not that it makes much difference when they'll certainly take word of what they've seen to the nearest village as quickly as they can walk, and I don't suppose ancient Greek is any nearer the modern than Anglo-Saxon is to English,' she said, apparently more possessed by scholarly curiosity than shock.

'See Greece and die,' observed Joe sourly. No one replied, it wasn't the kind of remark which could provoke response when fifteen men, women and children lay dead in the fuselage behind them, and most of the rest needed urgent hospital attention.

The storm had passed and daylight revealed that they had crashed through scanty pines and slid along a rock ridge, scattering wreckage in every direction. They had been very lucky. To the west more trees covered steep hillside, while to the east the ground fell sharply to a distant valley. Beyond again, interlocking hills parted to give a glimpse of black and distant mountains. Except for their own voices stillness was absolute; no glimpses of smoke, nor any movement on a single scratching of track which was visible far below.

Anne walked with Stephen to a rock bluff which gave a good view into the valley, and stood staring down at it. There was intense cultivation but nothing else. 'It's a long way away I know,' she said at last, 'but if there was any traffic on that track, I think we'd see it.'

Stephen nodded. 'Odd, isn't it? If we'd crashed in the Macedonian mountains you'd expect it to be deserted, but a lot of people work cultivating that valley. We ought to see something: a tractor, a house, an early morning bus.'

As he spoke they saw a column of black dots winding up the track, dust unrolling behind them.

'The army. Those old men must at least have had a telephone in their village.' Anne stared about her almost disbelievingly, at rocks and a clearing sky which promised a hot day; it was hard to accept that not a single villager had come to offer help. Silence was suddenly oppressive, the trees hostile. They must be watched, their distress known, and the only reaction was troops and suspicious waiting.

When they returned to the Dakota another passenger had died and, as horror rubbed raw again, Joe needed to be physically driven into helping carry the body out of sight. Anne felt numbed beyond reaction after the dreadful night, beyond even memory of bloodstained fumbling in the dark.

'They could land a helicopter here easily,' said Green angrily. 'It'll take hours for troops to climb up in the heat.' He was unhurt, his son Willie concussed, his wife dead; he did not seem to mind much and Anne could not decide whether he had been unable to absorb the fact of her death, or did not care.

'However long they take, you can double it for the journey down with stretchers, supposing they bring any,' said someone, and after that they sat in silence.

The soldiers arrived three hours later, by which time two more of the injured had died. Anne felt no relief when she saw them, only anger because they had taken so long; she had a splitting headache and was so dizzy with thirst that it was difficult to focus either eyes or mind on what was happening. She stayed sitting in shade under the crumpled wing while Joe trudged over to the knot of brown-clad figures panting after their climb. They stood a long time gesturing together while nothing further happened: Anne could hear Joe's voice rising, he would welcome the release of violence.

She scrambled from under the wing and stood to watch, mind jolted out of apathy: it wasn't possible for men to climb three hours to an air crash and then stand in distrustful indifference, fingering guns.

'I've been thinking about the map of Europe,' said Stephen behind her. 'I rather fancy we're not in Greece at all.'

As her lips shaped questions there was a sharp order and the soldiers fanned out, half a dozen coming directly towards them. Most of the survivors were too far gone to notice much when an officer shouted and uholstered his revolver, only five could stand and stare at him in astonishment: Anne, Astell, Green, Pamela Cuffley, the woman who had attempted to use her Greek, and a Pakistani oil technician called Nahadu Khan. Joe was still where he had met the soldiers, a rifle in his back.

The officer reeled off a series of questions, emphasizing each with a jerk of his revolver.

'No savvy,' said Green loudly, following the cherished principle of shouting at those who do not understand English. 'British, see? We crashed.' He waved his arm in unnecessary explanation.

The officer gestured again, the jerks of revolver unmistakeable. Hands up.

'For God's sake,' said Green in disgust. 'Why the hell should we? The bugger can see we've nothing but ourselves and a junked aircraft.' He whirled his fingers and made a buzzing noise. 'Helicopters. People too ill to walk. Doctors.'

The officer's eyes flickered but he gave no other sign of having understood, the soldiers at his back like painted images, old-fashioned rifles at the ready. They wore crumpled brown uniforms, and Anne had already seen the red star and curious design of crossed pickaxe and rifle on their caps.

She felt an insane desire to laugh, although nothing which had happened to them was amusing. Retribution had been ten years in the making, but fate had made sure that when it came it would be well-shaped to its purpose.

If they found out about her; why should they, after all?

Green's protests died as they were pushed over to join Joe at gunpoint and left waiting in the sun while the Dakota was searched. One of the soldiers gave such water as they had brought to the injured; they weren't deliberately callous but accepted with peasant fatalism that there was little they could do.

'Willie,' said Green in anguish. 'He's not badly hurt but needs attention.'

Joe spat. 'They all need attention.'

'Were you carrying anything which could justify suspicion if they find it, and slow things up?' Stephen was standing, hands in his pockets, watching the search as Twodex was hauled out on the grass. Of them all he seemed the least worried. Of course he didn't know any of the injured, but there was an absorbed, speculative look on his face which Anne could not place.

Joe shrugged. 'There's a couple of packing cases I'd prefer they didn't examine too closely.'

'Taken on board in Turkey?'

He hesitated, glancing at the soldiers guarding them, who stared incuriously back. 'Yes.'

Drugs, thought Anne. Of course, he'd never resist charging the company while carrying on his own trade as well. And that, surely, double-dug the pit they had fallen into.

'It's none of our business,' said Green hastily. 'You were hired to fly us out of Haibuk, the rest is your concern. If you were carrying a cargo the authorities object to, you'll be questioned and quite right too. The Greeks are strict on drugs, or so I've heard. But if you're lucky the company might pull strings to keep you out of jail since you have crashed while doing them a favour.'

Joe laughed. 'Oh, sure. Oil companies understanding pounds and dollars and not gratitude at all. They'll pretend never to have heard of me, you'll see. The bastards may grease a few palms in private for you lot, but this whole deal will be one item which won't appear in the press if they can help it. And I don't fly for an outfit which is going to publish its loss.'

'They couldn't fix this for you, anyway. You realize that we must be in Albania, where even Russia has no strings to pull, much less an oil company?' Anne turned to Stephen. 'Isn't that right?'

'Yes.' He smiled. 'A place quarter the size of England, sealed up so tight in prejudice and fear that they possess neither friends nor allies whose influence might be begged or offered. Not Russia, not China any more. Certainly not us.' He looked at the rifle held by the nearest soldier. 'A good symbol, don't you think? Out of date because no one will sell them anything better, but stuck in your back the moment they see you. I'll lay odds we're lodged in a prison cell and not a hotel tonight.'

Later, he and Joe argued over whether he had won his bet, since they weren't in a cell, but locked in a bare room under guard. The atmosphere remained very hostile, grunts and jerked weapons the only reaction aroused by questions.

They had been forced to walk in overpowering heat down the hillside, the injured slung in cloth since there were no stretchers. The dead were left behind; the soldiers had some kind of greyish powder they gave to ease pain but the journey was a misery, the men who carried them in relays not unkind but very rough. They would expect no better treatment if they were hurt, so could not conceive of its possibility. The six unhurt survivors were not prevented from helping but the steep climb in the aftermath of shock, without food or more than a mouthful of water, reduced them to a state where they were scarcely able to help themselves.

Anne was reeling with exhaustion when they reached the trucks in the valley below, and only struggled back to awareness as the trucks ground up tight bends to a walled town which looked as if it had stepped from a medieval scroll.

'Gjirokaster,' grunted one of the men, when Stephen made interrogative gestures, the only word their captors spoke to them during the whole journey, and he was cursed for it.

The town was built on a series of spurs, streets so narrow that a laden mule caused a traffic jam and their trucks were confined to a single wider street where vines and eaves almost closed overhead. Anne retained an impression of faces up-turned in the dark and a tiny square lined with tables and plane-trees; of donkeys grotesquely loaded and crumbling whitewashed houses. Then their truck climbed to where there were a few modern buildings and pulled up in front of an un-mistakeable police station.

The injured had disappeared, taken to hospital they hoped,

but Green's pleas to see his son were met by shaken heads.

Kicks on the door of the room where they were kept eventually produced a bowl of soup and something resembling porridge. 'It's all your fault,' said Green resentfully to Joe. 'Drug-smugglers couldn't expect much consideration after all, and that aircraft of yours—'

'You were pleased enough to see him at Haibuk,' interrupted Stephen. 'There's no purpose in blame now. It's happened and that's all there is to it.'

'It's nothing to do with me, and so I shall tell them,' snapped Green. 'Sooner or later they're bound to send someone who speaks English.'

'Oh yes, I should think they'll do that,' Stephen said, and laughed.

Anne rested her aching head on her knees, she seemed to have been sitting on hard floors for a long time. Albania. It was beyond belief that fate should have been so cruel. Could they find out about her? Would they search tangled wreckage thoroughly enough to uncover her papers, where her vulnerable lack of nationality was clearly set out?

Yes, she decided bleakly. Probably they would.

The outside world had been so long shut out from this claustrophobic fortress of a country that an air crash was apparently regarded more in the light of an invasion than an accident; the Albanians showed no sign of being satisfied until they had unravelled every twist of what must be a plot against state security. And infuriatingly, there was a great deal for them to discover: not political schemings, but passengers snatched illegally from revolution, cased drugs, and undesirables like herself. She looked up and stared at Stephen Astell until he turned, attention caught by the intensity of her gaze.

'Don't worry,' he said after a moment. 'I expect they'll let us go in the end, but it doesn't take much imagination to guess what Albanian bureaucracy must be like. Patience is going to be the watchword.'

'I suppose so, but I was thinking that each of us has something we'd rather they didn't know. Even Nahadur Khan came to the Gulf on forged papers and shouldn't have been in Haibuk. Green won't want them to know that he is senior amongst us in case he's held responsible, you—'

'I notice you skip over Miss Cuffley. I can't imagine her life beset by anything worse than mild tut-tuttery when she attempted to extend the best philosophic principles to her filing system.' She was asleep on a bright wool rug in one corner.

'You,' Anne said firmly. 'You ought to be more worried than you are. What are you intending?'

He grinned. 'Nothing. I'm not the macho type.'

No, he wasn't, she thought, looking at him. A thin, clever face to match the sensitive hands she had noticed; a scholar's high forehead and contemplative eyes. All the same, he was intent on something. 'Everyone else is horrified to be here, you don't mind, or not much anyway.'

'It's an interesting place to come,' he said mildly. 'A showcase for Stalinism thirty years after the maestro died, a medieval barony set into twentieth century Europe where one man has ruled unchallenged since 1945, quarrelling with every ally he's ever had. He even broke off relations with China because he liked the Gang of Four.'

Anne stared at the picture on the wall, the slogan which even ignorance could interpret: *Long Live Enver Hoxha!* People who lived without leaders staring at them from every flat surface didn't know how great a burden of boredom they escaped, the mental indigestion induced by seeing the same features everywhere. 'You aren't a historian, are you, or one of those crackpots who counts everything well lost in the cause of abstract truth? You're a surveyor, or so you said.'

'A mineral consultant, yes. All the same, there are other things in the world besides rocks and strata.'

It was on the tip of her tongue to ask him about Twodex. He would not have left Haibuk without it, whatever the threat, now he seemed unworried by the thought of it being impounded by Albanian police. Of course, he might simply be resigned, having no choice.

They were kept at Gjirokaster for three days; nothing particular happened. There was ample cold water and nauseating toilet arrangements, occasionally they were allowed to walk in a tiny yard filled with orange and pomegranate trees.

'I view the police of Gjirokaster more kindly after enjoying their courtyard,' observed Miss Cuffley, in the detached voice of one giving honour where it is due. 'I must think our own police superior, but Ealing Police Station had nothing so beautiful as pomegranates when I went there after my handbag was stolen.'

She looked faintly surprised when even Nahadur Khan burst out laughing.

The fourth day, everything changed.

Feet rattled in passages where there had been only the scrape of hobnails, leisurely shifting balance. They were not allowed into the courtyard, yet their unappetising gruel was actually hot when it arrived. The rather attractive girl called Liri who escorted Anne and Miss Cuffley to the toilet marched alertly and in silence beside them instead of offering Albanian words for whatever they pointed to, and dissolving into giggles when they attempted to imitate her.

'Someone's arrived with the power to put 'em all in a labour camp at the first word out of place,' said Joe. 'Us too, I expect.'

'I hope he speaks English,' said Green. 'I must get out of here and see Willie. They can put handcuffs on me if they like.'

'If he doesn't speak English but seems an educated man, I will try both Greek and Latin on him with various pronunciations. Albanian was part of the ancient province of Illyria you know, and their language has been preserved through two thousand years.' Miss Cuffley at least was awaiting interrogation with keen anticipation.

The sense of unseen harassment mounted through the day, without anyone coming for them. Liri was in tears when she brought food, shouted commands grew louder and more clipped, the burned-straw smell of local cigarettes disappeared altogether.

In late afternoon there were purposeful stampings in the corridor at last, the door flung open to reveal an armed escort and one of the policemen they had come to know, his uniform straight and uncrumpled. He beckoned Green and jerked his head.

'Don't be so bloody anxious to see Willie that you say whatever the bastards want against the rest of us,' called Joe.

Green stared at him in dislike. 'They can put you in prison and welcome; I shan't lose a single night's sleep if you rot there for the rest of your life.' He went out.

Joe rubbed his face, stubble rasping. 'Anyone would think I wanted to crash. I'd flown that same Dakota for fifteen years, it was like losing family for me too.'

Anne shrugged and did not answer. The room was stifling, the experience of being confined with ill-assorted people an unpleasant foretaste of what might be in store for her during the years ahead. She went over to the mesh-covered window and stared at sky and stuccoed wall, which was all she could see.

'Have you a good story prepared?' asked Stephen quietly behind her.

'No. Have you?'

He laughed. 'I don't need one.'

'Nor do I.'

He looked at her thoughtfully. 'If you say so.'

She bit her lip, feeling very much alone. They were all to be interrogated separately, that much was clear; she must regard everyone as an enemy now. Stephen she could not estimate at all, Joe would split like bad fruit at the first pressure; Nahadur Khan and Miss Cuffley were probably both too naïve even to see any traps which were set for them.

David Green did not return, but two hours later Liri came for Miss Cuffley. At this rate it will be the middle of the night before my turn comes, thought Anne. The time of lowest resistance when interrogators come into their own.

She could not rest, wandering around the room although she knew she was making tension worse. Anything was better than trying to improvise answers to the kind of questions she had cause to fear.

'Sit down,' said Stephen, when Nahadur Khan went. 'Anyone watching would be wondering about you by now.'

She looked around nervously. 'Do you think they are?'

'I don't know. Come and rest while you can.' He pulled her down beside him, their backs against the wall. 'Cigarette? I

34

kept two, and this seems as good a time as any.'

She nodded, although she did not smoke, and found it soothing. 'I'll be all right. I think it's only tonight I really grasped that all this had happened.'

'We're all frightened of the unknown. It would be odd if we weren't.'

She took a deep breath. 'It isn't unknown to me, that's why I'm scared . . . terrified of falling into their hands again.' She clung to him fiercely, fingers digging into flesh; he was no longer a man she knew slightly, but simply another human being on the edge of cataclysm.

He held her, speaking gently, stroking her hair, although she had judged him as a man who was awkward with women. 'You have been a long time from whatever you did before. Tell them of Haibuk and remember that Albania isn't the usual communist state. There's precious little fraternal love for foreign comrades here, and probably no access to KGB records or whatever else you fear. Now, think of something else, or you'll blurt out secrets at the first question.' He jerked his head at Joe, watching them morosely from the shadows. He probably could not hear low-voiced confidences, but would save himself at the expense of others if he could.

So they talked of England, remote at first with the beat of cicadas outside, but in the end it was Albania's immediacy which crumbled as they talked of places both had known, of London on a winter's day with scarcely a tourist in sight, since most foreigners thought of it as swamped in fog from October to April and seldom saw the splendid fabric of its streets and squares against a cold sky. Of Cambridge, where he had recently held some research appointment and she once worked in a hospital; of plays and bookshops, and walls without framed portraits of party leaders.

Stephen was called next. She walked with him to the door, and kissed him before he went. 'Good luck.'

He nodded, hands on her shoulders. 'I'll say what I can to help if the chance offers, don't look too surprised if you find you have qualities you never suspected.' He grinned. 'Although I think you have a few of those anyway.'

Endless, endless waiting then, with nothing but her

thoughts for company. She would certainly be next. The Albanians had a choice of charges against Joe without even trying to discover more; he would be kept until last, a common criminal lacking importance to minds honed on politics. It was the kind of thing she knew by instinct, had absorbed in childhood without even noticing it.

At last, more feet in the passage and Liri waiting for her at the door. She looked tired, heavy-footed as if she had stood throughout the night. She did not say anything, but smiled timidly for Anne alone when she thought the guards weren't looking.

A long passage, freshly scrubbed, more evidence of upheaval at Gjirokaster police post. Anne could feel her stomach tightening, and she stared with hatred at pictures of Party Leader Hoxha. Personality cult, she thought disdainfully, long-forgotten party hackles rising; the absurdity of such a reaction could still arouse amusement and unexpectedly she was smiling when Liri ushered her into an office, guards halted with much clashing of heels behind her back.

The room was high-ceilinged and airy, windows open to chill dawn mist. Across an uncluttered desk sat one of the most beautiful men Anne had ever seen.

4

Really beautiful.

She stared at him in astonishment; she had never imagined such perfection of bone and feature existed outside Greek sculpture.

He was slim-wristed and long-fingered, sitting with relaxed grace as if he had just commenced work instead of having spent the past twenty hours grilling police and prisoners. His eyes were light-flecked in an otherwise dark complexion, and set into sockets like hammered bronze; his face suggested the touch of an artist who relied on sweep and line for effect and emphasized only the long thin line of mouth, the long thin line of narrowed eyes.

He held motionless studying her, impassive yet vital, then inclined his head in an oddly formal gesture. 'I apologize for keeping you waiting. I came to greet unexpected guests to our People's Republic, and discovered that the affairs of Gjirokaster's police also required attention. I am Millosh Kaderi, from the government in Tirana. Please sit down.'

Anne sat, impressed despite herself. His English was excellent, his voice soft and without violence. 'We are pleased to see you, having become weary of one room and our own company.'

'One room and the use of the courtyard sometimes,' his tone had not changed, but the police commander standing beside her shifted. He understood English too, then.

'We are grateful for the courtesy extended to us,' replied Anne quietly. 'I am sure a People's Republic would not censure those who offer hospitality in its name, even if only to unwelcome guests.'

'Who said you were unwelcome? It would seem to me that we have been more fortunate than you under the circumstances.' He picked up a paper but made no pretence of studying it, eyes tight on hers. 'Do you agree, Comrade Storost?'

Blood drummed in Anne's ears, sight dimmed, mouth dried. She had feared but not truly expected it. In such a crash as they had suffered there must be hope that the small clues which could betray her would be overlooked; but now they knew, this man was not the kind who might be fooled by bluff or lies. 'I left East Germany a long time ago and though my father was in a high position, it wasn't political when I did. I'm Anne Storey now, and have been these ten years past.'

'Indeed? I have found no evidence of it, only of Anna Storost, Shoqë. That means Comrade in Albanian,' he added, 'I thought you might like to start acquainting yourself with the language.'

'Why? You haven't any reason to hold me!'

'You think not? Our relations with the Democratic Republic of Germany are difficult and would be improved by a gesture of goodwill.'

'I'm not important enough to constitute any kind of gesture, certainly not a goodwill one.'

'I think you are wrong. Your father is dead now, but was a People's Minister. You left the country illegally and no state takes offences against its sovereignty lightly, especially from those within the Party hierarchy. And all officials enjoy ruling off debit entries, for their own satisfaction if nothing else, don't you agree, Shoqë?'

'Don't keep calling me that! I am no comrade of yours, but a British citizen fortunate enough to survive a crash in your country. I demand to see the British Consul.'

'Britain does not have diplomatic relations with Albania, nor are you a British citizen if it did.' He shook his head regretfully. 'No consul, no means of pressure from your new capitalist friends, no British or any other imperialist in the whole of our republic to run squealing to the press. We answer only to ourselves for what we do.'

Anne moistened her lips. 'You know I'm no use to you, whatever you may say. My own people would take me back if

I was offered to them, but it wouldn't be something they'd feel obliged to pay for. They wouldn't care enough. So why keep me simply for spite?'

'You tell me, Shoqë. You knew that if we found out about you, then you wouldn't be released.'

And of course, she had known. She had defied the system and understood very well that once back amongst its cogs she would be remorselessly shredded; and Albania was a country of immutable cogs and patterns. Here the Party was led by a native prophet, Enver Hoxha, Stalin still patron saint; life so petrified that change was unthinkable. She had erred, she must be punished. It was as simple as that.

She nodded. 'Yes.'

'That is settled then.' He shuffled papers aside. 'I will arrange transport for you to Tirana. Now I should like to ask you about this unfortunate flight which ended in such trouble for us all.'

She thought his questions would never end. There wasn't much to tell, nothing to conceal when he knew so much already, but he took her over each detail several times. She couldn't make up her mind what he was looking for, or whether he was just an intelligent man starved for outside information in the prison of his small country. He knew about the drugs but was not much interested; they were useful as a weapon against them if he needed it, otherwise they represented the dross of the capitalist system and as such were beneath the attention of a People's Republic.

He was intrigued by Stephen's Twodex though, and returned to it several times. He disbelieved her when she said that she knew nothing of it, and eventually she realized Stephen must have given the impression that she had helped him in some way. She wished she had time to think, with no time at all to think under ruthless cross-examination. Brain spinning, sun bright outside, voices calling in the street; what happened if she pretended that she had helped Stephen, when they had failed to concoct any story which would hold together? What if she denied everything, and was tortured for information she did not possess? She cursed Stephen now for thinking that he could help in a situation so far outside his experience. He might be brilliant in his Cambridge laboratory and still be lost in matters she understood by instinct. She had no illusions about the methods Albanian police would use against her if they wanted to; even Joe possessed a government which would note his plight though they could not, or did not want, to help. She was no one and had nothing.

It went on and on. She couldn't keep her hands still any longer, felt sweat salt on her lips. Still Millosh Kaderi faced her, lightly erect, making few gestures, placing questions precisely into each chink of doubt.

'I helped him with calculations sometimes,' she said at last in desperation, plunging recklessly. 'I am trained in radio-diagnostics as I told you, that is my trade and all I know. I was on a year's contract to Haibuk to set up the new unit they wanted for research, and the company agreed to sponsor my British naturalization if I went. It seemed a worthwhile trade-off to me, although Haibuk is a dreadful place for a woman. You're allowed to walk in the park during the heat of the day when the men don't want it, and that's all. The rest of the time I worked or went to the same parties in the same houses in the compound.'

'If you are a radiographer, why did you help with Astell's calculations?'

'The computer,' she said, gambling heavily now. She took Kaderi very seriously but did not think an Albanian official, however astute, would know much about scanners or computers. She wished she knew what the hell Stephen's machine did. 'We had access to one for our research, and he needed to use it sometimes. I allowed him to, although I shouldn't have done, and let him run some programmes as if they were mine. It saved him waiting until he got back to London to check his results.'

'What did he need to put on your computer?'

'I don't know. He paid me, that's all. I wasn't in his confidence.'

Kaderi looked away from her for the first time and stared out of the window, considering. With difficulty Anne looked away too, down at her tight-locked fingers. She knew she looked exhausted, she must also appear defeated. If Stephen had said anything which exposed her as a liar, then Kaderi ought to interrogate him again instead of thinking her at fault. Surely though, Stephen must have been wary in what he said and was not a stupid man.

'Think, Shoqë Anna, how much trouble you would have saved us if you had confessed the truth immediately. Once you knew that you must stay you should have admitted to your greed at once. Or has sufficient socialism survived from your youth for you to feel ashamed?'

'Perhaps,' said Anne, enormously relieved. It was true that some chord was touched by the attitudes and smells of socialism. Crude soap, no perfume and moral earnestness all swept memory back. She was devastated by knowing that the rest of her life must now be lived surrounded by slogans which were always white on a red background, yet a faint tug of kinship also remained. She had been shaped by such simplicities, by a life where slogans always were white on red and not red on white; by Party discipline and clearly marked ways to virtue. This was right and that was wrong; no argument, and genuine moral shock if you strayed.

Kaderi smiled unexpectedly. 'Life is seldom so fixed in its ways as we assume, Shoqë, and Albania possesses a pleasanter climate than the Democratic Republic of Germany.'

'You aren't sending me back?'

'We will see. Tomorrow, Tirana. The day after, who can tell?'

Anne slept as though stunned through the rest of the day, then lay all the long night thinking bleakly of the future. She was quite alone, had not thought to ask Kaderi what had happened to the others, the few Albanian words learned from Liri useless for questioning her guard.

The police post hummed efficiently around her, so she assumed Kaderi was still there but did not see him, nor anyone except her escort when she was bundled into the back of a military truck the following morning.

She felt encouraged by being out in light and air again, sun hot on her skin, the wind visible as it turned olive trees inside out, from silver to green and back to silver again. She gazed around eagerly, forgetful of jarred bones and staring soldiers:

everything she saw was strange enough to fascinate though the pulse of life was often achingly familiar. Children in red scarves singing choruses and trooping purposefully along the road; exhortations precariously balanced on public buildings and trailing exclamation marks; red stars, drab clothes and headscarves, uniforms wherever there were people; loud-speakers drumming Party purposes into passive ears from streetside and rooftop, LONG LIVE THE PARTY ENVER carved into bare rock above. The sun and beautiful, unclut-tered beach; cicadas, vines and ragged hills, these were dif-ferent; otherwise she might have been back in the East Berlin of her childhood.

The soil was cultivated right down to the road's edge, mostly by women bending in the heat. The sea when it came into sight was Mediterranean blue, Greek Corfu looking close enough to touch. She stared at it, and then at snow-tipped mountains enclosing Albania to the east, thinking of escape. Thinking too, that escape would be very difficult.

First she would need to understand the language, steal or earn money, buy clothes. Even dirty and dishevelled as she was, she looked quite different from Albanian women, would not last an hour without suspicion. Also, everything was guarded. She was astonished to see youths standing with rifles in empty fields, sitting armed on bridge parapets and outside shops as if war was expected that very day. In one village boys with red armlets manned a road-block carrying axes in their belts. Anne wondered sardonically whether they were expect-ing Russians or Americans, Greeks or Yugoslavs to invade. Axes did not seem out of place in such a setting, but how extraordinary to live always in a white heat of paranoia, expecting attack from all the world. Compared to Albania, East Germany was an object lesson in co-existence and relax-ation.

She waved at some children fluttering red, then the lorry slowed as they passed a refinery, the soldiers chattering and pleased by this symbol of achievement, giving her a thumbs-up of personal pride when she smiled too.

A horn blared and a white car passed them out of the dust which had masked it; Anne glimpsed Kaderi's impassive profile and the soldiers fell silent, straightening guiltily as if he sat beside them. Only then did Anne realize that his was the first car they had seen since they left Gjirokaster. Oxen, a few tractors, a bulldozer and dozens of donkeys, but a single car in fifty miles.

They pulled off the road under some trees at the next village, Anne delighted by a chance to climb down from the truck. She felt breakable, as if the flesh had been worn off her bones, but in some strange way no longer quite so alone. By joining the soldiers in pleasure at their refinery, she had subtly become a comrade again and they shared limp-papered cigarettes with her as they stood stretching in the shade.

She was not immediately aware of talk dying away but turned to find Kaderi standing close, and felt a tiny frightened pain at the back of her eyes at the thought that he had planned this. The truck had been stopped so she might be grilled again at a moment when he judged her to be off-guard. Comradeship was an illusion after all.

'Will you join me for a cup of coffee?' he asked.

'Do I have any choice?'

'Of course. There are always choices are there not, even if some are more difficult than others?'

Just what might that mean? she wondered, and went with him anyway. It seemed childish to refuse when the rest of her life was at his disposal.

He led the way down a cobbled lane, plastered houses either side, the occasional woman standing in a doorway watching them out of shuttered eyes. The sea glittered at the end of it, and the same magnificent sweep of empty sand she had seen from the road; a few tables were set out under a tree, checked cloths curling in the wind.

He seated her courteously, then went in search of service leaving her alone. Anne looked round carefully but couldn't see anyone watching her, he had waved the soldiers aside when a guard tried to follow. She felt nervous and uncertain, as if being left alone was some kind of test he expected her to fail. Beyond the sea's dazzle people went about a life she had come to take for granted over the past ten years, and Kaderi had left her as if she could simply get up and go wherever the fancy took her.

On impulse, she stood and walked across the beach, refusing to turn and see whether anyone followed. The sea trembled with heat and the only sound was a tiny splash of waves. This was perhaps the only time she would have to decide for herself whether to accept whatever she was offered in Albania and find some satisfaction in belonging again. Or was this no longer a possibility after ten years of a different existence? Must she now remain unreconciled to confinement of mind as well as body, whatever her wishes in the matter? Escape was scarcely an option if she faced her chances squarely.

'There is something about the sea which makes it easier to clear the mind of confusion,' said Kaderi.

Anne jumped, she had not heard even a squeak of sand as he came. 'Perhaps because it's the only view in Albania not set about with barriers.'

'There is comfort to be found in barriers, when they keep the unwanted out.'

'And here you are content, if only others would leave you alone for ever?'

'As you say, Shoqë. Here we are content.'

'Then why not lift the barriers and see what happens? I lived within sight of the Berlin Wall once, built to keep our own people in and not the unwanted out.'

'It didn't keep you in,' he observed drily. 'Have you ever seen cattle escape from a field, or has all your life been lived in cities? They push through the first gap they see, then panic at unfamiliarity and wander looking for a way back which they cannot find. Let us go and drink our coffee while it is hot, and you shall tell me truthfully how much you enjoyed life in the west.'

He was a very good listener when he chose. It was part of his trade, after all. He sat without looking at her directly, motionless beauty of bone giving his face its own familiarity now. There was relief in talking too, to someone who understood the opposite of everything she had encountered these past ten years. For in the West people congratulated her on her escape; commented on how pleasant she must find it to travel where she pleased. When she searched for lodging, a job

44

or training, they pointed to her new-found freedom to do whatever she liked. Then closed doors in her face because she was East German after all, one couldn't be too careful.

'There is—was—so much that I enjoyed,' she said unhappily at last. 'I feel disloyal to be saying this to you. It is wonderful to be free and men aren't cattle as you suppose, panicked by the first unfamiliarity. You, for instance. You must often find Albania a prison, when a fool could see that you have enough ability to succeed anywhere you chose.'

'Thank you, Shoqë. But I am needed here, and personal success is an illusion when the Party and the Revolution is the cause we serve.'

She stared at him, her mood shattered. 'I'm glad we've had this talk. You've just reminded me of why I left East Germany.'

'Why?'

'Because of the way in which ideals I was brought up to love were used. To hide violence, greed and fear. For the Party's sake, men said no matter what they did, and even thought they meant it. You are ambitious and must be cleverer than most others here, so don't pretend that power isn't something you enjoy and intend to grasp; in fact it must mean more to you than most men, when so many satisfactions are lacking here which elsewhere you'd take for granted.' She smiled. 'I'm not cattle you see and say what I think, since I don't care what you do now I must stay. I believed and was betrayed.'

'You dramatize yourself and others. How old are you?'

'Twenty-nine. Why?'

'Nineteen when you left the Democratic Republic. It is surely you who are putting high words to base motive, not I. At such an age a girl escapes for some kind of romantic yearning and not politics at all; self-deceit comes later, when you judge the motives of others by your own petty treasons.'

She flushed, heart thumping. This was a duel she could not afford, nor could she refuse it. 'What is it you want of me?'

'For you to face your own truth. Then I will accept your help because you wish to offer it and never need to look over my shoulder afterwards, wondering whether I can trust you. You feared whips and cellars when you were brought to me last night, I could see it in your face, but what you truly have to fear is yourself. And me.' He stood lithely, every movement studied, each gesture serving his purposes though she could not guess at them. Even the way his eyes were on her body now, and the softer line of his mouth while his glance lingered there.

She did not see him again after he walked with her back to the soldiers waiting by their truck, and in the evening she came to Tirana.

5

She did not see Kaderi again for ten days, then he came and took her out to dinner. Unescorted as before, although previously she had been locked into some ministry guest room and closely guarded on the few occasions she was allowed out. She had asked for an Albanian grammar and was also given Party Secretary Hoxha's speeches to provide practice in the language and ideological education; yet decision was as far away as ever, fluency in Albanian as useful to a comrade as an eventual evader. It was the devil of a language, too.

'How do you like our city?' Kaderi asked while they were quickly and deftly served by a girl who looked as if she had lived on bread and macaroni all her life.

'I haven't seen much of it. The view out of a back window, and a few walks around the main square and avenues.'

'And your impressions?'

Anne laughed, it was marvellous to be outside without a gun at her back. 'Clean, no traffic problem, no temptation to buy anything. The same blocks of flats you find everywhere from Manchester to Teheran. The way everyone stares.'

'You do not look like anyone they have ever seen, Anna.' He showed as little emotion as ever, probably planned the warmth in his voice.

She nodded, feeling depressed again. Even if she dressed as Albanians did, they would still stare. Grooming, attitudes, instinctive grace of walk and gesture, all marked her out in a land where almost the only visitors in their history had been enemy soldiers or a few technicians. 'It's quiet enough to hear each footfall too. In London, the crowds are so great you never hear feet on the pavement,'

'How strange. Your friend Astell said much the same.'

She looked up quickly. 'Where is he? Haven't—are the others still here too?'

'No. Only him, and the pilot of course. He has a trial to face. The rest were flown out yesterday.'

'They've all recovered? Willie—'

'Some were still ill, but wished to go home. We were content to see them leave, when several needed expensive care.'

'Except Stephen? He didn't go?'

'Astell? He is here in Tirana.'

He wasn't on any company list of fugitives, she reflected, remembering how he had appeared out of the desert on that last morning in Haibuk. 'Did he want to stay?'

'What makes you ask?'

Anne remembered sensing that Stephen was not too displeased to find himself in Albania, but decided against mentioning it. 'I simply wondered why he wasn't flown out with the rest.'

'How are you liking our national dishes? The fish especially is good here, don't you think?'

'No,' she said flatly. If he could change the subject, so could she. 'You don't know what real fish tastes like. Come to England one day and try Dover sole; you'll never like Mediterranean fish again.'

Unexpectedly, he was angry. They ate in silence, the insult as personal as if Albania manufactured its climate purposely to produce indifferent fish. Anne was surprised by such a childish reaction in a man she had thought detached from pettiness, but refused to feel that she ought to soothe his pride. She murmured an excuse eventually and went through to the back, where she had seen other women disappearing; past the scrape of guitars and hollow bang of drums, the passage beyond reeking and unpleasant although the public areas of Albania were spotless. Beyond again was a yard, unlit houses etched against pale lemon tones lingering in the sky.

Why shouldn't she simply go?

Walk across that yard and disappear into the tangle of lanes she had glimpsed on her walks?

Without more reflection, she stepped briskly into the street;

she was being absurd, but her sense of oppression lifted with each step, lips curved as she thought of Millosh Kaderi sitting at their table waiting for her to return. He would never think that she could be such a fool as to walk out without money, in light shoes and possessing only a stumbling knowledge of Albanian. Well, she would show him, quite what she wasn't sure. But at least he would look the fool, not her.

She stopped at the first corner. Here, darkness truly began. Rough cobbles underfoot as planned streets ended and the jumbled growth of generations began. She stood irresolutely, biting her lips. She had acted on impulse, knowing she was bound to be caught, yet sensing also that Kaderi would end by dominating her will entirely unless she laid claim to it herself before too much time passed. Through small-paned windows she could see Kaderi still sitting inside the restaurant. He was smoking, smiling slightly to himself.

Anne stared at him, thinking furiously.

He had expected her to go. If she didn't when she could, then he won anyway. If she did, then speedy recapture emphasized his hold on her and made her receptive to whatever deal he proposed. Unless she was simply to play his game for him, she needed to stay free for several days and make him sweat.

Or preferably make him look ridiculous, the mind of a fanatic being more vulnerable to ridicule than obstinacy. Unbidden, a truly splendid idea slid into her mind.

She felt laughter in her throat, but forced herself to think hastily through the possibilities. She did not have much time but it was worth trying. First though, she must shake off the watchers Kaderi must have left to wait for her: one of her few words of Albanian was Sigurimi, the title of the State Security Police frequently visible in smarter uniforms than mere soldiers, but even more dangerous in shadows behind your back.

She turned and ran. She gave no warning at all, one moment standing still the next running hard, and as she hoped, her followers were taken by surprise. She swerved into the dark lanes she had seen, choosing turnings at random but keeping direction clear in her head. She moved easily, at Haibuk there had been little to do in her spare time except use the company's recreation facilities, and behind her she could hear pounding feet and confusion instead of the smooth shadowing the Sigurimi had expected.

Darkness was intense, the surface underfoot very rough. Once she went sprawling and would have fallen more often except that the narrowness of twisting passages enabled her to save herself. She refused to slow her headlong flight, speed her best weapon. Tirana was not large, sooner or later she would come to one of the avenues radiating from the main square, and she needed to cross its treacherous spaces without allowing her pursuers an instant in which to raise a general alarm.

A laugh snatched at her throat again, they would not dare abandon the chase without referring back to Kaderi, and had not time to do so. Situations changed but orders were orders, and his subordinates would not be accustomed to using their initiative.

She could tell from the temperature when she reached central streets again. Cobbled lanes trapped heat from the day; wider avenues sloping uphill were cooler, and lined by villas surviving from a time before egalitarian flats. She ran under shading trees, breath stabbing now. A gate open on her right. She took a chance and plunged into undergrowth which had once been a flower bed and lay gasping, waiting for pursuit to pass.

It came after a considerable pause, two men cursing and calling to each other. One put a hand to the wall just beyond where Anne was hiding: she could see him bent over, holding his chest. He was solid from years of diet unsuited to pelting down dark alleys, and when his comrade shouted at him he merely groaned and swore some more.

Anne willed him to move, conscious that the permanent patrols she had seen in all the main streets would soon be warned to look for her.

The other man came back, saying something in a savage undertone, and the two stood arguing. Anne caught the word Kaderi; she wasn't surprised that it was taking them a while to summon courage to report failure to him.

They went at last and she stood at once. There was too little time left to find a safer way out over the villa's back wall, so she turned directly towards where the main square must lie.

At this time of night Tirana was a ghost town, few lights, nothing to do or buy, its citizens shut away from sight. Anyone walking would be regarded with suspicion.

Some scruffy hens in a yard started squawking as she passed and she ran again to leave them behind, voices calling across the street behind her. Tirana was more like a series of sprawling villages jointed by avenues and punctuated by concrete blocks than a capital city.

The main square at last. She stood in shadow and stared at its emptiness: even in mid-morning it was a matter for remark if two cars crossed it at once, at night there were red-lit slogans, some street-lights and a huddle of police fingering rifles. Nothing else at all.

She had to get across and could not spare time for another detour. A pale slip of moon showed above the roofs, light sharpening every moment.

She needed a diversion of some kind, but could think of nothing. A single car drove across the square and all the policemen turned to watch; a car still something which most Albanians had never been inside.

Anne felt her muscles tense as she realized what she must do. Next time a car passed she must trust that watching cars was a sport Albanian police did not tire of easily, and slip across the corner of the square.

She waited a long time. How absurd to be standing in the hub of a nation's capital at ten o'clock in the evening, waiting for a car to pass. Headlights at last, and the sound of an engine coming fast.

She took off her shoes and waited, hand on warm wall. The car whipped past, and stopped in the middle of the square. Kaderi got out.

Now was her chance, while police were at attention and Kaderi blinded by his own lights.

She sprinted across spilled red from illuminated exhortation, not pausing or looking back. If she was seen then her plan was ruined anyway, and recapture on Kaderi's terms a matter of minutes.

Another street, a jumble of café tables to negotiate, the functional concrete of official buildings close again, shadow reach-

51

ing out to receive her. She leaned against a wall, panting and triumphant.

After a moment voices roused her. Kaderi was directing police with unslung rifles to stand at each intersection of the square; she had only just been in time. She caught a glimpse of his face before he drove off again: set tight, mouth and eyes cut deep into a bronze mask.

As soon as her breath steadied, Anne withdrew noiselessly around the corner, slipped on her shoes and walked boldly across to the guard on the side door of the official building where she was lodged.

He was very young and eyed her figure hopefully.

Anne made a gesture of pushing at the door. 'Let me in, please. *Me dhotem atje, ju lutem.* My room is in here.'

For an instant he hesitated, staring at her. Somehow, she smiled, while tension screamed that this was madness. Someone would come; the boy would send for his sergeant. Then he smiled back and stood aside, swinging open the door. '*Me kenaqisi, Shoqë.*'

Another guard stood outside the door of her room, but he was unsurprised to see her and came respectfully to attention. She had left earlier with Shok Kaderi, a man who punished sloppiness in guards, it was not for him to wonder whether she was a prisoner or Kaderi's woman kept discreetly close. The outer sentry might well have thought it odd that she returned alone, but Kaderi's power was too alarming for a recruit six months out of training to consider checking eccentricity. Not for the first time, Anne wondered just what Kaderi's official position was.

She flopped on her bed, utterly exhausted.

Since her guards had accepted her return as normal they would report it to their superior without remark. Her knowledge of bureaucracy suggested that at the least it would be several hours before routine guard reports filtered through a dull-minded system and the Sigurimi became aware that the object of a city-wide search was comfortably inside one of their own ministry buildings.

Anne chuckled aloud; for all that time Kaderi would be turning out men to search for her.

6

In fact she had judged Albanian bureaucracy by that of Britain and the German Democratic Republic, and it was two days before Kaderi came into the room and stood looking at her. 'You have enjoyed your little escapade, Shoqë?'

'Yes, I have,' she smiled and stood, looking across at him.

As usual, his face gave nothing away but the stiff way he stood, the burn in his eyes, betrayed both fury and humiliation. 'I hope then that you enjoy the next two days as much.'

He turned and went out.

She had expected retribution and thought the risk worthwhile. Kaderi wanted something from her and his choice of pressures was therefore limited; he had intended to demonstrate the hopelessness of escape while at the same time exposing the nerve of comradeship, the web which bound her to the past. Unless he abandoned his plans completely, he could not simply order her to be beaten up, whatever his desires in the matter.

Two guards took her down several flights of stairs, and logic about what Kaderi could and could not do vanished abruptly when she was hustled into the cellars. The building was full of preoccupied clerks and could not be a prison, but being taken under guard into cellars spelled one meaning only to those in the hands of the security police.

She was pushed into some kind of stokehold, containing a boiler which might have been manufactured to drive a transatlantic liner fifty years before, pipes, some empty filing cabinets, nothing else.

One of the guards jerked her arms roughly behind her and snapped on handcuffs, shoved her hard and slammed the door.

A moment later the light went out.

Two days, Kaderi had said, and he was a man who would keep exactly to the minute of retribution she had earned.

She stepped carefully across the floor, feeling her way. She edged round one of the filing cabinets and pushed hard enough for it to fall with a crash, then sat on it, arms awkwardly behind.

Soon, her shoulders began to ache.

The darkness was so thick it became an animal to be fought, pressing against her eyes and into her lungs with dirty, fume-laden air. The earth tipped and swung, balance easily lost when nothingness surrounded her.

Two days.

At least she knew some end was set to it, and somehow time would pass.

No, that was wrong. She must force time past, fighting panic with colour from her mind, with stories, thought and plans. Decision, too. After this their score would be levelled, and she thought Kaderi would not wait any longer but face her with his proposition while filth and disorientation drained her of will.

She shrank from any man seeing her as she would be at the end of such an incarceration, and him especially. Millosh Kaderi dominated others by the power of his will, and was also a man to whom few women could remain indifferent whether in love or hate. And Kaderi she must hate, whatever happened.

She lost count of time, of course. It became very hot. The boiler was not alight but the pipes were too hot to touch, so she sweated until her skin dried out and she lapsed into a dehydrated daze. It helped a little. More time had passed when she woke on the floor, pipes and stonework cold.

Very cold, in fact. She shivered, stomach snarling, mind swooping crazily.

She judged Kaderi unjustly only in one respect. He did not come himself to see her foul and reeling at the end of her imprisonment. She was aware of the stabbing pain of light and an indifferent woman offering water; cool to drink, hot for washing. Fresh clothes, food, and a bed.

Anne woke with a sense of having slept a long time. Her brain was clear and she felt ravenously hungry. She was back in her own room and lay blinking gratefully at sunlight before climbing out of bed and going over to the window. She took a deep breath, feeling warm air moving softly on her skin; everything the other side of the black time in the cellar seemed impossibly remote, as if she had been born again.

Which possibly Kaderi had intended.

There was no guard on her door and the woman who brought food told her that Shok Kaderi was expecting her at six o'clock.

'He is coming here?'

'No, Shoqë. You are to go to the Ministry of State Security and ask for him. See, it is across the square and down that street with trees.' She spoke quite good English.

'I am to go alone?'

'Of course. Why not? Our streets are not dangerous as I read that they are in capitalist states.'

You must hand it to Kaderi, decided Anne clinically. I gave him the hell of a runaround and tore up all his plans so he could only regain ascendancy by force, now he has the nerve to use the same gambit of trust again.

And this time of course, it was going to work. She had made her gesture, could not escape in Tirana again. She would have to decide whether to do what he wanted, or not, under the disadvantage of having walked voluntarily to his office.

Damn.

He also scorned to keep her waiting. A thick-legged secretary escorted her through corridors lined with more photographs of Party Secretary Hoxha, a huge painting of him dominating the stairwell. He was waving benevolently and holding a bunch of what looked like plastic flowers, the cut of his suit reminiscent of Chicago gangsters in the nineteen thirties. Godfather, thought Anne sardonically. Well, yes, I suppose so.

Kaderi stood when she came in. 'Sit down, Anna. Cigarette?' He sounded exactly as though they resumed a briefly interrupted conversation.

She sat. 'I don't smoke.'

'You will. It is a very common habit in Albania.' He studied her across a desk swept bare of papers, Hoxha staring into space above his head. The room was empty except for bright Albanian rugs and a massive antique cupboard. The effect was rather pleasant.

'There isn't much else to spend your money on, I suppose.' She hoped to annoy him, but failed.

'We do not require much money for our socialist way of life, Shoqë.' He smiled. 'Congratulations, Anna. I am almost relieved to discover that you have emerged from your cellar as unrepentant as you went in.'

'I would have been happy to relieve your mind even further by not going there in the first place,' she retorted acidly.

'I also would have preferred to know the trick you played on me. Come, Anna, you would have been astonished if you had not been made to pay for what you did. Only in the West have they forgotten that wrong-doing must be punished, and see what troubles it brings them.' He stood and went over to the cupboard. 'Have you tried our raki, or don't you drink either?'

'I drink, but would prefer wine.'

He brought over a glass. '*Per shandatin tuaj!* To your good health.'

Anne drank, the wine rough but quite good; she certainly preferred being softened up to threats and confinement, but did not doubt it was part of the same. 'You are about to offer me a choice, aren't you?'

'Directness has some virtues,' he observed. 'Yes, I am, but matters are becoming more complicated every day.'

'What matters? I've had plenty of time for thought, but can't see how I might be sufficiently important for you to waste time on me.' This office and the attitude of everyone she encountered confirmed what she had already guessed: Kaderi was too important to waste effort on trifles.

He walked over to the window and stood looking out, lashes dark shadows on high-moulded cheekbones. In profile his pure features were even more remarkable, and showed none of the ruthlessness which was visible full-face. That severe beauty might have belonged to an artist perfecting his masterpiece; uneasily she thought that perhaps it did, Albania his design

56

and she his offering to its need.

'What do you know of our country?' he asked at last.

'Nothing. It is small and poor and has quarrelled with everyone, including me when I crash by ill-fortune in its mountains.'

His face lit an instant with amusement. 'So we have. But we are not poor, Anna, we would be safer if we were. We have minerals in our mountains which the world covets. Before, we could quarrel with whom we wished because no one really cared what happened to us, now they do. They are poring over old maps and wondering just how much we have of what they want. The world is running out of minerals and a great deal of what remains is to be found in the Soviet Union or South Africa, either of which could use them to create a crisis overnight. Nearly all the world's tungsten is in China, and without it you couldn't even manufacture a screwdriver which would not snap under strain. Zimbabwe and South Africa have ninety per cent of the world's chrome and you don't need me to tell you how easily that could be out of reach. It's impossible to refine oil or design high quality aero engines without it and we have most of the other ten per cent.'

Anne stared at him. 'The remaining ten per cent of the world's chrome?'

'And a few other scarce minerals, quite which and how much we are not sure ourselves and I wouldn't tell you if we were. But the Italians opened up the chrome mines long ago and we export considerable quantities now: chrome is the one major mineral which neither the United States nor the Soviet Union possesses in significant quantities. Revolution in the Gulf brought you to disaster in our hills, it has also brought chaos to the world's oil markets and threats of intervention by West and East. What will happen do you suppose when the world discovers it has run out of silver in just ten years time, of zinc in forty, will soon exhaust known platinum reserves and cannot even manufacture aspirin without it? Albania won't be a country no one has heard of then.'

'You have all these minerals here?'

'No, but we certainly have some which the world is gasping for, as well as excellent harbours and short distances.' He paused and then added deliberately, 'We also have a leader who will soon die, and when he does then the great powers will seize their chance to stir up trouble, hoping for their advantage. The First World War was provoked not far from here, because other nations could not keep their fingers out of our affairs, and the pressures are greater now. The Third could very easily begin here too.'

'But wars aren't like that any more! Who would risk atomic war in Europe for the few mines and minerals Albania may possess?'

'Wars have not recently been like that, because politics have been more important than the grab for goods. Do you really think America would refrain from intervention when their economy shatters for want of a few tons of platinum or vanadium? Or the Soviet Union see all their great armies rendered useless because they cannot mass-produce steel tough enough to forge a pair of pliers, let alone a tank? They would both invade first and explain later. Yugoslavia, too. They hate us, and in places their frontier runs only metres from strata their geologists study through binoculars. When Hoxha dies they will all play on our uncertainties, the winner try to take over, the loser perhaps refuse to accept defeat. Either way, we lose. Again. You say we quarrel with everyone, but at least we have been forty years our own masters after living the rest of our history as other men's slaves. You can't be surprised if being trapped in our own country is a price we willingly pay for the pleasure of refusing to be pawns again. As you willingly paid the price of two days in a cellar for the pleasure of defying me.'

'You have no friends because you have crushed Albanians with the harshest rule in Europe, when even East Germany made a show of disowning Stalin and his methods.'

He turned. 'Yes, of course. Don't be foolish, Anna. You have lived ten years in the West but should be intelligent enough to realize that the same standards do not apply everywhere. Our people are strictly ruled but make no mistake, they would fight to the death, to the ruin of our land again, if others tried to take anything which is ours.'

'I don't see why you are telling me all this,' Anne said frankly;

she did not doubt his sincerity, only the purpose of it.

'Because I can't obtain what I need in any other way. Believe me, confidences break the habits of a lifetime.'

She was sure they did; she stared at him, waiting.

'You see, Anna, there are two pieces of information which will at least help us to prepare for the future. We need to know the precise state of our Party Secretary's health. We also require an accurate estimate of our mineral resources, and very quickly too. You can help us with both, if you will.'

Her brain zig-zagged, and for a moment she wondered whether he had mistaken her for someone else. 'I can? How?'

'You are a radio-diagnostician, a good one presumably since you were appointed to establish a research department at Haibuk. We have electronic-diagnostic equipment in the hospital here, and Party Secretary Hoxha is anxious to undergo tests for his health. You are not a doctor, but technicians are often shrewder than their masters realize. In the course of such tests you could probably estimate how long he has to live, and we will be better prepared for the crisis his death will bring us.'

'Why hasn't he already—he must have seen specialists, what do they say?' Every instinct warned against getting involved in Albanian politics.

Kaderi avoided her eyes. 'An Albanian would not pronounce on the Party leader's health. The Communist Party in Albania is the Party of Enver Hoxha, and as such lives for ever.'

'But . . . no one can set precise dates to such matters. If your diagnostic equipment is used correctly and it is modern as you say, the readings will tell much of what you want to know. You can't imprison a machine when it tells you that Enver Hoxha is mortal like the rest of us, so no one need risk his life by dabbling in the treason of facts.' She kept her voice neutral, but wondered what he really thought about the stifling harshness inflicted on Albanians by their rulers. Her resolution hardened; she felt sympathy for him in spite of everything, but after ten years in the West, his assumptions were no longer hers.

'I am willing to risk my life in such matters since I must

plan for the certainty of crisis.' He turned, face lost in the dazzle of light from outside. 'The equipment we have at our hospital is American, captured in Vietnam and given as a personal gift to Party Secretary Hoxha by Chairman Mao. Unfortunately, Chinese technicians understood it as little as we did, and were anyway almost immediately withdrawn when China became revisionist. It has gathered dust in the hospital ever since.'

Anne wanted to laugh, and knew he would strike her if she did. 'Is it in crates, or what?'

'No. It was re-assembled and connected but never worked reliably.'

'What make and type of diagnostic machine is it?'

He came over and took a paper out of a drawer. 'A Bell-Simpson Audiotronic Scanner VI. Do you know it?'

She nodded, it was not in fact a very sophisticated piece of equipment. Reliable and useful, the kind of thing you would expect to find in an American military hospital, when the most advanced gadgetry would be kept for Stateside research units. 'I'm not a mechanic though. I can use it medically, but if it has been unused for several years then you'll need a good electronic engineer to check it through.' And to check its re-assembly, she reflected, thinking of semi-skilled Chinese and Albanians heaving it out of crates.

'We have one looking at it now, but he knows nothing of medical applications.'

'Oh?' She had not expected Albania to have an electronics engineer of sufficient quality to tinker with the kind of circuitry Bell-Simpson used as a matter of course. Their Audiotronic Scanner was only relatively unsophisticated.

'Mr Astell. He was trained at Cambridge, I understand, and only recently completed an assignment to research.'

'Oh,' she said again, smiling openly now. 'What a very fortunate crash it was for you, to be sure.'

'I told you so at the time if you remember, although Mr Astell is less capable than I had hoped,' he added severely. 'It is easy to see that Western universities have serious shortcomings.'

'Tirana university too, since you need to employ Mr Astell,' she said caustically. 'I don't suppose he's ever attempted maintenance electronics on war-looted equipment before.'

Kaderi tensed, head thrown back as if instinct alone would make him call for a guard to kick her into a suitable frame of mind. 'Be careful how you exploit your position, Shoqë. You have already discovered that I can punish without damaging your usefulness to me.'

'You can't check my results though,' she said shrewdly. 'You need my goodwill if you are to feel confidence in them.'

There was a long silence, then he inclined his head. Although a man who was used to taking what he wanted, he could still accept what he must with dignity. 'What are your terms?'

'My freedom afterwards.'

'No, not until after Secretary Hoxha dies, supposing my word has any value then.'

'Why?'

'You will possess too much information for our safety. After you have trained a technician to use the hospital machine, then you will help Astell with his calculations. I understand he can adapt the computer attached to the Bell-Simpson for his purposes, and you allowed him to use something similar in Haibuk. He says that he needs you to speed up the mineral survey which he is going to do for us.'

She kept her face blank, for he was watching her closely. She knew nothing of mineral surveys out thought Stephen was talking nonsense for his own safety. Perhaps for hers, too. 'We make the Bell-Simpson work and then carry out a survey? What terms has he made?'

'The same as you. Freedom when it is done.'

'And you refused him too. At least you were honest enough not to pretend you would let us go once we possessed such information.'

'What is honesty in such matters? I have sufficient intelligence to know that neither of you would believe such a promise. You may have confidence in those pledges I do give though: freedom to work inside Albania, and follow your own speciality with such resources as we can spare.'

'What is the alternative?'

'I dislike unnecessary threats, but you are only of use to us working. If you refuse to work, then you are parasites and better shot. But I do not think that Mr Astell anyway is a man who could long endure idleness in the dark.'

Anne shivered; nor would she be able to endure it either. 'If we carry out your survey, you would let us move about freely afterwards? You wouldn't send me back to the Democratic Republic?'

'You would be watched, naturally. But yes, within our frontiers you could go where other citizens may go; and whatever you decide, I will not send you back.'

'Whatever I decide?'

'The art of negotiation is to concede something, is it not? You are medically trained so probably will not refuse help to a sick man, and the fact that he is our leader will make no difference to you. The survey is another matter, so I must offer something in advance.'

He was clever, the phrase about medical obligation slipped in so deftly that she accepted it without question and only later remembered how she had seen it as politics before, and been determined not to be involved. She nodded. 'I agree to do what I can with the Audiotronic, but success will depend on what state the machine is in. As for the rest . . . I shall have to talk to Stephen before deciding. How long will it take?'

'The survey? That depends on how quickly Mr Astell can make his Twodex serviceable after its shaking in the crash, and whether winter slows travel in the mountains before you have finished. Only six to eight weeks, I understand. It is very modern equipment.'

Really, there was no choice. She wasn't even sure she wanted a choice; if Kaderi was right then a future crisis could very easily explode here, with incalculable consequences. She had an obligation to help prevent it if she could, and also craved for certainties back in her life again, needed time to come to terms with her own confusion.

He had been watching her, motionless and intent, now without a word spoken he came over and stood close. 'Thank you, Anna. You will not regret it, I promise.' He kissed her, but held her slightly away from him instead of closely as other men did. As if emotion must be kept from contaminating Millosh Kaderi.

His mouth was fiercely demanding though, tearing her senses loose. The contrast between what she sensed in him and the chill detachment of his body was both tantalizing and disturbing. She felt herself yielding to him, wanted very much to yield to him, and at the same time was conscious of a mischievous desire to destroy the barriers this man set about himself, to force admission that even he was vulnerable to the passions of mankind.

His grip tightened even while he held her from him and when he drew back he stared at her as if it was the first time he had truly noticed her. A considering stare which marked how candidly she returned his gaze when forty-eight hours of blackness in a cellar had not helped his cause at all. Now he saw a delicately boned face alight with feeling, and aroused responses unshadowed by resentment. Laughter and mockery too, both unfamiliar to Millosh Kaderi, and . . . sympathy. He was jolted when he recognized that for what it was and turned away. 'I have appointments now. You are free to go where you wish in Tirana and I will take you to the hospital tomorrow.'

'Then I think that as a gesture to my new-found liberty, I should like a key on the inside instead of the outside of my door, if you would arrange it, Shok Kaderi.' Her voice was light; it took a moment to grasp that she was teasing him. Here, in his office in the Ministry of State Security, where fear was grained into the plaster.

'I will give orders for it,' he said thickly. 'Possibly I may come tonight and discover whether you wish to use it.'

He had intended to leave subordinates to deal with her now most of his purposes were gained, and have nothing more to do with her at all.

7

Kaderi drove Anne to the hospital quite early next morning. It was a largish square building, stucco flaking off, paint bleached by the sun, the driveway pocked by holes as if a minor war had recently been fought there. Calling it a hospital did nothing to inspire confidence in whatever practices were carried out inside.

Anne stole a glance at Kaderi; he was frowning, the sculpted mask imperfect. 'You do not look as if the night will join your happier recollections,' she said, annoyed to find she minded.

His mouth twisted, eyes on the road although driving was simplicity itself in a city almost without traffic. 'No, I don't think it will.'

She bit her lip, absurdly hurt. She did not care to examine her motives in leaving her door unlocked last night, yet she had done so, and he came. Then he was not like Millosh Kaderi at all; uncertain and hesitant at first, later a splendour of man in darkness, astonishingly tender in the dawn. He left while she slept and now was jailer again, behaving as if she had sold herself to someone of his acquaintance he disliked.

He drew up in front of the hospital and came round to open her door, but the courtesy was meaningless. He would order her wired for torment and flick the switch without change of expression she thought, and shuddered, unable now to understand how she could have found pleasure in the night.

Kaderi led the way through the hospital, brushing aside nurses lined up as if for inspection and a halting welcome from an elderly sister with moist, frightened eyes.

'They look as if they expected you to bring an execution squad,' Anne said sharply.

'I might yet do so, if word of our purpose in repairing this machine leaks out. Any rumour that we fear for the Party Leader's health must come from here, and the whole hospital held to blame. You and Mr Astell may be too valuable to execute at present, the same would not be true of some gossiping ward orderly. You speak to no one unless you wish to have their deaths laid at your door, do you understand?'

'I understand,' she said numbly. God, how many kinds of fool was she?

He paused, hand on a door handle. 'Last night is not amongst my happier recollections because it must remain something set aside. I shall not come again because I dare not.' He kissed her on the lips, passionless but holding her closely to his body, distance lost between them.

Without waiting for a reply he opened the door and ushered her before him into a large room, littered with a formidable collection of electronic and mechanical gadgetry.

Stephen Astell looked up from the floor. 'Ah, the sorcerer's apprentice appears at last. How are you, Anne?' He stood and looked at her carefully.

'Well, as you see, Mr Astell,' replied Kaderi placidly. 'My part in the bargain is fulfilled for the moment, is it not?' He looked completely in command of himself, the moment before already vanished.

Stephen looked at Anne interrogatively. 'You have been well treated?'

She nodded, unable to enter a discussion on her treatment, and saw his face tighten. He was no fool, and her self-command was less complete than Kaderi's. 'You're sure?'

'I'm sure.'

He sighed. 'Well, I suppose you know your own business best.' He stared at Kaderi, eyes slate-hard and contemptuous. 'You have your methods well-chosen for any eventuality, haven't you?'

'I am not skilled in riddles, Mr Astell, only in conducting state affairs efficiently. Does the machine work?'

'No.'

For the first time, Kaderi looked disconcerted. 'Explain yourself.'

'You claim efficient conduct of affairs, so I gave you an accurate answer. You would not understand any technical explanation I cared to make but I am perfectly willing to waste time in trying, if you wish.'

Kaderi shifted involuntarily, hand moving to where he undoubtedly carried a gun. For several breaths violence was close enough to touch. 'You take pleasure in exploiting your position, Mr Astell. Remember that you have a long time to live in our People's Republic once your value to us is less obvious. We do not like individuals who claim privileges for themselves. How long before you are able to make this Bell-Simpson work?'

'That will depend on the facilities of your physical research laboratories. I have made a list of equipment I require; matters would have been easier if the machine had not been uncrated by maddened gorillas using sledgehammers.'

Kaderi took the list without a word, and a few moments later they heard his car door slam.

'He must have slid down the banisters,' observed Stephen. 'Cigarette?'

Anne shook her head. 'Why did you set out to infuriate him?'

'I felt like it. Any objections?'

She shrugged. She had not expected Stephen to be perceptive enough to recognize any link except that of jailer and prisoner between her and Kaderi, or to resent it if he did. 'No, except that we're likely to be here a long time, and Kaderi is a powerful man.'

'He is head of State Security, the Sigurimi his personal command. It doesn't make me like the bastard any better, but perhaps you feel differently?'

'No,' she said again, feeling sick. 'It makes me feel . . . I suppose he told you about me, where I came from ten years ago?' He nodded, eyes on curling cigarette smoke. 'Well . . . I grew up fearing security police; the higher your family is in a communist hierarchy, the more you have to fear. They are only a word to you.'

He crushed out his cigarette. 'These damned things burn like bonfires. We'd best get to work then, I suppose.'

She touched a console of switches absently, feeling chilled and alone. Memory of Kaderi lingered on her body, a reluctant understanding too of some of the imperatives which drove him, even while revulsion was roused by what she knew he must have done, and was. These were contradictions which no one bred in England's comfortable tolerances could grasp.

She and Stephen worked well together though. Electronic theory was beyond her but she was deft and quick, well-trained in diagnostic techniques and interested in everything. The work was also complicated enough temporarily to banish other problems from her mind, and Stephen an exacting taskmaster. A truckload of equipment arrived during the afternoon, hauled upstairs by reproachful students whose courses had been disrupted when their laboratories were swept bare.

'My God,' said Stephen once. 'I wonder what I shall find when I need to use their physical laboratory at the Research Institute. The Eskimos must have a few things more advanced than these.'

Everything came from different parts of the world too, in varied sizes and circuits, labelled in exotic languages. Mostly they had formed part of distant Russian and Chinese aid, some useful but often surplus junk palmed off on people who were not expected to understand what they were given.

Anne was amused to see that, for all Stephen's show of indifference, the scientist in him was aroused by such a challenge: he did not have the true researcher's itch for perfection, rather he was an engineer who found it impossible to keep his hands off botched work.

They had one wing of the hospital to themselves, wards cleared so their wires could trail down passages from improvised switchboards, a pleasant bedroom each overlooking the mountains circling Tirana.

They worked for a week, Stephen often departing under escort to some laboratory where Albania's atomic research was conducted. Since technicians there became hysterical if he saw the simplest data, his work went slowly and was punctuated by extremes of exasperation. Anne rested whenever he was away and slept like the dead at night, avoiding thought.

'Well,' he said eventually, 'we'll probably kill Party Secretary Hoxha when we wire him to my circuits, but I suppose we'd better start full tests and hope to God it works.'

Kaderi came sometimes, saying little, prowling restlessly. 'What do you think, Mr Astel?' he asked now. 'In non-technical language, of course.'

Stephen scratched his jaw, stubble rasping. He looked exhausted, being the kind of man who found it hard to rest once he was engaged on a project. 'I can't tell you. There are a great many areas I've neither the skill nor facilities to touch. I expect it to work after a fashion, whether it has the accuracy to give the kind of data Miss Storey needs for diagnosis, I've no idea. Nor shall we know until Hoxha dies and proves us right or wrong.'

The muscles of Kaderi's face tightened at this flippant reference to his Party leader. 'If it does not work, Secretary Hoxha will be exposed to humiliation when he agrees to come here for no purpose.'

Anne met Stephen's eyes, and for a dreadful moment both nearly laughed. Kaderi glanced from one to the other, suspecting something wrong, but unable to see what.

'Come back tomorrow,' said Stephen at last. 'We should be able to advise you then on whether to risk humiliating Party Leader Hoxha.'

After Kaderi had gone they went for a walk before starting work again. Both felt jaded and preoccupied, stiff from long hours crouched in awkward positions. A guard followed them, a patient plodder of a man who kept his fingers on both trigger and safety catch of his sub-machine gun, as if he feared he might not react quickly enough should they decide to run. He fiddled with them constantly too.

'I wish to God he'd blow his own feet off and be done with it,' said Stephen irritably. 'It's bound to happen sooner or later. I'll tell Kaderi that his half-trained goons will shoot Hoxha by mistake unless he's careful, then we might get one who could be relied on to fire when we escape and not before.'

'When are you going?' Anne spoke matter-of-factly, knowing he had not chosen the wrong words by accident.

'I think that depends on you.'

'Me?'

'Hasn't it occurred to you that all I need to do is carry out a mineral survey which records very few resources in Albania beyond those already known, and I will be released? Accidentally, perhaps, to carry more conviction, but allowed to go nevertheless. Kaderi and his colleagues want to be left alone. What better guarantee of that than for the West to know from me there's nothing worth a crisis here?'

'And if you do find reserves of value?'

He glanced at the guard, out of easy earshot but with his gun trained directly on their backs. 'Christ. Kaderi promised us the same freedom as other Albanian citizens, I suppose this is what he meant. I'd be a fool to find anything of the sort, wouldn't I?'

Anne thought about it carefully, spine crawling. It was difficult to think of anything except that gun. 'You said escape depended on me. I can't see how, if that is what you think Kaderi intends. I can't check your results any more than he can.'

He slipped his hand under her arm, 'I wasn't implying that I didn't trust you, quite the reverse in fact. But Kaderi needs to inform East as well as West if my survey shows few minerals. I would serve his purpose in the West, you in the East.'

She stopped dead, staring at him. 'No! He would never . . . he promised that whatever happened he would not send me back to East Germany.'

'For God's sake have a care!' He jerked his head at their guard. 'If he panics we'll be blown in half. Keep walking and remember he has only two thoughts, to shoot or not to shoot. Do you seriously believe that Kaderi would hesitate for a moment, if sending you back helped Albania and his power?'

She hesitated and then shook her head. She thought perhaps he might not want to do it, but of course he would. 'If you find minerals in quantity he won't send me back.'

'Nor me. You see the difficulty, don't you? You are safe, at least to live in Albania which apparently you don't mind too much, so long as I find something. I will probably be allowed to escape if I don't.'

'And Hoxha's health?'

He shrugged. 'I doubt if Kaderi minds the world knowing such diagnosis as we can make, he probably wants it for his own purposes in the Central Committee. Although I agree with him that the worst crises are those which occur without warning. It's only in Albania that such speculations might trigger a struggle for power before Kaderi is ready to take over.'

She wanted to stop and think, to break away from his voice and be alone, but his hand kept her at his side, their pace desultory; two acquaintances taking the air with their minds at ease. A cold wind was blowing from the east, mountains stark against clear blue, peaks sparkling with early snow. 'Can you fix your survey results how you want?'

'Yes, in fact I can't do anything else, although that is strictly between you and me. Twodex is a completely new development in mineral surveying and needs a computer to process its findings, my own London terminal for preference. I have all my Gulf material stored in its memory at the moment for precisely that reason. I can handle random checks manually, but it would take years to do a proper profile that way, and they haven't a single computer in Albania that I've seen. By guess and falsehood I could produce something which looked reasonable in several months' hard labour; an accurate plot would take a few days in London.'

'And Kaderi has no idea of this?'

He shook his head. 'That maggot Green told him I'd been doing test surveys around Haibuk, on contract to the company. Once Kaderi knew that there wasn't a chance he'd let me go, and Albania is such an intriguing blank on everyone's geological map I wasn't sorry to have a chance to fill it in. So I spun what tale I could, and waited until I had some idea of what Kaderi wanted, and why. I said I needed you because—'

'Because I'd told you they had some hold on me, and you thought it might prevent them from forgetting me in a cellar.'

'I wish to hell I hadn't now. This Audiotronic thing saved you instead, where the survey makes everything more complicated.'

'There's no point thinking of it,' she said philosophically, 'and Kaderi could still have used me if he'd wanted to. You would have known nothing of it, but I'd have been dead just the same. Never mind, perhaps Party Leader Hoxha will have a heart attack when we wire him to your circuits, and minerals be forgotten in a fever of Albanian politics.'

'He easily might, but I don't suppose Kaderi would let it throw him. He'd hush up Hoxha's death if he had to gain time to complete the survey. It's always a help if you're in a position to shoot or imprison as many nurses, undertakers and officials as you please. He could do it for quite a while, if he wanted to enough.'

Anne shivered. He could, and would if the need arose. Then, whatever they found, she and Stephen would know too much ever to leave Albania alive.

8

Hoxha looked a very sick man when he shuffled into the room four days later, scarcely recognizable from the virile portraits littering Tirana. He was in his mid-seventies and appeared ten years older, eyes sometimes sharp but often wandering, voice husky and skin hanging in loose folds. Political activist, guerrilla leader, founding spirit of his party and state, Enver Hoxha had been ground down to pith by strain, hard work and too much power.

Kaderi stood in the background, eyes darting, saying nothing. There were only two personal aides attending Hoxha besides bodyguards on the door, and Anne wondered whether anyone else in the government knew of this attempt to discover a term to their leader's life. She caught Kaderi's glance resting on her once and smiled involuntarily, to be disconcerted when a flicker of surprise was his only reaction. Could he really compartment sensation as well as mind so easily? Anne feared and disliked everything Millosh Kaderi stood for but for her the tug of pleasure still remained, and reluctant understanding also of some of the compulsions driving him.

Hoxha was a bad patient, wanting every process explained to him, constantly calling to one or other of his aides as he remembered things he must do, or failed to remember something he had already done. Anne grasped enough staccato Albanian to gather that there had been a derailment on the rail link to the copper mines, someone called Tomas was causing trouble and new packaging for talcum powder needed designing. A weird mixture to anyone unfamiliar with states where no detail was too insignificant for a leader's attention.

'For heaven's sake!' snapped Anne eventually, exasperated.

'Millosh, tell him he must be quiet or half the readings will be worthless. How can I take electric pulses from his brain when it's as busy as a coat full of fleas?'

Kaderi came over, mouth drawn into what might have been disapproval but possibly was amusement. 'Do you speak French?'

She nodded, mystified. 'A little.'

'Tell him yourself, then. You are the expert and will not suffer for your frankness, I promise.'

Hoxha enjoyed speaking French, she could tell. Far in the past he had lived in Paris and the language made him feel young again. He lay back obediently and closed his eyes, co-operated in the long series of tests even when his weariness became obvious. Stephen was checking and writing down readings, aides curtly ordered out by Kaderi although he remained himself, watching every detail.

'Well?' said Hoxha when it was over. 'Perhaps you know more than we do about packaging talcum powder?'

He had taken up the conversation exactly where he left it two hours before.

'No, I'm sure I don't,' said Anne blankly. Patients usually asked immediately for the results of their tests.

'Come, mademoiselle. You buy it in your Western shops, do you not? Well then, not a single Albanian has seen any, so you must know more than us.' He wagged his finger at her, pleased by dialectic success.

Anne admitted that under the circumstances, perhaps she did.

'Tell her to design something suitable then, eh Kaderi?' He sat up grunting, hands to his tie. He looked ill but completely serious. 'Send it to me direct when you're satisfied. I don't like anything I've been shown so far, and it's important to give pleasure with a luxury purchase. Don't you agree, mademoiselle?'

'I suppose so,' Anne was torn between amusement and astonishment.

He went out of the room and bodyguards closed about him.

'Well?' asked Kaderi quietly. 'What is your judgement?'

'On packaging talc?'

'That too, since you have been asked. On the Party Secretary's health first, however.'

Anne went over to the console and stared at Stephen's precise figures: the Bell-Simpson was also a scanner and produced sectional analysis of a patient's functions and so far as she could tell from those, the machine was functioning with reasonable accuracy. 'I need time to consider the results in detail. A specialist would normally interpret them, I'm only a technician.'

Kaderi came across the room and gripped her arms, forcing her to face him. 'Listen to me, Anna. Most doctors inflate their importance by delay and long words. I do not require either, but a simple verdict which you are well able to give from your experience. I watched you at work, how you looked, which tests you repeated, which ones you found disturbing. You have an expressive face.' He smiled faintly. 'To those with sufficient understanding to interpret what they see, of course.'

She flushed, his eyes grasping at her senses. She had been wrong before; he was unable to wall off sensation or understanding any easier than she, only to hide it better. 'If you can read me so easily, then perhaps you should also tell me what I learned of Comrade Hoxha.'

'Very well. You are going to tell me that he has not long to live.' He spoke with careful deliberation and released her, standing back. As if he wanted her to feel safe to say what she wished, since he had spoken of the Party leader's death first.

She nodded. 'I'll work through the results of course, but the brain reactions were disturbing, most heart readings in the danger zone. Co-ordination was below what one would expect even for a man of his age and muscular condition. No doctor nor machine manufactured by man can give exact dates but if I had to guess then I'd say he has between nine and eighteen months to live. He is tough, and of tough ancestry; it could be more. For most Westerners, I would say less.'

'Will he be able to rule effectively during that time?'

'You can't ask Anne to hazard such a judgement,' interrupted Stephen. He had been standing, hands in his pockets, frowning heavily while he listened.

Kaderi ignored him. 'Your opinion, Anna, please. I will not repeat it.'

'Comrade Hoxha is my patient,' said Anne unhappily. 'I should speak to him, not you.'

'And you think such knowledge would benefit him? You will be visiting him tomorrow and may answer his questions as truthfully as you wish. This is one he will not ask.'

'Nor could I venture more than a guess in answer.'

'A guess is all I require.'

'Or you will have it beaten out of me!' she flashed. 'What good would that do?'

'No good at all. Yes or no, Anna.'

'For God's sake!' said Stephen angrily. 'I'm no diagnostician but I can see missing circuits when they are pushed under my nose. Hoxha's scarcely generating enough power to keep his systems going, it'll take more and more effort to do so until one after another they start shorting out. Which goes first, I can't guess and nor could Anne. As an engineer I can tell you the end of the process though, his circuit-breaker will trip when there's no longer sufficient power to keep it in place. And that will be that. Of course he can't govern properly; if you had any rational system for handing over power he would be retired already. You haven't, so he isn't. Every communist state I've ever heard of has a leadership petrified by old age because you flatter yourselves that you've grown out of murder at the cabinet table, but still can't think of any other way to get rid of unwanted rulers.'

Anne wished she'd had the courage to say it first. 'In medical language it would be the same verdict.'

'Thank you, you confirm my own judgement. Which makes it my problem again.' Kaderi struck a match and set fire to a corner of paper. They watched figures shrivel and flames dull the aluminium console as he fed printouts into the blaze. 'So we will dispense with written analysis of such a matter, which by your own words is liable to error. I have faith in the first reactions of experts in their field. Which brings us to you, Mr Astell. When will you be ready to commence your survey?'

'Two or three weeks, providing you have calibrating equipment of sufficient quality, and reasonably good geological maps of Albania.'

'We do not have time for unnecessary detail.'

'I can be persistent too, and careful. Call it Cambridge training if you like. Two or three weeks.'

'Winter is coming. Mountain travel is very difficult then.'

Stephen shrugged. 'Then we'll have to wait until spring.'

'No,' said Kaderi softly. 'I don't intend to wait.' He went out of the room.

'One day he's going to stand by while his guards beat you into mush,' observed Anne dispassionately. 'Can't you see that he's used to nothing else? It's remarkable that he's able to deal with you on your own terms at all, when Sigurimi in a cellar is the only reaction he knows to opposition. Why must you provoke him so? And don't tell me again that you just felt like it, you've been long enough in Albania not to behave like a damned fool.'

'At least you've no illusions about your friend Millosh. Would you enjoy watching when his guards lay into me?'

She felt very tired suddenly, exhausted by pressures she had thought left behind long ago, by hatred and double-dealing. 'You're welcome to think so if you wish.'

He held her then, as he had once before in Gjirokaster. 'I'm sorry. I didn't think it, nor ever would. I provoke him because I hate the bastard. He can't touch me now and I'm no fighting man, but one day I'd like his throat under my hands and he knows it. It's a fine, uncivilized feeling to have when you're his prisoner, and one I don't intend to give up.'

She stared at his sensitive scholar's face, at the mocking gleam which told her that he was laughing at himself, at the absurdity of planning to destroy a chief of Sigurimi with hands trained for quite different arts; he was nursing his intent carefully though, and intended to carry it through if he could.

'You have decided to run for it?' she said at last.

He nodded. 'What alternative is there?'

She broke from his hold, and began wiping up ash with impatient, clumsy movements. Winter was coming in the mountains but they had no choice but to run when their chance came, however slender it might be. If they stayed, then one or other would certainly be in prison for the rest of their life, more probably executed as the pressures on Kaderi mounted.

'You told me you would be safe if you produced a negative report,' she said, keeping her voice low, although Stephen searched the room each day for bugs and Hoxha's visit surely was something Kaderi wouldn't want recorded.

'I have some natural instincts left even after four-fifths of the twentieth century have passed. I also value my ease of mind and would not want to lose it, thinking of you in an East German jail while I walked out free.' He glanced through the window at snow-capped mountains. 'Which is a pity when you think about it.'

'What if I don't want to go?'

'Because of Kaderi?'

'No,' she said evenly. 'Because here I might have a place.' Which wasn't strictly true; instinct told her that if she stayed then involvement with Millosh Kaderi was something she could not avoid.

'Then the issues would become even more complicated than they are already. You have a right to choose your own life – and death. For you must know it wouldn't last. You don't believe or behave as a good comrade should any longer, or hadn't you noticed? Kaderi knows, and in consequence has discovered how damned dull well-drilled comrades are. You're dangerous though. You could get him shot too, if he cared for you at all. Do you think he does?'

She found herself subjected to the exacting scrutiny he would use on a botched job, precise thinking being something he was used to pursuing through many blind alleys. 'I don't know,' she answered honestly.

His expression relaxed. 'Nor does he. Think about it carefully, and then hope that neither of you will ever be driven into the disaster of finding out. Now, I really think we should give some thought to packaging talcum powder, what do you say to stripes in the Albanian national colours?'

She laughed, and they both turned to the task of transferring equipment from the hospital to the University physical laboratory where Twodex was kept under guard. But to her surprise, the first thing Hoxha asked when she was shown

77

into his presence the following day, was about talc. He seemed disinclined to discuss his health, probably he was realistic enough to know most of what she could tell him; instead he worried about the many problems facing the nation which was uniquely his. He might last longer than she had thought, Anne reflected, so long as no one took power away from him. Idleness would kill him in weeks.

'You see Mademoiselle, the Albanian people have sacrificed so much for the future,' he explained. 'We thought the time had come to indulge natural cravings for a sign that reward is not impossibly remote. Some coloured pencils are to be made available for children to buy, a consignment of Italian tools for the men, and I wanted some personal indulgence for the women.' He put a finger to his nose and pulled down his lips, for an instant a benign old man accepting the follies of mankind. 'I lived in Paris and remember what women like. Powder, I said. Nothing useful just this once. But it must be well packaged so they feel they are buying luxury, don't you agree?'

'Yes,' said Anne, feeling enormously sorry for both Comrade Hoxha and the people of Albania. 'Yes, of course.'

'Come then, mademoiselle. What do you suggest?'

'Gold paper?'

'Too expensive. It must seem luxurious, but not bourgeois. Definitely not. This is a People's Republic, mademoiselle.'

'Mr Astell thought that perhaps Albania's national colours would be appropriate.' Anne could not resist the dig, and was unsurprised when Hoxha considered the idea seriously.

'Sound, quite sound, but I cannot be entirely happy about it,' he pronounced eventually. 'Some members of the People's Committee are outraged by the idea of putting luxuries on sale, and they might consider the national colours provocative under the circumstances.'

'Flowers,' said Anne desperately. 'National flowers of Albania printed on the box.'

He pursed his lips. 'It would need several different coloured inks to print. An attractive idea though, almost Parisian, but—' He paused, frowning, then his face cleared. 'I have the answer. You and Mr Astell shall both submit designs, as our own artists are doing, for the People's Committee to consider and make recommendations. Then I will decide.'

Anne left the villa feeling dazed, ceremonial guard clicking heels behind her. Hoxha was not remotely senile this morning, simply preoccupied with one particular problem: it could just as easily have been the supply of goat cheese or a matter of peace and war. When a leader dealt with everything in a country, relative importance became a matter of opinion. The leader's opinion. After all, the powder was to be a reward for an eternity of deprivation, so who could maintain that the design of box was a triviality?

She laughed aloud as she walked through the sparse streets of Tirana with a guard at her heels; the drab uniforms, bicycles and white-fezzed men around her seemed almost familiar. What on earth would Stephen say when she told him to leave his work on Twodex and turn his mind to the design of talc packaging?

9

The truck wound slowly through a barren landscape. Rocky slopes trembled in late autumn heat while shaded grass remained furred with damp, the sky a thin, translucent blue, more reminiscent of northern frosts than Mediterranean sun.

Anne and Stephen sat uncomfortably wedged either side of Twodex's canvas-wrapped bulk in the back of the truck, facing four glum soldiers. It was difficult to think of anything but vertigo as serpent-twists of road coiled ever more steeply behind them. A hidden valley came into view, dappled with vines and figs, then they climbed again, road roughening all the time, the smell of hot metal alarming.

'Do you suppose we're going to use this same truck up and down every hill in Albania?' asked Anne.

'I expect so,' replied Stephen lazily. His legs were awkwardly cramped when four small Albanians sat quite comfortably opposite. 'A good few of my survey traverses can only be done on foot though, they'll be able to repair it while they wait.'

Anne studied Twodex with misgiving. 'It looks heavy for carrying up mountains.'

'It is. It's designed to be portable though, and so long as they're trailing along, our guards might as well do the work.'

Something in his voice made her look at him sharply. He was staring out of the truck at rock and burned-yellow grass; she knew that one day he intended to slip the guard set on them, now she realized that he meant to take Twodex with him when he went. The results of such a survey would be hot information in the West.

He had worked for three weeks on Twodex in Tirana, refus-

80

ing all but the most elementary help, now they were on their way to start his survey.

Apart from the journey along the coast from Gjirokaster, this was the first time they had been out of Tirana and the prospect was not encouraging. The few villages were sparsely poor, full of watchdogs shaking chains and not much else. They would starve if they attempted to escape here, stand out instantly as strangers under the most casual of scrutinies.

'We'll never do it,' said Anne aloud. 'Not here, anyway.'

Stephen's eyes flickered but he chose to misunderstand her, although their escort looked blank-minded. 'There's a great deal of preliminary work in a survey like this, but we'll manage it, don't worry. Kaderi tells me this is the wildest part of Albania, so we must hurry to finish before the snows; the central area has copper and chrome mines with galleries near the surface. We can use those for surveying in bad weather, and in many ways it's the most hopeful area.'

'You're not only doing this because you must, are you?'

'Information is my business,' he replied cryptically, and would not be drawn further.

He had already told her that he had been researching into mineral survey methods when a change of government policy abruptly withdrew funds from his project. All his findings were classified as secret, but his laboratory was closed and surplus equipment sold, his own contract terminated. He had not said how he managed it, but within a few months he had bought at knock-down prices all he needed to reassemble Twodex and finish the testing programme at his own financial risk. Anne gained the impression that he found duplicity and profit pleasant after several years of squabbling over Whitehall red tape. Easy too, since he possessed the kind of brain which functioned best under pressure and was not a civil servant by temperament or training.

He had originally been an electronics man and worked his first assignment in mines safety systems; since then he had become interested in the whole field of minerals and their extraction. The research appointment had simply been a means to an end and once Twodex was developed he had never intended to stay in an atmosphere he disliked.

Kaderi met them when they climbed down from their truck in the evening, which was a disagreeable surprise. If he proposed to supervise every stage of their survey personally, then vigilance would be maintained no matter how far they went into the mountains.

They found themselves in a tumbledown village where the wind beat off black peaks all around, the sun a ball of blood in a cold glass sky. 'I have arranged quarters in the police post for you,' said Kaderi, snapping his fingers at the soldiers as an order to pick up Twodex. 'The tavern will be overfull of soldiers and fleas.'

'You're a long way off your beat, or do you frequently need to check on your hired help in the mountains?' Stephen's dislike showed instantly.

'Not often. I find the threat to come myself is usually sufficient. There are a few things not completely understood between us however, and the night before you begin work seemed the best time to remove any confusion from your mind.' His voice was cool but menace unmistakeable.

Thitji police post was small and coldly stuffy, Albanian cigarette smoke lying like sea-mist in the corners of its single room. Kaderi turned out any police who seemed idle and set the rest scurrying for food. He wore a peasant-style shirt and goatskin jacket, but the edge in him was as sharp as ever: remote mountains provided no illusion that he was less dangerous than before.

The food was plentiful but unpalatable. Sardines, cubed peppers and apples, chalk-white goat's cheese and maize bread full of grit. A bowl of meat floating in yellow grease.

Anne felt sufficiently queasy after the journey to find eating an effort and conversation lagged uneasily, Stephen monosyllabic, Kaderi impassively watching them both.

Eventually he leaned forward and put his elbows on the table. 'Well, Mr Astell, we have business to transact.'

'I thought it long since transacted and my options closed.'

'We made an agreement, yes. Now I wish to be informed on precise details. I have placed teams with markers on the summits you indicated, sent others ahead of your track. What is your procedure to be, exactly what results can you and your equipment guarantee?'

Stephen flicked desultorily at pepper-pips on the plank top, then arranged four in a line. 'I intend to use the same method as the Romans when they engineered their roads across wilderness: smoke on a couple of peaks you can fix, keep them in line and you have your traverse approximately where you want it. Eventually we shall have a series of dashes between known dots, not a continuous survey, which would take too long. When I unscramble the results, they should show us where to look more carefully next time around.'

'Next time?'

'Twodex is a quick way of discovering where to look more closely, where not to waste your time. Anything which shows promise will have to be redone, in more detail and under good conditions. If the results are still positive, then there's no substitute for old-fashioned core-drilling before you invest large sums in extraction. Ten, twelve thousand feet of four-inch core; a job which only a handful of men in the world have sufficient skill to carry out successfully.'

Kaderi looked taken aback. 'You told me you could survey for likely minerals within weeks.'

'So I can, that's the measure of Twodex's worth. Without it, you make an informed guess and drill cores one at a time with only hunch and experience to suggest what you will find. It was different when extraction meant five hundred foot shafts or opencast terraces, then any moderately intelligent geologist could bet on a likely result. But nowadays you can mine economically at a depth of fifteen thousand feet, which means a crippling loss if you get it wrong. Twodex can give information which will save years of work and millions of pounds of investment; it isn't a substitute for the preliminaries of extraction itself.'

'How does it work?' asked Anne curiously. He would be using it in front of Albania's security services tomorrow, so a basic explanation would not hurt.

His eyes flickered to her and then back to the pips again. He was not precisely unfriendly, but wary as he had been each time he studied her and Kaderi together. 'On sound of such high frequency it is virtually without waves, as laser light is.

83

It's probably easiest to think of it as a sound laser in fact, although you need special listening gear to hear anything except a thud when it fires. Lacking waves such sound can travel thousands of feet into rock: laser light triggers equipment in space on the same principle. In space it is the initial energy to generate the laser which is important, the material it penetrates is nearly constant, so flow remains negligible. With the earth's crust matters are somewhat different, each strata and compacting of it varies the flow of sound, so you can build up a profile reading at depths where drilling is prohibitively expensive, especially if the result is negative. The theory is known; where Twodex makes a new departure is in relative ease of handling. Microchips and a good few other developments make it possible to back-pack its recording gear and store sufficient energy for five shots at a time. Before, you would have had to manhandle half the Cavendish laboratory up every hillside to achieve what we hope to do tomorrow.'

'Five shots,' repeated Kaderi. 'You mean that after five – what do you say, profiles? – into rock, your machine has to go back to Tirana?'

'To a powerful generator, yes. I've improvised the other equipment I need. Don't be such a bloody ungrateful bastard. In a single day we shall store information which would take a year to gain by conventional means; a day to shift camp and perhaps two more to reset Twodex depending on your generating capacity, then the same again. When we reach the central mining area where I can work under cover and with plenty of power on call, matters should be even quicker.'

Kaderi thought about it, staring at Stephen, the planes of his face like hammered bronze. Then he turned his head and looked at Anne. 'It seems to me that you have been dishonest with me on several occasions, each explanation I receive being slightly different from the last. I do not now see the need for Anna to accompany you in the field. She is better employed adapting the hospital computer to your needs, so it is ready when you need it.'

Anne tried not to let her dismay show. She was quite incapable of tampering with computers.

Stephen shrugged. 'The explanation I have given you now

is a gross over-simplification. Twodex also requires two people to operate it correctly.'

'Very well. I will draft a skilled engineer to assist you.'

'No. I am doing this because I now know too much of such matters as Party Leader Hoxha's health: you would shoot me if I refused. But you can't force me to do it in any way except my own, since once I have agreed to carry it through you need me both mentally and physically fit. Afterwards too, my knowledge is of the kind which Albania needs desperately if you decide on deep mining. So Anne stays here.'

'Why?' asked Kaderi mildly. 'I am sure she is able to do whatever you require, but so could others similarly trained who would be more used to harsh conditions in our mountains.'

'Because that's the way I want it, unless and until she desires to return to Tirana of her own free will.'

'Why?' Kaderi asked again.

Stephen smiled, eyes cold. 'Because you are also an untrustworthy bastard. You could fill me with tales of how splendidly Anne was doing while I finished your survey, and ransom her back to me calculation by calculation when I had finished.'

'You could still falsify your figures.'

'So I could, but I just might not think too clearly under the circumstances, and falsifying calculations on a third-rate adapted computer is the kind of thing you need all your wits to hide. It would also take the hell of a time, and if you drafted in most of the mathematicians in Albania eventually they could trace out what I'd done. Like this, the day anything happens to her I reverse the charge and blow Twodex apart, stored results and all, and the devil take your mathematicians afterwards.'

Anne listened, heart slamming; these two were inextricably tangled by events but what each really wanted was to kill the other. Stephen had never dealt with a man like Kaderi before and detested the stereotype brute which was all he saw; Kaderi used men as he chose and brutality was the only reaction he knew to defiance. Yet both must set aside instinct, manoeuvre for advantage, do what they were forced to do so long as compulsion lasted.

And she was part of it all. Torn in understanding, straddling both their worlds, knowing also that the edge which lay between these two was lethally honed because of her.

'Tell me, Mr Astell,' said Kaderi slowly. 'Would you agree that you have been well treated since you crashed?'

'Apart from the major matter of my freedom, yes.'

Kaderi looked at Anne reproachfully. 'You did not tell him, Shoqë. I thought perhaps that you had not.'

'Told me what?' asked Stephen sharply.

'I found it necessary to place Shoqë Anna two days in a dark cellar with her hands restrained and no food. She deserved it because she held our People's state lightly, the results also were entirely good since all her illusions were stripped away in this one short time. I am surprised she did not tell you.'

Anne flushed; she had not told Stephen because her relationship with Kaderi was something she did not want to probe. 'It wouldn't have done any good if I had.'

'On the contrary, Shoqë, you might have saved us a great deal of trouble. Mr Astell apparently possesses even more dangerous illusions than you, which would have been dispelled by accurate information. He is used to handling facts, I understand. Now he must learn from his own experience.' His voice was even but for the first time the effort needed to control his temper showed. Anne was reminded of the other passion she had discovered in him, also held in by will, but in the end he had surrendered to it and not dared touch her since. One day Kaderi might forget the constraints of policy and kill Stephen simply because he wanted to; she did not wonder yet whether he might also forget the dedication of a lifetime and love for the same reason. 'Take off your coat and shirt, Mr Astell,' he added now, enjoyment no longer masked.

Stephen neither moved nor looked at Anne, but he had the withdrawn expression she had seen when he was absorbed in calculation, and she knew he was considering the reasons why she had kept silent over her imprisonment.

Kaderi said something rapid in Albanian to a policeman on guard in the doorway. The man called another and came to stand behind Stephen.

'Take off your coat and shirt,' repeated Kaderi, 'or he will do it for you and tie you outside naked for the night.'

Stephen hesitated, then stood and took them off. He topped his guards by several inches but looked slight beside their bulk. He was in hard condition though, about forty Anne supposed, and Kaderi a few years older although it was hard to tell when his face was so ageless. The soldiers and Sigurimi were squat mountaineers mostly just out of their boyhood; obedient, tough and primitive.

Kaderi put a round black box on the table; it measured about four inches across. 'Do you know what this is?'

Stephen glanced at it. 'No.'

'Albania is not offered much by the outside world, but this is a miniature transmitter and a gift from the International Wildlife Research Foundation. We have a breed of wolf in our mountains which is nearly extinct and they want us to monitor its breeding activity.'

Anne stared at him, brain racing, feeling her body shiver. God knew what he intended now. Stephen looked defenceless and already cold, facing Kaderi in the squalid room with a policeman at his back, a sharp line of sunburn separating neck from white skin below as if he was decapitated.

'And your Central Committee did not fancy carrying monitoring devices in their pockets, or is their species of predator unhappily not extinct enough to monitor?' He spoke flippantly though, hands relaxed on bare table boards.

'It is unwise to bait those on whom your life depends, Mr Astell.'

'Even more unwise not to, surely. Unless one wants to co-operate in creating a world run by Sigurimi and their like.'

Kaderi's hand closed on the box, knuckles white. Gone was the beautiful, emotionless mask he had held in place easily before. 'This is designed to be harnessed to anything from bear to mountain goat and transmits a signal every few minutes, so their wanderings may be charted. It is virtually indestructible but we have added an outer case to be sure. I propose to attach it to you, Mr Astell, for you are an untrustworthy bastard too who would like to steal information we cannot afford to share. Since I also give you credit for being a clever bastard I don't doubt you could destroy it, given time

87

and tools. I intend to deny you both, and so long as you carry it then regular signals will make escape impossible.'

'No wonder Albania receives few gifts, when misuse can be taken for granted,' commented Stephen acidly.

Anne stared at the box, it was quite bulky and had four metal rings welded to the edge. 'How . . . what are you going to do?'

'Chain it to him tight enough to keep his hands off it.' Kaderi nodded to the man waiting at Stephen's back. 'Go with Nako, Mr Astell, he has a blacksmith outside. I advise you not to give him any trouble, since he will be your personal guard these next few weeks and knows only one way of enforcing obedience. There are a dozen other policemen in this post, not to mention myself.' He added something to Nako in Albanian and the man grinned, lips drawn back from uneven teeth. He wasn't a boy like the rest, seamed face thrust out between thick shoulders like a gargoyle's head from stone.

'It wouldn't take all those people to hold me down,' observed Stephen mildly. 'I am sure an attentive fellow like Nako could manage very well on his own.'

. Kaderi was silent a long time after he had left, regarding the backs of his hands pensively. Anne watched him, mind shuffling through a wreckage of shredded hopes and growing menace. Only now that Kaderi had removed all possibility of escape was her own mind functioning clearly again. Once choice vanished, a future for ever in Albania became insupportable, particularly when she had learned th se past ten years how different life could be. Yet, in spite of everything, she had only to look at Millosh to recall how the alloy of their bodies had flowed together, feel the touch of his hands and his lips on hers.

'Escape in these mountains is difficult at this time of year and I do not think he would try without his Twodex – and you,' Kaderi broke his silence. 'Even so, I have respect for his intelligence and he could cause a great deal of trouble if he attempted it. But harnessed to a . . . a bleeper, is that right? . . . it is impossible.'

Anne thought so too. 'What if he simply refuses to work?'

'He can't, I would have him shot if he did. Equally, I cannot damage him so badly that he is incapable of doing what I want, nor rouse such antagonism that his will is tougher than before. I need to master him in many smaller ways until defiance becomes unthinkable, and I will do it, never fear. I made a serious mistake in misjudging his attitude to you.' His tone was clinical, but he was watching her now and smiling. The physical pleasure they had gained together strengthened him and weakened the Englishman; she might have been Astell's ally and instead her senses were in pawn to him, Astell already isolated. Kaderi moved to sit beside her, feeling well content with her and with himself. He wished that was all he felt.

Nearly half an hour went by before Nako brought Stephen back. He was still stripped to the waist and shuddering with cold: a blast of wind accompanied them into the room.

'It is done, Shok Kaderi,' said Nako.

The casing was fixed to Stephen's chest by steel links anchored to rings on the box, crossing above his spine and fastened to a metal belt both front and back.

Kaderi went over and ran his hands carefully over links and joints, while Stephen stood looking resigned. Kaderi nodded, satisfied. 'Tell the smith I am pleased with his work. You are fortunate to find such a craftsman in our mountains, Mr Astell. Many would have bruised you severely before they had it tight enough.'

'I certainly mustn't put on any weight while I'm wearing it.' Stephen went over to his shirt. He would not look at Anne; for all his show of indifference, she thought he disliked intensely the humiliating position he was in.

Kaderi nodded to Nako and he moved with surprising speed for such a bulky man, seizing Stephen by the crossed links at his back and shoving roughly so he fell.

'I have not finished with you,' Kaderi spoke without any tone of brutality, as if their eyes were deceived in what they saw. 'I do not see how you can interfere with that box when the seal is so tight against you, but you'll have no chance to try. At night you sleep as you are, without shirt or covering, so your guards may see everything you do. Nako has orders to make sure you do not freeze.'

Anne started to her feet. 'You can't! He won't last a week in these mountain huts, where it's so cold at night he'll never be able to rest! For God's sake, it's not much above freezing in here now.'

'I respect Mr Astell's stamina more than you do. If he prefers it, I will strip you instead and fasten this box's fellow between your breasts while Nako watches.' He smiled, quite pleasantly. 'Scarcely a threat, is it? Since he dare not call my bluff, knowing I would do it if he forced me and the fault be his.'

He turned and went out.

10

Anne was unprepared for the sheer exertion of surveying in mountainous country without even goat-tracks to ease their way. If they did discover a precipitous path or rope-hung bridge, then it was rarely along the line they must take, and Stephen was uncompromising over the matter of base-lines and triangulations. At least the weather remained favourable although it was the end of November: clear and crisp by day, clear and cold at night, the distant rim of snow creeping inexorably down the high peaks towards them.

Twodex was only just portable. Relays of soldiers sweated under its weight and that of Stephen's listening gear, routine the same day after day. A long morning scramble to some point only Stephen was certain of and for which he would accept no substitute, while everyone else slid and swore behind him over a concertina of tumbled hills. Sometimes Anne stopped with breath burning in her lungs and looked out over them, feeling the same kind of exhaustion as a swimmer after too long battling in choppy sea. By nightfall she was scarcely capable of swallowing ill-prepared, indigestible food before falling asleep with her head on an unscrubbed table top. She felt ashamed when she woke, knowing that Stephen could not rest so easily, but was too tired to stop herself. Nako kept them the width of a room apart at night and stripped Stephen of everything but trousers the moment he had eaten, carrying out his orders to keep the room temperature above freezing but no more: apparently he felt the contemptuous dislike of a tough peasant for a man he considered an over-civilized weakling and took pleasure in petty tyranny. When Stephen was sufficiently tired or acclimatized to sleep, Nako often woke him to test fastenings and belt although he could see they were intact; if the cold was sufficient to set Stephen pacing until he reeled with weariness then Nako would go outside half a dozen times to urinate and insist his prisoner came with him into icy darkness.

Only Kaderi possessed authority to change Stephen's handling and Anne tried everything she knew to send him word of what was happening, since she could not believe he had intended this. But no one would consider forwarding a private message to the Chief of Security, even if they had not been completely indifferent to the whole matter, perhaps came to enjoy the baiting as it gathered momentum. Nor could she fathom Stephen's attitude and often had to fight against exasperation. He accepted without protest whatever interpretation Nako placed on his orders, which served to increase his contempt, and seldom spoke except to give orders over the survey. Then he was as precise and exacting as if he was not acting under duress at all, nor being deliberately debilitated to the point where any independent judgement would become impossible. So far as Anne could see he made no attempt to tamper with the casing on his chest although the chafing discomfort of it eased as he lost weight he could ill afford.

Any attempt she made to help him simply aroused Nako into inflicting further humiliations on Stephen: Anne suspected that Kaderi had given orders for her to be treated with care and felt more wretched in consequence. Especially when Stephen accepted her passive complicity in his regime, the lever she represented against his will. He did nothing which might place her at risk, yet never seemed to consider that the same constraints prevented her from offering more than the smile or touch which would have shown her sympathy if he had noticed them. Instead, when the panting confusion which afflicted their daily expeditions allowed her to approach him, he turned aside solicitude with some comment which came close to suggesting that she was Kaderi's hireling. She saw how weariness bleached his face and forgave him every time, but eventually hurt kept her away and their days passed in the same silence as the nights.

Anne usually operated the firing sequence on Twodex while

Stephen stood some fifty yards away listening through earphones to ultrasonic echoes; when he was satisfied they moved on and the whole weary business began again.

Then, in the second week of December, the weather changed. They had spent two days in a valley of the upper Drin, where a two hundred foot waterfall leaped over rock to block the end of their traverse. There was no bridge over the river nor way up the rock face, which meant a long diversion if Stephen held to his line. They watched anxiously as he used his theodolite like a telescope to scan the far side of the valley, seemingly unaware of collective longing from twenty or so people that he would be satisfied with the results he had. Anyone would think that he wanted Albania to be the richest country on earth, thought Anne resentfully. Twodex had been playing up too; after four weeks without serious hitch, that day only two shots had fired correctly and then Stephen had been dissatisfied with his readings.

'We'll have to go back,' he said now, continuing to study cataract and rock through borrowed binoculars. 'Down to the main valley until we reach a bridge and then up the other side. I'll work on Twodex tomorrow and we'll return the following day if I can fix it.' Like Anne, he spoke adequate, ungrammatical Albanian by now.

'What if your machine isn't repaired, Shok Astell?' The captain of their escort took no part in Nako's activities and treated Stephen with such consideration as he could, but he wasn't Sigurimi and was powerless against their orders.

'Then I'll have to go down to the laboratory in Tirana. I'll tell you tomorrow and you can contact Kaderi for permission.'

'Shok Kaderi,' said the captain automatically. 'I think delay may be forced on us. I do not like the turn in the weather.'

Wind had been gusting into their faces as they climbed, the sky glazing, peaks hiding clouds which now boiled into view. Before they were half way back to where they had left their trucks snow was falling, the ground treacherous underfoot. Soldiers cursed and fell, unbalanced by the heavy equipment they were carrying, while Stephen called for extra care with Twodex.

The valley funelled wind; Anne felt her teeth chattering as

their pace slowed, the snow wetter as they lost altitude. She tripped into a narrow gulley, slush soaking inadequately proofed clothes, only to be hauled to her feet and sheltered from ice-grained wind as Stephen held her.

'Bear up,' he said, and kissed her. 'Another couple of hours and we'll be down.'

She clung to him thankfully, although his clothes were soaking too, his face rimed with sleet. 'I thought you'd written me off as Kaderi's stooge for ever.'

'No. Listen, we've only a couple of minutes. When they cased this damned bleeper to me I'm fairly sure they put in a microphone as well: one of our escort is carrying a recorder so I expect some pipsqueak Sigurimi sits up at night listening to what's been said the day before. But with this storm and masked in a gully, they won't pick up much until they realize they've lost us and come back.' He tightened his arms still more, so she could feel hard-angled casing through his clothes. 'Just to be certain, I'm making sure you help to muffle it some more.'

She kissed him impulsively. 'So that was why you—'

'Why I've been so damned disagreeable, yes. Not to say I didn't feel it anyway. I think I've seen a way we might escape through this way but not in weather like this. We need to leave this valley as a gap in our survey and come back later. March, I suppose to be safe. It's a great deal of time to gain when I can't do Kaderi's calculations for him in worthwhile detail, so you must help keep things slow when we go into the mines or further south. Use any excuse, providing it doesn't arouse suspicion, as I have by putting Twodex on the blink today. Remember though, Kaderi is a very suspicious man. Clever, too. Keep as fit as you can, when we go we'll need to climb both fast and far.'

'What about you? They'll have worn you down long before March.' Her face was only inches from his, and she scanned it anxiously.

'Don't you believe it. They'll have me so well broken in to cold I'd be able to climb Everest naked. Their third-rate alps will be nothing to me then.'

She laughed shakily, the sound so completely unfamiliar it shocked her.

'Come, my dear,' he added. 'They'll be looking for us. Don't change from how we've been together these recent weeks, we've a long time to survive yet and our chance won't be easy when it comes.' He released her and led the way out of the gully, back into the full force of the wind.

They were chilled deep into heart and lungs by the time they regained their trucks, too cold even to think of danger on a skidding journey to the village below. By contrast, the police post where they were camped seemed wonderfully warm, though the stove in fact was quite inadequate. Anne had not spoken to Stephen again, but with new perception saw how he hung back at the entry when everyone else crowded round the stove, recognized dread of being stripped again, when before she had noticed only indifference.

Nako turned, grinning. 'Stay over there, and let's have a look at that box of yours.'

'He must dry off,' said the captain anxiously. 'He'll die if you force him to sleep like that.'

'Then he's best without his clothes as usual, and I'll see to that, eh Shok Astell?' He roared with laughter.

As the storm continued to blow it became rawly cold in the little room. Anne slept a little but this time awareness nagged at her through exhaustion. As the soldiers took it in turn to stoke the stove and huddled round it in reeking goatskin jackets, she sat feeling cold strike into her bones and watched Stephen across the room by the draughts of the door. He fiddled for a while with Twodex, presumably in an attempt to keep his mind occupied, but his fingers were too clumsy and soon he began walking. Arms folded, hands under his armpits, crude light of unshaded bulb on blue-white skin, feet dragging with tiredness. He might think he could beat cold by determination alone, but Anne doubted it; he was not a particularly strong man and looked much less fit now than when they had started. As Kaderi surely had intended. Anne faced it squarely now, and blamed him and not his underlings. Kaderi was expert in men's endurance and had calculated that the gain in breaking Stephen justified the risk that he might collapse or catch pneumonia before his survey was complete.

Half-fainting, he slept eventually and Anne went over to the captain. Whatever warnings Stephen had given her, this she could not bear to watch another day.

'Shok Captain, you must stop Nako. Tell Kaderi his prisoner will not live stripped each night in the kind of weather we are encountering now.'

The Captain stared at Stephen uneasily. 'I know, Shoqë, but—'

'But you are afraid to interfere, of the trouble Nako will make for you if you do.' His jacket was open and steaming as he sat in the place of privilege by the stove, and she slid her hand under it, began fumbling with buttons, her head at his shoulder. 'I swear that unless you do, I will choose my moment and make it seem as if you are pestering me. Nako will enjoy reporting that to Kaderi.'

He jerked free in alarm. 'You would not!' Every man in the escort had drawn his own conclusions about Anne's relationship to their Chief of Security.

'Why shouldn't I? It wouldn't be me who was the loser, and I intend to stay in this hut and refuse to go on another survey until Kaderi comes himself to see what is happening.'

'I can force you, Shoqë, you know that. And if I don't, then Nako will.'

'I don't think so; there isn't much you dare do to me without informing Kaderi, which is what I want. As for Mr Astell—' She glanced across at him, half-roused and shuddering again. 'It won't take much more to kill him, and that you cannot risk.'

It took three more freezing days before the captain's fear of losing his prisoner's life overcame his terror of lifting a telephone and asking to speak to the Chief of Security. He kept Anne on a bench away from the stove and on the other side of the ill-fitting door from Stephen, without food or water, in an attempt to alter her resolve. And all the time Nako nagged at him to allow tougher methods until he was almost distracted by the responsibility of it all.

In the end, he dared not wait any longer.

The snow had cleared although it remained bitterly cold. They ought to be on the survey again but Nako refused to allow Stephen so much as a shirt while they remained inside, roused him constantly if he dozed, and while Anne remained unfed Stephen refused to eat or work on Twodex, which ultimately panicked the captain when he realized that soon Stephen would be incapable of any physical exertion at all.

'I have spoken to Shok Kaderi's office,' he said, sweating with the fear of his own words. 'They will see that he receives my message. You must eat now.'

Anne shook her head. Her mouth felt strangely toughened, her spine as brittle as glass from long sitting on unyielding bench. '*Pastaj*. Afterwards. When Kaderi comes.'

'He may not come,' said the captain wretchedly. Whatever happened, he was in trouble.

'That's your business,' said Anne, and put her head in her hands, swooping dizzily down a slope of almost-nothing. She wondered how Stephen felt, who had been weaker than she when this last ordeal began, and whether he thought she was using this way to gain time; if that had been all then she did not think she would have had the resolution to persevere.

She must have lost consciousness for she was next aware of heavy jolting and balance queasily lost. She opened her eyes and stared at olive-flapping canvas before realizing she was in a truck descending so many hairpin bends that they could only be going down to the plain. She sat up dazedly, thinking of Stephen left behind to Nako's mercilessness and then relaxed; eyes closed in a skull-like face he was sleeping heavily on the steel floor beside her.

She slept too when the road improved, and woke ravenously hungry. She was in a small room, bare except for the bed she lay in, but gloriously warm while a blizzard swirled against the window. Only Kaderi could have authorized so great a transformation.

All the same, where was she? They must still be high for it to snow so heavily, and the room was bleak enough to be a cell. A woman who brought food pretended not to understand when Anne questioned her, and locked the door when she went out. She wore nondescript clothes and certainly wasn't a nurse; yes, a cell, thought Anne, alarmed. The room lacked a light-switch too, although there was a light, and she lay in the dark worrying.

She must have dozed again, for the next thing she knew was light cutting at her and she sat up in alarm, hands shielding her eyes.

'*Si o ndjeni veten?* How are you?' Said Millosh Kaderi. 'I hope you have your packaging for talcum powder ready to show Party Secretary Hoxha. He was concerned to hear you were unwell, and endorsed my decision to come here personally.'

11

'One cannot be too careful,' explained Kaderi blandly, sitting on the edge of her bed. 'We are not used to foreigners in our country and I would be suspect if I was observed dealing privately with two of them. The Party Leader's interest is invaluable.'

Anne pulled bedclothes up to her chin. Kaderi had turned on the light from some switch outside and was so disturbingly at ease that recollection of the night she had spent with him instantly returned. Yesterday she had hated what he was; faced with his presence she felt her body soften and blood pulse in her face.

'That's much better,' he said. 'You looked too pale before.'

'If I was, then it was through your orders,' she snapped. Whatever happened she must show neither fear nor the betraying pull of longing, though he could rouse both simply by being there.

'Certainly not. I ordered every care to be taken of you. Whatever happened was due to your obstinacy.'

'Or Stephen's?' she asked shrewdly. 'What did you expect? That he would grovel instead of lasting to the point where your orders risked the ruin of your project? I worked it out in the end, only I still can't see the point of it all. Nako would have enjoyed to have Stephen plead with him, call me stupid if you wish but I should be surprised if you found much pleasure in it.'

The beautiful, uncompromising face stared back at her. 'Thank you. You are quite right, as it happens. But I am alarmed to find out how I misjudged Mr Astell again. A scholar bred in England's softness should not have lasted as he did.'

Anne thought of the unscrupulous skill with which Stephen must have double-crossed Whitehall, and what little he had told her of a fairly tough life in mining: Kaderi had been unlucky in the scholar he caught. 'He did though, so what now?' She needed to understand Kaderi's purposes and he was more relaxed at this moment than she had ever seen him.

'Now I must change my methods, nothing else. You and Mr Astell know that in this one matter you have beaten me, Nako and his like must never guess.'

'Or the foundations of your state will crack, once Albanians discover that Sigurimi can be beaten?'

'No, Anna,' he said gently. 'Albanians will suffer unnecessarily when they discover afresh that the Sigurimi cannot be beaten. I do not often need to be harsh, because I am feared. When fear goes, harshness returns. You and Mr Astell are in a privileged position since I require your services, but you do Albania a disservice if you encourage others to believe that I have lost my will to be cruel when it is necessary.' He folded down bedclothes and opened the loose cloth of her state-owned nightdress, leaning to kiss the breasts he held.

Instantly, sensation leaped to his touch though she lay still, willing herself out of response. She remembered bitterly how when Stephen kissed her she had felt only relief at being sheltered from the snow; reason and perhaps even liking has little place in the alchemy one being may or may not impart to another.

Kaderi lifted his head, unsmiling, hands caressing as if against his will; perhaps he could control sensation no easier than she. 'You are bad for me, Anna. A lifetime of serving the state as best I can, of believing that foreigners would poison everything we hold dear, and now I find it hard to avoid risking the one for the other. You could get me shot, did you know?'

'Stephen said so once.' She had to make herself say it and disconcert him, keep longing somehow at bay.

His hands tightened abruptly, making her gasp, pleasure and fear merged so stillness was no longer possible. 'Astell. Again. So long as he remains master of himself, he's clever enough to outwit me. Well, we'll see. I've not finished with

12

nne discovered that they were staying at a military hostel in ulqize, and when she walked through the little mining town he could see spoil heaps which she was told came from hrome mining. This must be where they would be working ext; copper was extracted not far away and further south on, zinc and nickel, with heaven knew what other riches waiting to be found in the mountains all around. Anne knew hat Stephen considered it the most promising area for future discoveries.

He had been ill a week and slow to recover afterwards: Anne suspected that he was not so unwell as he appeared, but Nako's regime had left him so skeletally thin that Kaderi accepted the necessity of waiting. Perhaps for once was happy to accept it, and a further week afterwards while Stephen tinkered with Twodex, for during that time he came three times more to Anne's room under pretext of interrogation, the bitter flavour of danger intrusive now. In Albania of all places, where outsiders were almost unknown, a security chief who lept with one would be regarded as a betrayer of the state.

'You mustn't come again,' Anne said, caressing him. 'You atch everyone else, someone will be watching you.'

'Yes, of course. Me above all. I never gave it a thought efore but find it amusing now. Strange how love brings ughter in its baggage.'

'You mustn't,' she said, alarmed. 'A sense of humour is mething you certainly can't afford.'

'I can afford so little, and will be left bankrupt by the end.' e felt him laugh. 'There you are again. Words of capitalism ould never have used before I met you. Things are not so

him yet.' He moved and held her throat a mome
blood pounded and darkness gathered behi
Perhaps he intended to convince her that he co
life taken if it became necessary. More likely he
convince himself, and if so, he failed. For the st
they both had felt consumed them then; the gulf v
have set their lives apart utterly without significa

He slept in her arms afterwards, wrapped in t
peace she thought he had not known since child
watched him, and his face was no longer a mask she
read; perfection of bone remained but he had the loo
who lived again after long petrification. She did no
had cause to be grateful for what she had done to hi
position a man was better turned to rock.

He moved quite soon; time insistent for them b
kenaqesi madhe. My sweet love. In you I have found
my life lacked before.' He had not opened his eyes,
hated to face the world which waited for them both.

She held him speechlessly, they had so little ti
crowding in such fragments of grace and passion as w
for them. He took her again, this time with a delight
played on pleasure and disregarded scampering minute
left her with the same tenderness she remembered in
before and had forgotten when she faced the reality
power in freezing mountain huts.

When he had gone, she lay and thought of him. She
to feel ashamed. Not because she was unable to avoid re
ing to a man who loved her, but because she had felt
Kaderi, head of security, a man who inspired such
seldom needed to be brutal. Who must nevertheles
past filled with brutality to make him so greatl
although her mind refused the images of her thoug

She did not know whether she loved him, whet
possible to love such a man as he, instead she lay rer
how he had slept with his head on her breast and
name one of the many emotions she felt for him.

Pity.

He would not thank her for it.

simple as they were.'

'If it was possible . . . if there was a way . . . would you leave Albania with me?' She owed it to Stephen not to suggest that he might have found a way, and with Kaderi's conniving escape would be easy anyway.

'No. Never. You knew that though, didn't you?'

She kissed him, lips telling her that he was smiling. 'I was afraid I knew.'

'I believe in what we are building here. Without it I should lose myself, although you may think at the moment that you would prefer me quit of it. My family was slaughtered and I had killed my first German by nine years old, I've killed when I had to since. But whatever I have done, it has helped lead our people out of slavery in a single generation. If I threw everything aside for my own happiness, then I become a murderer and nothing else. Perhaps I am, but I should not like to think of myself as such.'

'I left East Germany when I thought I loved a man.' She could scarcely remember the blond young Englishman who had helped smuggle her out at a time when she was disillusioned by watching her father's Party manoeuvrings, only recall how she had discovered afterwards that she was incidental to her rescuer's enjoyment of adventure.

Kaderi stroked her hair. 'I guessed it was something like that. We leave what we do not love for what we do. If you had stayed longer it might have been different, but you had nothing staked in your land, no pledges given or blood shed. I have all of these.'

She would have pushed him away then, but he held her with his full weight, yet withheld passion while she lay taut beneath him, forced to put recoil into words since he refused to allow her body to speak for her. 'So you don't care for me at all. Since you stay here for what you love and I left my homeland for it, even though I found myself mistaken.'

'I love you, *kenaqesi*. Tonight I wanted you to know, beyond doubting. By not coming I love you more, not less. I keep myself from you while I say it, so you may one day accept how much you were to me. More than I shall ever be to you.' He moved then and they did not speak again.

Next day she went with Stephen to the mines.

Anne had visited him a few times while he rested and worked on Twodex, and told herself that he did not want to see her often. She had even wondered whether she should spend more time with him to allay suspicion which might be building towards Kaderi, and only then discovered how much she disliked being in Stephen's company. He saw too much, guessed too much about her. He ought to be immersed in technicalities, but wasn't like that at all.

Also, it was impossible to avoid the image of a Millosh Kaderi she detested when she saw Stephen, still weakened by a regime deliberately designed to break him, his ribs and shoulders chafed by chain, other nameless victims conjured into her mind by the fact of what had been done to him.

She felt him considering her as they were driven to the chrome mine, and remembered again the microphone he said he carried. Her stomach contracted with fresh fear: he might easily say something malicious about her and Kaderi. He had no reason to feel regard for a man who ordered him frozen and worn out by sleeplessness, in fact made no secret of his hatred. If he could bring trouble on Kaderi then he probably would, and reckon discord might help their escape. Any listener to bugged conversations would be under Sigurimi orders, but even Kaderi could never be certain to whom his men reported.

God, what a tangle.

What a country, too. How could Millosh love it, see his own image in it without revulsion? She looked out of the truck and began to wonder whether there was any way in which she might crack his resolution to stay, force him to look honestly at what he had helped to create.

Bulqize chrome mines were a depressing sight in winter drizzle. It had snowed frequently during the time they stayed at the hostel, now a dank thaw had set in and they might have been a thousand miles from the Mediterranean. Nako was still in charge of Stephen, the captain and escort reappeared out of nowhere, pleased grins and handshakes all round as if they were good friends. Anne felt no animosity towards the captain, and the rest were just boys: there was Nikoll who sweated even in the cold, Enver who liked to boast that he

104

shared the name of his Party leader, and Spiri who one night had admitted to apprehension because his mother had given him a Christian name instead of one off the party-approved list.

'I am a good communist, Shoqë Anna,' he said, fixing her with anxious eyes. 'Yet I respect my kin and they would think me less than a man if I changed my name through fear. You'd expect my mother to have more sense, wouldn't you, than burden me with such a choice? And for nothing, after all.'

'Perhaps for honour,' suggested Anne. 'The easy way would be to change it.'

'I don't want to do that,' he said sulkily. 'The Party list is all very well for clerks, but depressing when six men out of twenty are named the same.' He would not have said it to a comrade who might have reported disloyalty he did not feel, but by some obscure process of thought felt safe with her.

He grinned and gave her a conspiratorial wink now, whispering as they walked to the mine office that he had not yet changed from Spiri.

Nako had not changed either, a brooding presence eyeing Stephen like a hyena waiting for its betters to finish feeding. Kaderi had ordered in the captain's hearing that Stephen's clothing should be unfastened at night but not stripped from him as before, one wrist cuffed to Nako while he slept. 'You may check on him as often as you wish,' he added, 'but Shok Astell must sleep sufficiently to keep his strength for the work he has to do.'

Kaderi only glanced at Anne before he left for Tirana, expression inscrutable, and gave no orders concerning her, so she was treated with the same consideration as before, more protected than a captive.

The mine manager produced massive plans of the workings under his control, and everyone else dozed in pleasant heat while he and Stephen discussed possibilities. Anne gathered from what she could understand of it that the mines here possessed both opencast and underground workings.

'Christ,' said Stephen when they finally went to look. 'I never thought to see ore hand dug into wheelbarrows. The last chrome mine I worked in was Rhodesian, where they have grabs to bite out fifty tons at a time.'

In spite of miserable conditions and weather the workers seemed cheerful though, watching them with open curiosity, anxious to explain what they were doing as if shovelling dirt was a complicated process. Criticism was not quite justified either; on lower, richer terraces they found a bulldozer and trucks run on pulleys. Where a cable had broken bullocks were being used in its place, but everyone was working steadily.

'Do you often use animals for haulage?' enquired Stephen; his Albanian was improving rapidly.

'Quite often, Shok,' replied the drover, rubbing his beast's muzzle affectionately. 'The winding gear is Russian you understand, and the motor Chinese. Both have left us and good riddance, but spares must be hand-forged even if we are able to discover just what is needed. Beasts are simple. You feed them and they work.'

'Like men,' said Stephen caustically.

'Yes indeed, Shok. We are cared for now and happy to work. My kin remember times when they starved at this season.'

'It's a different life,' said Anne quietly. 'What matters to you has no significance for him. For his grand-children perhaps.'

Stephen's eyes flickered to her and back to the bullocks. 'If you say so. I wonder what the hell their underground workings are like if this is standard on the terraces.' He turned to the mine manager. 'What is your safety record?'

'Very good, Shok Astell.'

'How many fatalities this year?'

The man looked uncomfortable. 'That is state information.'

'Sounds unpromising,' commented Stephen, in the voice of one who had expected no better. 'I'm damned if I'm going to get myself killed surveying through galleries which would send a nineteenth century mines inspector into hysterics. Unless Nako goes first, of course.'

Nako scowled, Stephen's easier conditions filled him with rancour even though he realized that his patience was unlikely to be tested for long.

The underground workings divided into several sections: some were adits driven from the face of the hill, elsewhere shafts had been sunk from which a series of levels radiated. As they went deeper it became pleasantly warm, but increasingly ill-lit, the air heavy, shafts and levels less symmetrical. The soldiers peered about them, silent and fascinated, their boots sometimes echoing in abandoned workings, then in the next section all sound was swamped by the clatter of hoists and drills. Anne had never been down a mine before and felt as they did, interest making her forget the extraordinary sequence of events which had brought her a thousand feet underground in an Albanian chrome mine.

Stephen went ahead with the mine manager, saying very little, listening to explanations, occasionally studying rock or writing something in a notebook. The same professionalism which he had retained under extreme stress in the mountains re-emerged at once in surroundings where he was expert, the manager's voice becoming defensive as his explanations shattered against a wall of criticism all the more obvious for being unspoken. The Italians had started mining here fifty years ago and cared nothing for Albanian lives . . . the Russians had decided to sink a different shaft and were desperate for whatever they could extract . . . the Chinese despised the Russians too much to continue their workings and opened up quite a different system.

'Yes, well, it may be politics but it sure as hell isn't mining, and I thought I'd seen some crazy concerns in my life,' observed Stephen at last. 'That being so, I'd prefer everyone else to return to the surface if we're to go on. Except Nako, who I'm sure will wish to come; I'm quite happy for him to disappear under rock.'

He had spoken in Albanian and Nako gave a growl of fury. 'I will report your insolence to Shok Kaderi, and he will let me repay you.'

'One day I expect he will. Report to him by all means, then perhaps he will come himself and be under rock with the rest. No wonder accident figures are state secrets.' He turned to the captain. 'You know your way back to the first level?'

'Yes, Shok Astell.'

'Take everyone with you and wait there until the mine manager and I return.' He glanced at Anne. 'I mean everyone.'

'Why go on yourself if you think it is so dangerous?' demanded Anne. 'What does it matter to you?'

'Call it sheer bloody-minded curiosity if you like, the bane of my profession. Kaderi knows the feeling too, you must ask him about it when next you meet.'

She was so coldly furious that she followed the captain back up the shaft at once, creaking cage-lift giving a disagreeable feeling of insecurity. She frowned, trying to remember. Where had the soldier been standing who carried the box which Stephen thought was a recorder? and how easily would it pick up voices against the clang of shovels and tip-trucks?

They waited a long time before Stephen, Nako and the manager reappeared, filthy and soaked. 'We'll have another look at the plans tomorrow,' Stephen said briefly. 'I'm not working on the lowest level, that's certain. A shift only needs to sneeze at the same time to bring down a hanging wall, and no one knows what effect an ultrasonic shot might have in such conditions. If you had the sense of a gut-shot rabbit you'd refuse to let men work there,' he added to the manager.

'I go there myself, it is my duty to the people. We have no help from anyone now and must manage as best we may.' He looked with affection at wet walls and dull lights; he knew nothing else and was proud of his mine, resentful of criticism.

Stephen stared at him, mouth compressed in a tight, angry line. 'Someone else besides Italians doesn't care about Albanian lives apparently. They at least were conquerors; what excuse do you offer for yourself each time you check an accident list?'

'The need of our people, not the profit which kills men in your Western mines,' replied the manager simply.

Stephen's eyes narrowed. 'I can tell you one thing, this place would be closed down by any self-respecting capitalist company. I'll use the upper levels and plot my course tomorrow, but it's going to be a slow process. You can tell Kaderi that I will fire my shots at shift-change only, when there is no one on the lower levels.'

'You can't,' said the captain, aghast. 'Shok Kaderi expects you to finish here in a few days. Like that it will take weeks.'

'I can and will. For God's sake man, I'm a mining consultant of nearly twenty years' experience. There are always stresses in mined rock which no one can calculate until they snap into balance again, but what can be established is the damage those stresses cause when they adjust.'

The manager licked his lips. 'You think your machine could cause such a pressure break?'

'I tell you, I don't know. In a mine with recognized safety standards the risk would be minimal, but then they'd insist I cleared the lower levels for experimental work. Here I can't begin to judge risk or anything else, only look at what I see. Under no circumstances will I use Twodex while there is a shift in the galleries below. If you don't clear the drifts at shift-change, then you'll have to stop work while I do it.'

They argued and pleaded, following him in plaintive groups when they regained the surface, trotting sometimes because he was taller than they and anger lengthened his stride. Secure in Kaderi's certain displeasure at his prisoner's defiance, Nako felt free to enjoy himself again; the need for patience had lasted an even shorter time than he had expected. He fastened the handcuff tight enough to swell Stephen's hand, and scraped back clothes so he might as well be naked. They all slept uneasily in the pump-shed at the mine and each time she woke Anne heard movement where Stephen was, as he was kept relentlessly awake.

Not again. She couldn't bear the whole miserable business again. She began to long to go down to Tirana where surely it would be warmer, see Millosh and start persuading him that his dream was worthless. She did not feel particularly sorry for Stephen, rather was angry that he should force conflict on her yet again. The mine looked squalid rather than unsafe to her, and the men working there would not be so cheerful if accidents were frequent. If Stephen chose this way to gain time that was his affair, he could not complain of the consequences. All the same, she loathed Nako and lay planning what she would say to Millosh so he would see the wilful cruelty of a man he trusted.

With luck she might manage to have him severely punished: most Albanians were as ordinary as people everywhere, but he symbolized to her everything detestable in such a place. She refused to accept that Kaderi also was a symbol, and could have controlled Nako with a word if he had wished.

Next day the same gloom clamped over the spirits of their party as over the spoil heaps of Bulqize, made worse by squabbles and recriminations. No one stopped Anne when she went for a solitary walk past tumbledown, badly repaired cottages, slogans the only relief from drabness. There were new concrete flats and official buildings near the centre of Bulqize, by the mine only some processing sheds looked recently constructed. The pot-holed streets were running with water, the people glum and bad-tempered, heads down in dowdy clothes. With a sense of shock Anne realized that Christmas and New Year must have passed without a single thing to mark them: no lights or decorated shops, no change in routine, no greeting or different food.

She returned to the pump-shed feeling as depressed as the Albanians looked; their life and regime would appear more cheerful in the sun, even if not changed at all. Stephen looked up as she came in; there was blood on his face.

'What happened?' Anne asked sharply.

Stephen shrugged. 'Nako felt an urge to scratch while I was shaving.'

'Fleas,' said Nako complacently. 'When they jump you can't wait on some fool shaving before you scratch.' Stephen was still handcuffed to him, hand swollen an ugly purple.

Anne sat on a bench and put her head in her hands, feeling wetness on her fingers. There was no end to it, to strain and hate and torment, to double-dealing and divided loyalty. She could drowse at night and feel Millosh beside her, now reality shattered self-deception and she wasn't sure whether she could bear him with her ever again.

Despair only weakened, it was no help at all. She looked up, realizing that every man in the tiny room was watching her with a variety of emotions according to their natures. Satisfaction or embarrassment, sympathy or simple curiosity. Except Stephen. He was staring at the floor, face blank of any expression at all.

The next two days were much the same, but worse as tempers frayed. The manager came to plead with Stephen,

Anne's Albanian not sufficiently fluent to follow rattled technicalities. Once, Stephen went to his office which at least released him from the handcuff, but when he returned it was snapped tight again which meant he refused to alter his decision.

On the fourth day, Kaderi came.

He was blazingly angry, as Anne had never seen him before, and curtly ordered everyone into the mine. The descent was only partly by cage so Stephen had to be unlocked again, but neither he nor Kaderi spoke through all the long climb down. Anne watched them, fear a constriction around her heart; she could only hope that Stephen would be satisfied with the four days he had gained but he was an obstinate man and driven by hatred he usually managed to hide, hatred which must have been increased by the past few days.

In the furthest gallery of the second level, Stephen stopped. 'That's far enough. I'll take you down to the lowest level if you wish, Kaderi.'

'You mistake my purpose. I brought you here to do the work you have agreed to do, without more time wasted. We all go down with such equipment as you need.'

'Perhaps your underlings did not report me accurately. I refuse to fire Twodex while there is a shift below ground, nor will I use the lowest level for experimental work.'

Kaderi nodded to Nako and he came over grinning hugely, pulling a knife from under his goatskin jacket. He grasped Stephen's arm and doubled it behind his back, then drove the knife quite hard through clothes into his stomach. The captain made a single involuntary movement and then stood still, breathing heavily; the other soldiers watched, fascinated. They liked Stephen and had come to know him well, but he was set beyond the sheet glass barrier of state security.

Stephen leaped sharply, arm cracking at his recoil, mouth open soundlessly.

Kaderi nodded again and Nako twisted the blade, knee hard in Stephen's back to keep him still, then very gently he drove it deeper.

Anne ran to Kaderi, tearing at him, forgetting everything except the need to make him stop. She did not know what she said, said nothing coherent, anyway he did not look at her. Instead she felt herself held, then dragged away from him. She twisted round and saw it was Spiri grasping her; he refused to look when she shouted at him, as if she had never comforted him over a name he disliked.

She heard a grunting moan and knew Kaderi had nodded again; she was close enough to see sweat on his face, the way his hands trembled, clasped behind his back. This is what he does and says he seldom needs to do, yet does it all the same, she thought dazedly. This is what I wouldn't face before.

'Wait. Please . . . in the love of God—' her lips felt loose, words difficult to form.

'There is no God,' Kaderi spoke with even precision. 'Nor mercy for those who defy the state.' He turned back to Stephen. 'Well? I have been patient with you, but now is the time to choose.'

Arm doubled, legs straining against the weight in his back, blood pouring down his trousers, Stephen looked like a figure from Heironymous Bosch, wet rock and darkness the gates of hell. The whole thing had been so swift, the reversal of strategy savagely difficult to grasp.

'Stephen—' said Anne. 'Please. What does it matter after all?'

He shook his head, lips framing refusal without sound.

Kaderi's drawn breath rasped in tune with Stephen's, as if both were on the same rack of torment. The moment of choice for them both. Nod again and he lost Anne forever. Nod again and Nako would seriously injure his prisoner; change his attack to another, less lethal place than the stomach and it was defeat of a sort. He needed Stephen working, he also needed him too cowed to consider falsifying results. Surrender on any issue would serve his purpose and firing Twodex in the mine had seemed to offer the chance Kaderi sought. The first yielding of a captive was what counted, after that degradation became routine however long it took.

A knife sunk with no warning at all in a place so instinctively guarded as the belly was usually sufficient to crack most men; if that didn't work, perhaps nothing would.

Kaderi could not turn back though, he was committed now.

Grudging respect, the sympathetic griping of his own guts could not, must not, make any difference.

He nodded to Nako.

13

Anne tore at Spiri's restraining hands, and might as well have torn at rock. 'Millosh . . . stop him! You must . . . I can fire Twodex!'

For an instant Kaderi stood as if he had not heard, every muscle locked. Then he shuddered slightly. 'Wait,' he said to Nako. 'Tighter against his back and hold the knife where it is.' He turned to Anne. 'What do you propose?'

Her lips were too unsteady to fumble words together accurately, nor had she spoken with anything in mind beyond stopping Kaderi. 'I—I've fired Twodex most of the time in the mountains, while . . . Stephen listened to tell whether it was right. It's charged as usual for five shots now . . . I could do it if you wanted.'

'We need Mr Astell to read the results.'

'Not now. To reset Twodex and interpret them later, yes. For the moment they're recorded.'

'What does he listen to then?'

'I don't know exactly. Nothing, if the shot goes well. Occasionally he hasn't been satisfied and we've had to repeat in the same place. Not often though, ask the captain.'

Kaderi stood, considering. He needed the Englishman to capitulate; what Anna proposed was useless for his purpose. They were using the mine simply for convenience and shelter from the weather; only Astell's obstinacy had forced this confrontation and that was what must somehow be overcome. Otherwise he might as well gut the swine now and abandon any idea of a survey, since no reliance could be placed on such a self-willed, capitalistic sod of a man; Kaderi's fury blazed up fiercely again.

He hated seeing Anna plead for another man; on the other hand . . .

'Very well,' he said abruptly. 'Tell these men what you need and they will take it down for you. How long before you are able to fire the first shot?'

'Half an hour.' She had no idea what line Stephen had chosen or what significance there might be in his choice; he had refused to contemplate any line at all in the lowest level where she must go. Set Twodex up and fire five shots anywhere, it didn't matter so long as it stopped Nako from tearing him apart.

She stumbled amongst piled boxes trying to concentrate, aware of Stephen on his knees retching, hands to his stomach. Kaderi followed her everywhere, watching, questioning, the soldiers redoubling confusion as they backed into each other in an effort to keep out of the way.

The lower level was reached by a cage, which came up full of ore and descended empty. Safety gates clattering, lights brighter by its shaft, Anne stood and watched Spiri and Enver holding Twodex between them as they dropped out of sight with the rest of their escort and equipment. Only she and Kaderi were left waiting for the next load, and Nako standing over Stephen knife in hand. Anne felt nothing, certainly not fear, every reaction numbed by the horror of that moment when she had thought she would have to watch Stephen butchered before her eyes.

It seemed a long time before the whine of winding gear announced the arrival of another load, soon they would descend too and she wouldn't waste any time over what she had to do. Anne looked round and saw that Kaderi had left her side and was over by Nako, watching while Stephen was hauled to his feet.

She ran over, an abscess of terror gathered again. 'What are you doing? You said . . . I'm going to do it!'

'So you are, Shoqë. But before we go I want Mr Astell to understand the contrast between your courage and his cowardice.'

Stephen licked his lips, he looked white and dazed, make-shift padding thrust inside his trousers and held in place by a belt around his hips. 'What's happening?'

'Shoqë Anna has agreed to take your place and fire Twodex in the low level.'

Stephen stared at Anne, then fumbled back a step to lean against the wall. 'You mustn't.'

'Why not, since I couldn't stand by and watch you gutted? You know I'm able to fire Twodex as well as you by now.'

'No. Anne, I mean it. There's a shift of ninety men down there. Twodex will probably have no effect, but you haven't the right to risk it. For me, for you, anyone.'

Anne gaped at him, blood drained by shock. He meant it. This had been no delaying tactic absurdly escalated by obstinacy and violence; professional principle held him from taking unacceptable chances with lives he had been trained to guard. 'I have to do it now. Can't you see?' She spoke numbly, knowing he wouldn't see.

'If you are so certain of risk, are you content to cower here and allow Shoqë Anna to go in your place?' interposed Kaderi smoothly. This was the lever Anna had handed him, and he was confident it would work. The strongest men were flawed, you only needed to look long and skilfully enough to find their weakness, then the right pressure applied there snapped them apart.

Stephen shook his head in an attempt to clear it rather than in denial. There was a long silence. 'Wait until shift change. Then I will do it after the manager has reported that every man is cleared from this level and the one below.'

'No,' said Kaderi positively. 'That was one of the points in dispute if you remember, and we do not stop work at shift-change. The manager is worried where he was content before, all because you told him his mine is unsafe. It is no more unsafe today than it was before you saw it but he doesn't believe it any more. His anxiety will spread to his workers unless you yourself correct the impression you have given.'

Stephen smiled faintly, wits collected again. 'That was the idea. Your manager had no standard of comparison so was content with the inevitable. Now he wonders about the nature of inevitability.'

Kaderi took Anne by the arm, she could feel him trembling.

'Come then, Anna. You must not keep us all waiting.'

She found it enormously difficult to think. Black swags of rock pressed in on her, dust in her lungs and throat adding to the sense of suffocation; for the first time she visualized the enormous weight pressing down on her, looked with horror on man's puny efforts which kept a thousand feet of rock from crushing them where they stood. It suddenly became unthinkable to go lower still, to undertake risks she was incapable of assessing. Yet someone must fire Twodex or Kaderi would not allow Stephen to leave this mine alive, be driven into an action for ever unforgiveable.

The cage arrived with a roar, hoist spinning, bringing with it a gust of stale air. Its load of ore tipped into waiting trucks in an artillery of sound, surely the hiss of Twodex's firing was nothing compared to the everyday uproar of the mine. I'll do it, she thought, shutting her mind to the fact that she knew nothing of ultrasonics. She simply was incapable of standing aside and watching Nako's blubber-grin while . . . while he disembowelled Stephen where he stood. She stared at Kaderi through a fog of dust. He too was ground down by choices which were no choice at all; pity remained while much else which in another life might have grown between them, bled dry under Nako's knife.

Then, surprisingly, Stephen was in the dust-cloud too, leaning on Nako instead of led by him.

Kaderi smiled, relief obvious; his manoeuvre had worked as he had thought it would. 'Ah, Mr Astell. You have decided to assist us after all?'

Stephen nodded. 'Send Anne to the surface.'

Kaderi considered. The cage was empty, wheels silent ready for descent. 'No. You appear to need frequent reminding of your obligations, so her presence might prompt you to carry out what I require when your own safety would not.'

Stephen's lips tightened, he looked as if he was about to refuse again. Then, half pushed by Nako, he followed them into the cage.

It was large enough to hold thirty men, crunching with dust and faintly lit by a protected bulb. It lurched downward slowly, streaked rock visible through mesh sides. Kaderi still held

Anne's arm but tension had drained from him, his touch intimate, just as if he had not been using her only seconds ago as a tool for his purposes. He looked at her, lips soft, the prudence enforced by Nako's presence almost forgotten in the aftermath of success.

Nako himself was a deeply disappointed man. He had shoved Stephen roughly against steel switches and now scowled sulkily at the floor. He looked up as the cage halted with a jolt, but without interest; when Shok Kaderi stopped him he had been a finger's width from the downward slice which in the past men of his district had reserved for blood enemies. His heart beat strongly from the sensuous feel of it, and he made no attempt to think of anything else. Soon, he would finish what he had begun.

Kaderi also looked up when the cage stopped, he knew nothing of mining and was not at first surprised by seeing no obvious way out. The shaft hemmed them in, glinting in faint light. He went over to the sliding safety gate and shook it. 'What's happened?'

Stephen lifted his head; he had slumped on the floor when the hoist stopped, legs drawn up as if in belated self-protection. 'It feels as if the emergency chock has flipped for some reason.'

Kaderi went over to a red-painted lever set in a steel case, together with a lamp and tools. 'Is this the brake?'

'It's the emergency stop if something was wrong here, but this has been tripped in the winding gear. You can try, but it shouldn't make any difference.'

Kaderi knocked off the emergency fastening and strained at the handle: it refused to budge and Nako went over spitting on his hands.

'It's probably rusted solid,' remarked Stephen in a detached voice. Already the air seemed thick, the solid floor of the cage cutting off such circulation as they had felt on the upper level. 'There should be a handset to speak to the operator below, but of course there isn't.'

Nako grasped the lever and heaved, muscles bulging, but after a second attempt Kaderi called him off and examined the lever carefully. 'It seems set on some kind of notching, as if you should place it differently in an emergency and it's only like this when out of use. What do you think, Mr Astell?' His formal courtesy was grotesque, making the mind doubt what had gone before.

Stephen hesitated and then stood carefully; Anne went over and steadied him since no one else considered offering help. His skin felt clammy-cold, in the aftermath of shock. He moved awkwardly too, the knife had taken him somewhere low against the hip and Anne suspected that Nako had deliberately turned his blade to flay muscle without deeper damage, and so take his pleasures slowly.

Stephen ran his hand over the series of cogs where the handle was, and then grunted. 'Hold that clip down and tell Nako to put both hands on the lever; he's to jerk with all his strength when I say. It'll be very stiff.'

Kaderi moved aside, fingers fumbling with the clip, and Nako braced himself, pleased to show off his strength.

It was the last emotion he ever felt, for Stephen cracked his skull with a four-foot brace taken from amongst the tools.

As he pitched on his face, his weight came off the lever and it swung back like a spring; Kaderi screamed, crushed fingers streaming blood as the ratchet his clip had held in place reversed viciously.

14

'I'm sorry,' said Stephen. He was holding Kaderi's gun which he had taken from him while he was blind with pain. 'It was us or unjustifiably risking the lives of ninety miners in the low level. I didn't intend you to be here, but was driven into a corner by the end. You have a fair chance though, if you'll do exactly as I say.'

Anne blinked; she wasn't afraid – yet. 'You planned this?'

He gave a ghost of a smile; he was sitting again, legs drawn up as before. 'Kaderi was a fool to take me on my own ground. Anywhere but here he could have won, but any miner who knows his business would be able to take advantage of his ignorance here.'

Anne looked around: an oiled steel cable disappeared into darkness above their heads, Nako's corpse sprawled in a corner against Millosh Kaderi, whose mangled hand was clamped into the handcuff which still dangled from Nako's wrist. The slightest movement made him semi-conscious with pain and Anne had to steel herself to endure watching him. Of course Stephen was right to fasten him by his bad wrist instead of the good, but all the same . . . 'Couldn't you change the handcuff to the other side?' Her voice jumped uncertainly.

'No, and it's a damned sight looser than it was on me. If he keeps still it won't make anything worse.' Stephen's voice was unyielding and she could not blame him, his own arm fiercely strained from Nako's handling. 'Anne, listen. I shorted the controls, it wasn't difficult when there are God knows how many unguarded wires. The hand winch is solid with rust, they'll never shift it that way. We have a while to think. If you'll look amongst those tools there's a lever designed to take the clips off the safety hatch above our heads. Once they're off you can climb through easily, then you'll find steel footholds set into the side of the shaft. They were needed during construction so that's one safety precaution they haven't neglected.'

She stared at him, eyes enormous. 'How far to climb? You can't—'

'No,' he said gently. 'I'm staying here.'

'What do you think I am? Of course I couldn't go and leave you!'

'Anne, listen to me. I can't climb that shaft, but all I need to do is wait. The winchman knows the cage has stuck. It may take time while they try the usual routines to free it, but eventually they'll lash up a sling to bring us through that hatch. Everyone will be chasing their tails once they realize their chief of security is caught in one of their shafts.'

'What a damned fool you must think me,' she said contemptuously. 'Why would you force me to make a hazardous climb if all we had to do is wait? When they take Millosh out, the first words he's able to speak will order us shot for what you've done.'

'When you get up there I want you to go directly to the surface, take advantage of confusion and disappear.'

'It's scarcely a chance, is it?'

He shifted awkwardly and swore under his breath. 'Better than no chance at all.'

She went over impulsively and laid her hand against his cheek, the first gesture of tenderness she had offered him. 'I didn't mean that. I meant I didn't believe you. As you said yourself, you are on your own ground here. When I've gone you intend to clear up such evidence as you've left, then drop the cage. As you intended to do all along if I hadn't come too. Accident. It wouldn't be so difficult for me to spin a good tale then, would it?'

'God preserve me from imaginative women. Anne—'

'No, Stephen. Think of another way. This is your province, remember?'

They stared at each other, wills locked. Argument alone was enough to make air settle solidly into labouring lungs. In an hour, two at most, they would be unconscious unless help came.

Then she saw Stephen tense, next moment felt what he had sensed an instant earlier. The whole cage was shuddering slightly, scraping against its cables. Very faintly below they heard a shuffle of sound and air swirled up the shaft, dispelling suffocation for a moment; then it was followed by choking clouds of dust and an echo of shouts. The cage lurched abruptly and the light went out.

Anne felt herself slither as the floor tilted, then she slammed into mesh sides and lay retching on dust, mind fluttering. Another terrifying lurch, her head hit something and she spun into nowhere.

She groped back through darkness, troughs of dizziness waiting to bear her away again. After a while she opened her eyes but it made no difference, blackness pressed like cloth against her face

Cautiously, she stretched her legs, then arms. They obeyed reluctantly, so no bones broken. Encouraged, she considered standing and discovered that she was lying in the sharp angle of what she guessed was floor and wall; when she moved, the whole cage shuddered. She lay still again, heart thumping.

'Anne?' Stephen's voice. Thank God. She nearly cried from the infinite mercy of not being trapped alone in the bowels of the earth.

She wiped her mouth on her sleeve, had to before words would come. 'I'm lying against the wall.'

'Yes, I know. So am I. Move as gently as you can, but crawl until you reach a corner. Then pull yourself up so you're angled up the floor. We must get our weight as high as we can. If you stand where you are the whole thing could slip off whatever is holding it; crushed winding gear at a guess.' His voice was steady but oddly rough.

With extreme care Anne pulled herself along the wall until . . . she recoiled sharply, exclaiming aloud.

'What is it?' demanded Stephen.

'Millosh.' After her first horror at encountering his body, she felt carefully. He was breathing irregularly, stickiness which must be blood on his face. He was deeply unconscious

and when she felt further she discovered his handcuffed arm
had fractured as Nako's body was flung sharply aside. She
tried to crawl across him and then stopped, it was no good.
She could feel his familiar contours and there was a strange
quirk to his lips when she touched them. As if he knew she
was there, though she told herself it was a rictus of pain.

Carefully, she felt further and discovered Nako, flesh
already chilling. Just possibly he might have the handcuff key
on him, and she could make Millosh more comfortable.

The cage shuddered as she fumbled through his clothing,
hatred too fresh for her to feel anything except thankfulness
that he was dead.

'Careful,' said Stephen sharply. 'Where are you now?'

'Nearly at the wall, but Nako and Kaderi are in the way.'
Anne did not want to admit that she was wasting time making
Millosh more comfortable.

The key, at last. It was infuriating to have to do everything
by touch alone: if she dropped the key she would never find it
again. Stephen heard the click as the handcuff opened. 'You're
letting him loose?'

'He's unconscious,' she said defensively. 'The way he was
flung across the cage . . . his arm is broken as well now.' She
could feel angles of bone as well as the mash of his fingers,
they had nothing to fear from him at the moment.

'Let's hope he stays unconscious then. I'm going to brace
myself against the wall and stand, or at least I shall be lying at
forty-five degrees up the floor. Try to do the same, and feel to
your right until we touch.' He did not need to add another
caution: as soon as she moved the cage dropped fractionally
while they both froze, breath stopped.

Anne left Kaderi once she had his arm padded and folded
inside his coat; it needed the most enormous effort to force
herself to her knees, to her feet, to scrabble up the frighteningly steep slope of floor. Darkness confused everything. The
plan of the cage was clear in her mind, Millosh and Nako
behind her to the left, Stephen somewhere to her right, tools
clipped on the high wall ahead, but distances and dangers
loomed larger for being invisible.

How long it took she could not tell, but the moment came

when she felt something warm in cold darkness and Stephen's fingers fastened on hers.

'Steve,' she said. 'Has anyone called you Steve before, or is it always Stephen?'

'Often,' he said, and laughed. 'Formality hasn't quite fitted the bill several times in my life, but none quite like this. I'm going to work my way across to you and then you must stand on my shoulders and reach up for the tools. We've got to get that esape hatch open whatever the risks. There's a lamp with the tools too, if it works.'

They managed it after a struggle.

He lay braced on the floor while she edged up his body and stood, heart in her mouth, groping her hands up the further wall. Almost at once she felt that several tools had gone, but the lamp and a flat-notched lever were still there, together with a miscellaneous collection of spanners. She handed the lever down and fumbled with the lamp, it would be unbearable if it didn't work.

She found a knob and twisted, feeble yellow glow like a floodlight after such blackness. She turned to look down and gasped. She had thought that light would drive back some of the terror, instead it made it worse. The rock of the shaft was visible each side of the cage but beyond the bottom corner where Kaderi and Nako lay, only snapped wires and more blackness showed through mesh.

Stephen was saying something and she wrenched her mind from thinking about the tangle of wreckage which alone held them at an angle across the shaft. He was lying face down, head twisted to look up at her. 'There won't be much juice in that lamp, use it and then turn it off. Hook it to you if you can. D'you see the hatch?'

'Yes.' It was above and behind her in the slanted roof.

'Can you reach it with the bar? Slide the notch over the wing-nuts you see and heave. They'll be stiff, judging by all the Albanian machinery we've seen so far, but keep your weight evenly spread on my shoulders and hold the mesh with your other hand. If you slip—'

Don't worry, she thought. I'm no engineer but I can guess what the jolt of me falling to the lower edge of the cage would do.

The bar only just reached. It was neck-straining, muscle-trembling work leaning backwards as far as she could stretch to slot the heavy bar over nuts, and once she had it notched she lacked leverage to shift rusted threads. The fingers of her left hand clutching mesh were skinned, her shoulders burning, breath caught in a spasm of frustration . . . if only she had been an inch taller. She could not shift it.

'We'll have to change places,' she gasped at last; his shoulders must be agony under her nailed boots.

'No. I've only one arm with enough strength in it and if I couldn't hold myself to the mesh then I'm heavier than you when I fell. Hold very still while I'm not braced and I'll take off my belt and Nako's.'

He had been wearing a second belt to keep the pad in place against his stomach, she remembered. 'Steve . . . where Nako knifed you, is it still bleeding?'

'I don't think so. You and the floor are a good tourniquet. Buckle one belt to the mesh upright, and then the other to it. Take as many turns around your arm as you can in case your hold slips and see if you can shift the nuts with your extra reach then.'

She did not think she would ever manage it. The belts allowed her to lean further back but she was still at the very limit of her reach. Then, with almost her full weight on the bar, the nut gave sharply and only the belt twisted around her forearm kept her from falling. Now for the other one. This was diagonally across from the first and both she and Stephen had to change position, every move needing to be thought out and carried through with infinite precaution. Also they were very tired. Both had lived through a wilderness of emotions since they came underground less than two hours before, the air in the shaft was foul and becoming hot, Stephen's face pressed into dirt, Anne needing to wait before she moved as cramp attacked abused muscles.

At least the second nut gave without much fuss, or perhaps the desperation with which she threw her waning stength at it had an effect. At once she thrust the lever under the metal edge of the hatch and heaved; it lifted with a clatter and slithered across the roof, starting a miniature avalanche from the ore fragments caught there. Utterly still from shock and fear, they heard the skitter of sound fade down the shaft, the distant echo when the hatch landed.

'How deep is it?' Anne whispered, a normal tone seemed a temptation to the fates.

'A hundred feet perhaps from where we are. Enough. We'll make it somehow though. Shine the lamp at the hatch, they must use it to inspect the pulleys and there should be some means of climbing through, a hinged ladder perhaps. No self-respecting miner swings up seven feet on his arms.' He did not say, but without some means of climbing they were still trapped, the cage too steeply angled for them to be able to stand directly below the hatch.

There was nothing.

A tangle of wire glimpsed in the fading light of the lamp, the sheen of rock, and that was all.

15

Disappointment was crushing; the enormous effort needed just to remove a pair of wing-nuts had brought a disproportionate feeling of triumph when they succeeded, and obscured the fact that this was only the beginning of what they must do.

Silently Anne unbuckled the belts, crawled down from Stephen's shoulders and went to lie beside him in the grit. She turned out the lamp, partly to save its remaining power, partly because blackness suited how she felt.

After a while she saw the only way it might be done. 'Steve, how much strength have you in your arm?'

'Some, why?'

'How much?'

'Using it has helped. The hand is fairly sound, but I wouldn't like to trust much to the shoulder.'

'If I buckled both belts to an upright and used them to hold myself in a crouch on the floor, could you stand on my back and pull yourself through the hatch? Then you would probably find an end of wire to let down to help me up.'

'For God's sake,' he said, startled. 'I'm no lightweight, you know.'

'Not even after ten weeks of Nako?'

He gave a ghost of a laugh. 'I'm lighter than I was, I'll give you that. But no, we must do it the other way around. I could damage your back too seriously for you to be able to climb the shaft afterwards. Don't forget that we're still God knows how far down even when we do get out.'

'No,' she replied drily. 'I hadn't forgotten.'

'Well then—'

'I'm a good six inches shorter than you. I don't think I'd be able to reach high enough to pull myself up and crouched like a hedgehog on the floor there can't be six inches worth of difference in the step we shall offer. Your stomach too . . .' If he crouched tightly to give sufficient bow to his back, that slice would start bleeding again.

He lay quietly, thinking, hand resting in the curve of her shoulder. Darkness pressed in on them, so she made an involuntary gesture to push it away from her face. 'What happened?' she asked suddenly. 'I know you shorted the controls or something, but afterwards wasn't you, was it?'

'Hardly. We're in an earthquake belt here, that's one reason why I distrusted this mine so much. The manager told me they have at least a dozen tremors a year, mostly slight of course. Occasionally one causes a hoist to slip like this, or brings down a section of workings, yet there's scarcely a sign of safety factors being increased to take account of the extra risk. All the rocks here are full of stress, anything sets them off. Like today. Like Twodex could have done.'

'It's crushed in the lower level now I suppose, with the captain and the rest.' Anne had liked the captain and understood that Spiri could not have refused to hold her.

'Perhaps, perhaps not. We're in the furthest shaft here, and they've other ways out, it wasn't a severe tremor. But while the rescue teams are occupied there, no one is going to worry about a jammed hoist, although they certainly will once someone tells them Kaderi is in it.' His voice changed abruptly. 'Nako! If we can haul him up here, it'll help the weight and give us the extra height we need.'

In the end, they simply had to chance it and also set squeamishness aside.

They could not lift his body high enough up the floor and then secure it crouching below the hatch, unless they went down to where he lay and used all their strength. The hoist shuddered under their combined weight in the lowest corner, once a rock split off the wall and went hurtling away, striking sparks down the shaft: the quake had made the whole area unstable. A creaking rasp they had heard before became more obvious too. 'The cage roof,' said Stephen grimly. 'It's peeling back like a sardine can under pressure.' As if to add meaning to his words the cage settled heavily again, a row of rivets squeezing out and rattling on the floor.

'Oh God,' said Anne, 'it can't . . . not now.'

'Up with you then, and see if we've got him close enough.'

She ought to have been revolted by stepping on a dead man's back, and in some distant corner of her mind disgust locked tight and waited for a better time to pounce. For the present there was no thought at all, nothing except the heaving effort of reaching into that infernal trapdoor and scrabbling for unseen holds: wire, anything. Soon, she was conscious only of anger that Nako could not give her an extra inch.

Then she was through. She could not have done it without the spur of fear, nor without Stephen reaching out somehow to support a fraction of her weight.

The top of the cage was a tangle of wire and she slithered dangerously in her haste, pebbles falling over the unguarded edge to warn of her peril. On two sides the cage fitted tightly to the shaft, elsewhere a single unwary move could bring her to disaster.

She wedged herself against a pulley and began sorting out wire. It lay in unmanageable heaps and without visible end. The first loop she let through the trap unravelled with a horrifying roar above her head and was useless; Stephen needed some kind of stirrup to ease the strain on his shoulder and stomach as he climbed.

Eventually she found a section which was sufficiently pliable to twist around the pulley in the length she wanted and he managed quite easily then, coming through the trap with a rush and putting his arms around her in a spontaneous hug of relief at both being out of that hateful cage at last. Then he went to examine the shaft, while Anne peered back into the cage. Stephen had taken the lamp so she couldn't see anything, but Millosh was there and had not moved through all their long struggle. She hated leaving him more than she would have believed possible, and thought how extraordinary it was that even now she should be unable to shake free of the emotions he roused in her.

But they could do nothing for him now and if they could escape then the rescue teams would certainly make him their first priority. Stephen might not intend to tell them of Kaderi's presence here but she certainly would and to hell with the consequences afterwards.

Stephen scrambled back across the sloping roof and squatted beside her. The pulleys made a safe lodgement so long as the cage did not slip any further. 'What I thought was a safety ladder set into the shaft side is something rather less. Shaped rungs let into rock eighteen inches apart: I suppose ladders rust too quickly here to be worth maintaining. It's going to be the hell of a climb.'

'How far?'

'God knows. The lowest level is about two hundred and fifty feet below the second, where we entered the cage. By the sound of things dropping we're at least a hundred feet up, perhaps more. I don't think we can have less than a hundred to climb though, it took me quite a time to isolate the wires I wanted and short them out.'

Anne touched his arm; the lamp was a mere glow but she could hear drained weakness in his voice, guess his exhaustion from her own. 'Let me have a look at what Nako did to you first. Another five minutes won't make any difference.'

'I wouldn't like to bet on it. When this roof peels back just a little more the whole corner will crush and down she'll go.' They could feel the cage trembling. Once our weight has gone, Millosh will have a better chance, Anne thought.

But first she insisted on Stephen lying against the pulleys, and when she eased down his trousers found blood everywhere. Dried on thighs and crotch, wet on dirty cloth padding. She uncovered a long cut, shallow at one end, deep and torn above the hip, blood oozing sluggishly while she watched. She took off her shirt and tore it in half, folding part into a pad and pressing until he winced at the pressure: he could not afford to lose another ounce of blood.

She stared upward and wondered whether it was imagination which suggested a lighter patch far above. Could he possibly climb a hundred feet of eighteen inch rungs, and probably more, in the state he was in? She ought to leave him and climb alone but did not feel confident that, if she succeeded, he might not take the opportunity to crash the cage and give her a free run clear of blame. And the cage could crash of its own weight at any moment, taking him with it if he stayed.

She had brought Nako's knife in case it came in useful, and cut strips off the remainder of her shirt to secure the pad as tightly as she dared. Stephen's eyes were closed when she had finished and she rested thankfully herself, mind battered by a chain of disaster which seemed endless. Air. She needed air desperately. Her lungs were heaving, bursting, sweat wet on her face, the darkness growing whirlpools and spinning sense away.

Her head jerked painfully, she must have slept for an instant as the insidious relief of abandoning effort crept through mind and muscle.

The lamp glowed brighter for a moment, and went out.

'Stephen!' She shook him, urgently. 'We mustn't wait any longer.'

He stirred. 'The rungs are behind you. Have you still got the belts?' His voice sounded slurred.

'One. The other's round Nako.'

'Any more strips of shirt?'

'A few, why?'

'Plait them into a belt and fasten the one you've got to it.' His voice was clearer with the need to plan, and his hands brushed hers demonstrating what he meant, testing each knot himself. 'Now you've got this loose end of belt at your hip, when you need to rest you can twist it around a rung to take some of the strain, make resting easier. Keep your hand on the end you've twisted around the rung of course, as you can't fasten it.'

'What about you?'

'I've got this blasted chain round my chest. There's some ends of wire I can twist into a kind of hook for the same purpose.'

'I'll wait while you do it,' she said. 'You're going first, or hadn't you realized? I'm afraid of the dark.'

She felt him laugh. 'Liar. You're afraid I won't come if you go first. Don't worry, I'm coming and will do the best I can.'

'I'm waiting and you're still going first, but for God's sake hurry.' Urgency was driving now, the roof on which they crouched seeming as fragile as torn paper, the time he took to splice wire interminable.

Then they argued again, but he could not shift her. He was going first or neither went, and both knew why. With a strained shoulder and weakened by lost blood, his endurance was highly questionable; if he went first and fell then probably he would take her with him and this alone might drive him on when all else failed.

In the end, he capitulated. Every breath they drew of increasingly foetid air reduced their chances, delay the most dangerous choice of all. Higher, surely, the atmosphere would be better.

At first it was easy. The rungs were square in section, solidly set and took the whole depth of a foot; Stephen climbed steadily and economically ahead of her, not fast but without pausing.

Once started, Anne felt absurdly jubilant. Had she possessed breath to spare she would have shouted with pleasure as depth and darkness were trodden underfoot. Such confidence was out of all reason. Danger increased as dragged muscles and vertigo made their presence felt, and in such darkness she kept imagining that the shaft was tilting, thrusting her backwards from her hold.

After perhaps thirty rungs she began to tire. Eighteen inches was an uncomfortably high step each time, iron rough under her aching fingers, legs and back quivering with strain. Stephen too was slowing, twice she grasped at a rung and found his foot still there, had to wait and lose more strength until he moved.

She simply had to rest.

Five more steps, she promised herself, then I'll rest. She lost count, but next time she felt Stephen's foot still on the rung above she fumbled for the belt at her hip. But she had to clutch back at the rung before she had the belt safely wrapped, unable to hold her weight one-handed; when she tried again she could not secure the belt. Her fingers were too clumsy, her weight too great to hold for more than seconds.

Frantically she tried to hook an elbow under iron, scrabbling in panic while she lost more strength.

Somehow she forced herself to think, to stand square and rest as best she could. To struggle was death; even-paced steps up another sixty feet of shaft the only way to survival.

'Anne?' Stephen's voice above, sounding as strange as she felt.

She licked her lips. 'Yes.'

'I'm resting with my wire twisted round a rung. We must be nearly half-way.'

She knew they weren't, but perhaps he was just encouraging her. 'I—I'm resting too.' Best not to tell him she couldn't use the belt to help her. Very carefully, she tried again and this time succeeded in twisting it several times round a rung level with her waist. The relief was enormous as its grip redistributed her weight but the lesson of her struggle was plain: she would not succeed again. Next time she set off would be the last. She might stop but could not rest until she reached the top.

She heard Stephen move after a while, but waited until he was several steps ahead, overcome by reluctance to take her hand off the end of belt and allow it to twist clear. When at last she did, she could not move the loose end round to her hip and it snagged on the rungs as she climbed.

She had lost count again, but they must have climbed sixty rungs by now. Ninety feet. The head of the shaft could not be far away. Through the rasp of her breathing she could hear Stephen grunting with each step, close above her again, pausing at each rung. She wanted to scream at him, beg him to hurry, then felt wet on her upturned face and knew it must be blood dripping off his leg.

The gulf below was gaping, her eyes stinging with sweat, heart slamming, her one idea to breathe even though foul air offered no relief. She realized then that she could not go any further; no feeling of defeat, just simple relief that it was over. Stephen was stopped above her too, body hunched as if he lacked strength to lift his hands another rung and straighten.

She was seeing the shape of him. Shaft, rungs and him crouched above her, all were faintly bulked by light reflected from above. Triumph revived her but when she tried to speak her voice was gone. If Stephen did not move soon . . . 'Steve,' she croaked, 'Please . . .'

She could see that he was shaking, spasms tearing at his grip as loss of blood and foul air left his muscles unfuelled. Until the attack passed she must not urge him on. After what seemed an endless space of time he gathered himself and fumbled another couple of steps, boots grating as he groped for the next tread. Then suddenly the rungs were gone, smooth rock stretching ahead, a ladder alongside as the shaft opened out. They could see dull emergency bulbs glowing in the gallery they had left so long before. A metal plate projected on the far side of the ladder, cluttered with winding gear offering splendid handholds, the step sideways on to the ladder and its few rungs the last barrier before reaching safety.

Alone, Anne could have done it easily, strength reborn by the knowledge of how close success now was. Waiting for Stephen took her last reserves, the step over space to the metal plate an unimaginable effort, the hated rungs her friends now she must leave them for flimsy ladder and treacherous, grease-slicked metal.

Then she felt Stephen's hand reaching for her and sprawled over him into the safety of the gallery.

16

Anne woke in the same bed in Bulqize military hostel, and lay
quietly as memory slotted together again, wondering vaguely
how long she had slept. She remembered stumbling through
evacuated galleries searching for help, for Stephen as well as
Kaderi if the cage had not fallen; then there was a blank filled
only by anonymous faces and the feel of snow on her face.

She turned restlessly and cried out as abused muscles flared
their protest. She wanted to know what had happened, yet
when she tried to get out of bed she could not stand.

Much later a woman came in with food and told her that
Stephen was resting, Kaderi alive but very ill. 'Weak and
delirious, Shoqë, but the surgeon who set his arm says he will
live. Most of the miners are safe too, it wasn't a serious
tremor.' She dumped the tray robustly on Anne's knees and
went out. Those able to ask questions did not need cossetting.

Anne discovered that she was ravenous and felt much
stronger when she woke again. Moonlight filled the room and
she lay worrying about what would happen to them now.
Presumably Nako's death was accepted as an accident, but
Kaderi would soon change that when he recovered consciousness. Or just this once might he bend the framework of his life
and accept an explanation which avoided the necessity of
executing them both?

Anne shook her head and smiled wrily at the ceiling. She
didn't think so, although he might try to blame only Stephen.
One of his men had been killed and no one of his power and
conviction could compromise on such an issue, even if he
wanted to. Perhaps above all if he wanted to. She had come
close to loving the man Millosh Kaderi could have been but

not the man he was, and judged him without illusion.

Which meant they had to get out fast, before he recovered. For Stephen's sake if nothing else. She turned over again, wincing. If she felt frail enough to be a grandmother, how must he feel? Tomorrow she must see him. See Kaderi too if possible and discover how long before his doctors expected him to be lucid.

Next day she was still creakingly stiff but able to get up and dress, only to find Sigurimi guarding their chief and openly contemptuous when she asked to see him. A nurse with the speculative look of a born intriguer whispered that she had heard the doctors speak of a week's fever on the telephone to Tirana, and with that Anne had to be content. Two days, she thought. If they think he'll be ill for a week then I bet he's clear enough to tell someone to arrest us within two days.

She found Stephen in entire agreement with her judgement. To her surprise he was dressed, although he looked unwell and was limping heavily. 'I was coming this evening to warn you of how little time we have. Between us we've made Kaderi look a fool and I killed a man under his personal command.' He hesitated. 'You may be better placed than I am, but I don't think so.'

'Nor do I,' Anne squeezed torn fingers together. How merciless was life.

He looked relieved, having probably expected argument. Surprised, too. An Englishman could still expect emotion to blind her to Kaderi's compulsions, where Kaderi himself would accept that wish and action were set utterly apart. 'Tomorrow, I think we can risk it until then, take another twenty-four hours of rest when every hour adds to our chances.'

Anne remembered the microphone on his chest and reached out instinctively to see whether it was still there: it was. He was padded with bandages where his weight on the harness had split skin, but no Albanian doctor dared cut Sigurimi equipment loose.

Stephen smiled. 'It's all right. They'd hooked up a recorder under the shelf, but I've jinxed it so they'll think it's an electrical fault. We've time to fix what we must do.'

'Walk out,' said Anne unhesitatingly. 'No one's watching us although there's a guard on the corridor. Do you know what happened to the captain and the rest?'

'They're safe. Enver has crushed legs, the others no more than bruises. Two miners killed and a dozen hurt. Plus Nako. They were damned lucky if you ask me. I'm going to have a look at Twodex later, Spiri brought it.'

'We can't take it with us!'

'No, but I'll have a look at it just the same. My gift to Albanian progress.'

She wondered at his tone a little but made no comment. 'Do you think someone might authorize you to take it to Tirana for repair? We – I don't think we'll get far if we're forced to run from here.'

'It's a chance we'll have to take—me anyway. No one will authorize anything since we're known as Kaderi's business. As usual in such matters, they'll sit tight and wait for the boss.' He looked at her directly. 'If you come with me you'll be taking on a hell of a bad risk. I've twelve stitches in me which look like cobbler's darning; I can't go far and they'll know it. I shall have to hole up to wait for better weather and enough strength to climb those mountains. On the face of it you'd be safer if you stayed. Kaderi . . . he has every reason to protect you and precious few for saddling you with blame which is rightly mine. It's only instinct which tells me that such thought processes are wrong.' He grinned. 'Not Albanian if you like. Kaderi's a sophisticated security bureaucrat but he just might revert to an older culture and see what we've done as blood-feud. And blood demands blood. Mine if possible, yours if I'm not caught. Yours anyway if you connive at my escape, or if I stay and then you side with me.'

Anne nodded slowly, she had not expected him to be so perceptive. 'I know now that there's nothing for me here, there never was if I'd faced it honestly. So I'll take whatever chance remains and come with you. The point is, how?'

But no matter how often they threshed it over, the how remained elusive. They would simply have to walk out, wait for any split-second chance events might give them to get past guards, almost certainly downstairs as well as on their corridor. They would be without money, papers, food or more than the sketchiest idea of Bulqize's surroundings: the idea was madness if the alternative had not been a firing-squad. There was also the bleeper Stephen carried; unless he could fix it in a hurry they would be picked up within minutes.

Anne left him feeling intensely depressed, slept heavily for a while that night but woke very early, mind caught on a ratchet of despair. They must go, but deprived of proper food and medical attention Stephen would not regain much strength, and without strength they could not cross the mountains even supposing they could hide successfully for the month or so which remained before spring.

She curled into the bed like a hibernating animal, it was simply not worth the effort of battling any further. Surely they must be safer to stay and leave Millosh to decide their fate, for he would know he had to live with his decision afterwards.

It might even be the saving of him.

Resolution formed, she drowsed as light strengthened and snow fell outside.

She was wakened by the sound of boots in the corridor and a moment later her door was flung open to reveal half a dozen Sigurimi.

'Up and dress,' said their sergeant brusquely.

So they had not had two days' respite after all, and Kaderi's decision was made. Anne felt completely calm since there was nothing she could do about it, almost relieved the choice was out of her hands. 'If you'll wait outside I shall be with you in a few minutes.'

The sergeant spat. 'You can come as you are if you want, it's all the same to me.' He added something to his men that she did not catch and they sniggered, spreading out around the room so each could watch his fill while the sergeant threw her clothes on the floor one at a time for her to pick up.

It was absurd to mind, as if she was a girl fresh out of convent-school. She did though, very much, and most of all because this was Kaderi's ordering, his first thought on recovering consciousness.

As soon as she had dressed she was hustled along deserted

passages, hostel staff prudently hiding from Sigurimi. A military truck was drawn up in the street outside, Stephen already in the back, Twodex on the floor beside him.

'You all right?' he asked, and stood to help her up, fingers comfortingly tight on hers.

She nodded, throat locked on words.

He said no more, but held her hand all the long way down to Tirana.

Once there, they drew up in front of the kind of building all countries provide for government offices: the style varies but their dusty gloom and clutter of subdivided spaces transcends time and culture. It was heavily guarded, which was no surprise since Albanians guarded everything, and they stood a long time with rifles in their backs while authority was fetched, consulted, sent scurrying for more authority and returned with reinforcements. Eventually they were shoved into a room furnished with a table like an aircraft-carrier and nothing else, a pair of surly youths stationed by the door, fingering guns. Sigurimi of course, cut and cloth of their uniforms better than anything the army could show, arrogance in every gesture. They could not have been twenty but already everyone except superiors in their own service feared and stood aside from them.

Stephen eyed them with dislike and turned his back to lean against the table; the journey on steel truck-seats had tried him severely, new stitches draggingly uncomfortable on rough Albanian roads. 'Sigurimi Headquarters, do you suppose?'

Anne thought of Millosh's office where she had been before. 'I don't think so. Ministry of Justice perhaps.'

She saw the sardonic look on his face at the thought that any Albanian ministry should bear such a name, but he turned to the sentries. Information was worth the risk of a blow. 'Is this the Ministry of Justice?'

One of the boys snicked the catch of his rifle half a dozen times, to assert his power presumably, but eventually shook his head. 'The Ministry of Justice was abolished four years ago when Party Leader Hoxha called for economies in the administration of the state.'

Stephen gave a crack of laughter. 'What an inspired choice

139

for economy! I am sure Albania operates more smoothly without such a check on its actions.'

'Yes indeed, the Party had criticized its functions severely,' the guard replied seriously.

They lapsed into silence. Endless waiting dragged at nerves and conjured up a longing to be done with it all, though if they waited for a People's Court, then sentence was already decided. Anne felt a muscle twitch in her cheek and put up a hand to still it; the Sigurimi knew all about letting time work for them and were capable of keeping them here for days. The only surprise was that they were allowed to wait together. So far.

Feet often sounded in the passage outside, hastening past unaccompanied by the usual gossiping office voices. Once one of their guards dropped his rifle and the clatter made them all jump; he looked embarrassed and made them stand instead of sitting on the table so as to recover his self-esteem.

'Perhaps they're going to keep us here until Kaderi is fit enough to return to Tirana,' observed Stephen gloomily. 'He wants to see the colour of our blood for himself.'

Anne winced; unfortunately it was only too likely. 'Tell me, what were you doing when you were nine years old?'

He rasped his hand over unshaven chin, if he was surprised he did not show it. 'My family farmed – still farms – on Exmoor. Nine years old; it wouldn't be long after the end of the war. No petrol because we looked after our stock on horseback, so no travel beyond the nearest small town which was Dulverton. Plenty of food though, whatever the rationing system said. I used to fish in the Barle, poaching I suppose, and ride all over the moor. It's beautiful country. I love going there still, even if I never doubted that engineering and figures were my future rather than farming. At nine I'd just built my first wind-driven generator.' He grinned. 'It produced half a dozen sparks and a few faintly-glowing filaments. We used oil-lamps as long as I lived at home.'

Anne nodded; the tough, self-reliant country background explained a good deal about him. Only foreigners like herself subconsciously expected all Englishmen to come from London. Her mind swung back to the reason why she had asked: at nine years

140

old Kaderi had killed his first German and seen his family obliterated. It explained a good deal about him as well.

More steps outside and they both swung round, such a purposeful ring of boots and weaponry could only mean them. Their guards stiffened but the escort this time wore an additional splendour of red at collar and cuff; Anne's fear of immediate trial might not be so very wrong after all.

They were taken along chipped-paint passages and down a wide staircase into a marble hall, which once had been well-proportioned but was now disfigured by plywood hutches for guards and clerks. Oppressive red and black of Albania's flag everywhere, plaques of its crossed pickaxe and rifle symbol, then beyond again and into another passage. Scrubbed and gleaming this time and hung with the black double eagle of Skanderbeg, Albania's national hero, so many of them and such a blank of anything else that Anne felt as if she was entering a stage-set for Hitchcock's *Birds*.

Stephen's halting pace annoyed the guard, their precision lost as they had to keep shifting step and tripped over each other marking time. He smiled tightly and slowed still further, hand under Anne's elbow in a determinedly unmilitary gesture. Annoying Sigurimi was a pleasure he no longer saw any reason to resist.

Anne had felt quite calm, now she was very frightened. However much you tell yourself that you will accept the end when it comes, the mind refuses acceptance when the moment is here and now. A fly was crawling up a door where they were forced to wait again: how beautiful it was, how delicate the tracery of wing wiped nonchalantly on one leg. Strange if this should be the last fly she ever saw.

The door opened from within and an officer led them forward, guard firmly shut outside. A long table with about twenty faces gathered round it, all staring at them. More flags and eagles. Yes, a People's Court. At least Kaderi had not wanted to wait and see their blood himself.

'Ah, Shok Astell and Shoqë Storoch,' said Party Leader Hoxha. 'We wished to consult you again on this matter of the talcum powder, while the Central Committee were considering our production schedule.'

17

Anne and Stephen stared at him, utterly stupefied.

'We understand that you were involved in the earth tremor at Bulqize and regret it,' added a disagreeable-looking man lower down the table. 'However, the Central Committee of the Party has no more time to waste on this affair and we demand an answer now.'

Stephen cleared his throat. 'An answer to what?'

'These designs, of course. We have studied the question thoroughly and find that a compromise is necessary. Flowers are all very well, but the women of Albania must never forget our socialist purpose, nor the unceasing vigilance of the Party. The pencils which are to be made available to children will have "Long live the people of Albania and the Five Year Plan" stamped on them. Why not the powder? It should be packed in our national colours at the very least.'

'National colours!' spat a man seated closer to Hoxha. 'The carton should be printed with a message from the Party Secretary. National colours are unsuited to such a purpose.'

'You don't think that perhaps the Party Secretary's thoughts might also fall into the same category?' enquired Stephen in the voice of an earnest seeker after truth.

He was beginning to enjoy himself Anne could tell, while alarm bells still rang in her own mind. Absurdity trapped as easily as violence.

'Certainly not,' interrupted Hoxha, before anyone could risk their career on such a difficult point. 'There is no time or place unsuited to the encouragement and guidance given by the Party.'

Twenty hostile pairs of eyes swivelled instantly to Stephen.

'The home is the most suitable place of all for a personal message from the Party Leader,' said a thickset man with a face like carved oak.

Everyone nodded, the party line happily rediscovered amongst the hazards of a consumer-tainted policy.

'Then surely your problem is solved,' replied Stephen courteously. 'The Party Leader composes his exhortation, and the state printing presses set it up to the exact size and shape of the carton, so no millimetre is left uncovered. It should achieve a striking effect, especially if you employed inks of Albania's national colours.'

Murmuring began around the table, swiftly degenerating into staccato-sharp argument. Hoxha lifted a clip of papers and delicately let it drop; the inaudible sound silenced everyone. 'Mademoiselle Anna, I ask you. For this particular purpose do you not think that subtlety might be more effective than an approach used every day? I wonder whether perhaps a woman might read my words on her gift more carefully because she has enjoyed looking at flowers first. When she has done so, then she would see national colours and the Party's message. What do you think?'

He spoke in French and ill-humour immediately deepened around the table as incomprehension brought fear of some plot at the Committee's expense.

'Yes, Comrade Hoxha,' Anne felt obliged to attempt French too. 'The message should certainly be prominent and perhaps in stronger colours, but if the intention is to give pleasure then flowers would be very effective.' No one who retained a glimmer of prudence disagreed with a Party Leader on such an issue.

'You speak of gifts and rewards. Is this powder to be distributed free then? I understood it was to be sold,' Stephen had sensed the atmosphere and took the opportunity to return to Albanian, although clearly he understood French. The committee relaxed warily.

'Naturally it would be wrong to weaken our efforts to build a socialist future by diverting resources into free distribution of luxuries. As it is, we have had to re-schedule the Plan to allow for something which is, after all, a frivolity. The powder will cost fifty leks a half kilo.' The man who replied flicked a

143

glance at Hoxha and then stared at the table, tacitly expressing disagreement with the whole business.

'A half kilo?' echoed Anne blankly. 'You are never going to sell it in such . . . that – that will make a very large package surely? Fifty leks, why, that's worth nearly—'

'Three pounds fifty,' said Stephen. His face was still but she could hear laughter in his voice. Wages in Albania varied between two hundred and four hundred leks a week. 'When the Party . . . gives, it would not wish to be ungenerous as to quantity.'

'Certainly not,' said Hoxha. His prestige was involved in the talcum powder project and nothing short of a coup d'état could stop it, so he found some pleasure in old-style Balkan generosity. 'There is no machinery directly suitable for manufacturing such packaging, but we have a factory in Durres which normally prints cartons for figs. Could you adapt it to this purpose, Shok Astell, while Shoqë Anna draws her design to the size the machine will take? Powder weighs lighter than figs, so it will be half-kilo size as I said.'

Stephen hesitated; Anne was certain that he had never tackled anything remotely similar to adapting fig packaging to take talcum powder. 'If it is possible, I will certainly—'

Hoxha laid his hands flat on the table with a snap. 'All things are possible in the service of the Party. Recollect your position here as trespassers and imperialist spies, then see whether you are willing to accept this task.'

Menace slipped from its sheath and glittered coldly where affability had been before.

'I don't forget it, although not a trespasser by choice nor an imperialist spy except by your definition. But Shok Kaderi has ordered me to complete work urgently for him and will be angered to discover that I have not resumed it while he lay sick. Also, I am not a production engineer; Albania surely has many men better qualified than I for such a task.'

Suddenly they had been presented with a ghost of a chance. Anne could sense how Stephen chose his words with infinite care, though he looked guileless and anxious to assist. Yesterday they had been faced by the choice of waiting for a firing squad or running with scarcely a chance of breaking free, today Albanian politics had presented them with an opportunity to be exploited, where success might give them time to recover under the patronage of Party Leader Hoxha himself. Time for snow to melt in high mountain passes and for them to plan escape at their leisure.

'Naturally an Albanian could succeed in whatever I asked him to do, we train many excellent engineers every year. However, they are allocated to the Plan, and you could do this without the need to disrupt another project. As for Kaderi—' Hoxha glanced round the table, every eye fastened on him now. Normally Kaderi would be here and part of the struggle which age was fastening on Hoxha's throat, but few would object to strengthening their own position by humiliating the chief of security in his absence. 'Like all of us, Kaderi accepts the will of the Party. This project takes priority, and he must wait until you have completed it before claiming your services again. I will give orders for you to travel to Durres tomorrow.'

So, quite casually, was shelved a plan to survey minerals on which Albania's future and the ambitions of greater powers depended, in favour of a scheme to box talcum powder. Not urgency but the Party Leader's support was what mattered.

Anne could scarcely believe their luck as they were ushered from the meeting of the Central Committee with far more ceremony than they had entered. Unless Kaderi wished to launch his bid for power prematurely by defying the Central Committee, he would now have no choice but to wait and keep revenge leashed while they fiddled with fig-machinery. She felt stupidly delighted also that he had not planned the humiliations of the morning, although she knew he was capable of doing so. Whether he was also capable of revenging himself after weeks of waiting, after perhaps renewing a human contact with her which she knew was precious to him, remained to be seen.

'What I find so splendid about the Party is that you can always rely on it. Any eventuality and bingo!' Stephen smacked his fist on his palm for the benefit of the microphone on his chest, 'it carries through logic to an extent one would not have believed possible.' He doubled up laughing against a plywood hutch in the magnificent marble hall.

18

After bleak discomfort in the mountains and occasionally-thawed slop at Bulqize, Durres was a return to civilization. A tree-lined boulevard and stucco villas along the edge of the sea were pleasant reminders that they were after all in twentieth century Europe, the air sufficiently warm for it to be possible to imagine a Mediterranean spring in the not-too-distant future.

The town was built along a strip of land between what had once been salt marsh and the sea. There was the usual clutter of a port: storage tanks and cranes, factories making cigarettes and machinery, a refinery looking stark and very new, which reminded Anne of the pride her escort had felt when they passed a similar complex an age ago on the way from Gjirokaster.

'You have to admit that for a poor nation starting without even a railway, they have achieved a good deal,' she remarked to Stephen. They were walking along the deserted beach, the inevitable armed guards a few paces behind. They had not heard anything of Kaderi in the two weeks they had been at Durres, but one day the military guard had been replaced by Sigurimi, their rooms separated in the empty hotel where they were living, more guards placed in the one between them. Neither said anything but both guessed that Kaderi had returned to his office.

'Yes, they've done a certain amount. I would find it depressing, though, if I had to admit that progress could only be achieved by making talcum powder an affair of state. Automation one end of a factory and blokes running around putting white-hot metal into horse-troughs with tongs at the

146

other.' He hunched his shoulders into the wind, looking out over a grey sea towards where Italy lay, perhaps seventy miles away.

'And you don't admit it?'

'No. Do you?'

Anne thought about it carefully. Her trouble was that she saw too clearly the faults of both systems, understood that if the restraints imposed by want and fear were too precipitately removed, then people who had known nothing else would refuse to accept easier disciplines. Nor did deprived backgrounds breed leaders who had mastered the arts of moderation. 'I don't know. After being brought up to expect certainty in everything, I find I'm not sure of as much as I thought. Certainty seems like arrogance to me now, and violence gives me indigestion.'

He laughed and slipped his hand under her arm. 'Thank God for that, anyway.'

With contact, she was instantly aware of him; aware above all of pressures he was only just succeeding in holding under control. In the mountains and at Bulqize he had been too frozen and exhausted to find her proximity trying, since they came to Durres this was the first time he had touched her willingly. After they left the Central Committee building in Tirana, she had collapsed with delayed shock: a day which had begun when an armed squad watched her dress and ended with nerves as farcically loosened as they had previously been tensed, left her so shaken she could not stand. One moment she had been laughing with Stephen and the next tears were streaming down her face. Stephen had held her then, let her feel the tremble in him too and comforted her with his warmth. But he had not slept with her, although that was the release both needed: the shadow of Kaderi lay between them again the moment her attack had passed.

Stephen wanted her badly though, she could tell; he had been months now in Albania and without a woman until last week. Then Anne had been restless and early one morning saw an Albanian girl slip out of his room: she had been acting as maid in their hotel, was attractive and no peasant. Anne guessed she was Sigurimi-planted for just such a purpose, and hoped that Stephen realized it too: she ought to warn him but recoiled from interfering in something which was scarcely her affair.

After a moment Stephen dropped her arm, hands back in his pockets, mouth a tight line. 'I'm returning to the factory in an hour. They should have those parts welded up by then and I want another test run in the morning.'

'How long now?'

'For a full production run of cartons? Ten days, I suppose. I expect plenty of breakdowns though, it might be as much as three weeks before I have all the bugs ironed out.' He shook his head warningly and spread the fingers of one hand twice where the guard could not see. Eight days. Before eight days were up they must find a foolproof way out of Durres, a place where neither went a step without a guard nor covered more than a couple of streets without demands for papers they did not possess. At least both were fit again; Albania was a small country but the mountains enclosing it were nearly nine thousand feet high and most passes would be too heavily guarded to attempt. They looked longingly at an Italian ship loading in the port, but quite apart from strict security which sealed off the whole docks area, a solitary non-communist ship would be the first place the Albanians looked.

After Stephen left, Anne stood by the window of her room, fiddling irresolutely with inks and paper. Since she lacked anything else to do and needed to divert her mind, she had drawn and re-drawn her design for the powder carton and felt reluctant pleasure in the result. The fig machinery could only print in four colours so she had used delicate shades on a background suggesting mountains, intricate interlocking of each flower species providing variety the colours lacked. Stephen had groaned at the complicated setting-up required on antique machinery, but they needed as much time as they could gain and he adapted to what she wanted. The factory staff became intrigued by innovation too. Nothing defeated them, fig-packers brought in relatives who might weld plates or forge parts illicitly, pride growing in achievement, with the prospect of producing something attractive after years of sickly figs.

Only one problem remained insoluble: Albanian talc would be marketed perfumed with figs.

'I dare say it won't matter,' Stephen had observed philosophically. 'They've never had it before and won't again until long after they've forgotten the smell. We've scoured everything and the only difference is that now the powder smells of chemicals as well as figs.'

Anne had laughed but felt sad for women who would not know the scent as well as the touch – just once – of luxury. She picked up a pencil and turned as the door clicked.

Kaderi came in.

His arm was lightly plastered but not in a sling, face thinned so it looked like undercut carving. He studied her drawings and then stared at her, unspeaking. She had forgotten how still he could be. She had chosen also to believe that, because her last illusions were stripped away when he ordered Stephen knifed at Bulqize, the attraction he held for her would sour and fade, though understanding might remain. For understanding Millosh Kaderi, chief of security, was something you could walk away from if you wanted to enough.

Now he was in her room and made her instantly aware of how he looked and breathed and felt; life changed because of it.

She went over and stood close to him, not touching. He was not a man to touch without his own wish that she should. 'Your arm, has it healed well?'

What inanities came to the rescue when so much else must be silenced.

He bowed unsmilingly, a curiously old-world gesture which betrayed unease he did not show. 'Unlike Nako, I shall recover.'

'So has Stephen recovered when the next nod from you would have killed him,' she retorted, pleasure in him dimmed by reality again.

'I shall be waiting for him when Party Secretary Hoxha has finished with his services.' Unslaked fury showed; only vital strategies concerned with his succession to Hoxha's power could have forced him to obey the Central Committee and defer revenge by the short time their work at Durres would take.

'Millosh, please! You don't need to, no one else knows what happened! Why must you—'

'You know why I must and so does he. Not for murder, but because he attacked one of my men. It would make no difference if Nako had only been stunned.'

'And if Nako had not been yours?'

'I grew up in a village where blood demanded blood. Astell would be less of a man if he hadn't revenged himself when he had the chance; I don't consider him a murderer any more than he thinks of himself as such.'

'You wouldn't understand it I suppose, but he does blame himself. He said that a civilized man who was more or less chained to another for so long, ought not to have needed to kill. He saw it as defeat that Nako brutalized him while he could not alter Nako at all.'

Kaderi shrugged. 'Then he's a fool. Men like Nako do not change. But such judgements are unimportant since they cannot affect the issue.' He kissed her then, without any warning of his change of mood. 'I also resent the hold he has on your regard.'

She could love Millosh so easily and felt so much more than understanding for him: hate, pity, sorrow, generosity and hope. Above all hope rekindled, because whatever he said, he had come and loved her still.

They came together quickly and strongly, as if in celebration, incapable of subtlety. Afterwards, Anne held him tightly. 'Millosh, what are we going to do?'

He lay on his back, staring at the ceiling. 'Nothing.'

'Nothing? How can you mean that? I know what you risk each time you see me; you wouldn't do it unless—'

'Unless you had become part of my life. As much a part as bone and blood. There is nothing we can do, even so.'

'Of course there is something to be done, there always is if the wish is there.'

'No.'

'Why not?'

'Because I shall soon have Astell shot and should never be easy with you, nor able to trust you afterwards.'

'Let him go then! In Albania I can see that—' Anne swallowed, in Albania he could not allow anyone to defy the Sigurimi and live. Revulsion shook her and words dried.

'You see,' he said gently. 'There would always be others in Astell's place, tearing us apart. You cannot change and nor can I.'

It wasn't a question of loving or not loving, but simply that the cost of loving him was too terrible to be borne.

'You realize that one day you are going to have to kill me too?' she said evenly.

He shifted uncontrollably. 'No. No, Anna, never.'

He knew, and would not face it.

'Yes. Once Stephen is executed you can't let me go, nor be sure of keeping me safe for ever in prison, which would itself be a living death. If you can't hold me with love then there's no other way. And Millosh . . . nor will you be able to exist much longer with what you do, however you justify it to yourself.'

He did not reply, his hands like those of a drowning man as ecstasy vanished and crude fear was kindled in its place. Tenderness replaced by violence, glad yielding by the stirred dregs of disgust. No way of forgetting any longer that his nod had nearly killed Stephen, and soon he intended to finish what he had begun.

Anne bore it, knowing this was her last chance. At the end of it Millosh must have fought free from a hideous legacy or the bond between them broke. If he could change at all then she would stay, and the decision would probably cost both of them their lives. But no matter what happened she would never regret a risk so knowingly taken, for both their sakes and for Albania when Hoxha died. The same clarity of thought told her that if he could not change, then to stay as he was now would bring only misery and widening ripples of disaster.

He rolled away from her at last and stood looking out of the window. 'I can't let Astell go. I don't know what he has discovered on his survey, even whether he possesses any information at all which is of value. Nor have I any way of finding out since I cannot believe anything he says, either now or after I have extracted whatever he chooses to tell me under pressure. And once he has been interrogated then he certainly can't be released. I mistook the kind of man he was when I ordered him to make this survey, and now he also has the power to make my country absurd before the nations of the world.' He flicked his fingers at the drawings for the powder carton, voice dry and toneless. The Central Committee of the Party would not waste time on such nonsense once he controlled it. 'I told you, Anna. In this we are both trapped and both the losers.'

'If it was just Nako, could you forgive?'

He came over and kissed her, without passion. 'For you, perhaps. For myself, no. It doesn't arise anyway. But whatever happens, remember I was honest with you. Astell could be dead and you never know how or why: it is always easy to keep Sigurimi business secret. If I deceived you into thinking we might have a future together then it could have been a long time before you discovered actions of mine you considered unforgiveable, which circumstances occasionally force me to commit.' He turned and went out.

19

The first production run of talc cartons at the fig factory was a disaster. An uncontrived, unqualified disaster. Ink smeared, guillotines sheared the Party Secretary's message in half, the bold red and black in which his words were printed made Anne's design appear insipid, the truck bringing powder from Tirana was diverted to carry steel rods to the port.

Dramatic scenes occurred as humiliated workers blamed each other; only Stephen's Sigurimi guards appeared unmoved. After Kaderi's visit they followed him so closely that he tripped over them every time he turned, fraying tempers further.

'Party Secretary Hoxha will be displeased,' observed one, picking up a smudged carton. 'Shok Kaderi won't have to wait much longer for his turn. Our sergeant has orders to inform him the moment matters are completed here, but it would seem that the Anglez is too incompetent to be worth preserving much longer.' They knew Kaderi's feeling towards his prisoner, but not the cause of it.

Anne had gone down to the factory to watch, her part was done and she felt miserably restless, the sense of impending crisis overwhelming. The worst part was not being able to talk to Stephen: the desperate gamble of escape must be accepted within days and they had not concerted any plan at all. One or other of Stephen's guards checked the box on his chest several times a day, the factory workers sympathetic and murmuring as they came to know and like Stephen. Another reason why Kaderi would soon be able to persuade Hoxha that it was dangerous to leave them in Durres any longer.

Stephen appeared remarkably unruffled by it all. For three

days he worked his way through every faulty setting in the factory, Anne hauled out of bed at three in the morning to advise on inks.

'For heaven's sake, anyone would think you really cared about packaging socialist talc,' she said, irritated. He knew perfectly well that Millosh waited for him at the end of it all.

'We mustn't disappoint the Party,' replied Stephen cheerfully. 'Tomorrow we'll have a full production run again and this time I think it'll be okay. I've told everyone I'll be down to throw the switches myself, are you coming to witness our triumph too?'

They were walking back to their hotel very late on the third evening, guard at their heels as usual.

'I suppose I might as well be in at the death,' said Anne bitterly.

He glanced at her. 'Never accept sentence until you're sure the firing squad's using live ammunition.'

'They are. Did you think for a moment that they – he – wouldn't?' She didn't care who heard.

'I certainly don't propose to stay and find out. Come to my room when we get back to the hotel.'

She stared at his hidden microphone in frantic warning. How could he have forgotten after so long?

He smiled. 'Don't worry. They have to play back the tape to hear what we've said, and no translator will bother to sit over it until morning. We shall be gone by then.'

Tonight. After all the months of strain, of being torn by wanting and not wanting, tonight they would be committed, the faint hope that Millosh might change be lost for ever. Once they ran every soldier and Sigurimi would shoot on sight.

Stephen was watching her. 'You want to come, don't you? It's long odds against success, but we've nothing to lose. Stay here and we're shot anyway.'

She nodded, Kaderi had warned her plainly enough. No logic could explain her obstinate belief that when the time came he would not be able to kill, knowing he destroyed her too. 'Yes, I want to go. When?'

'Once we're back at the hotel go to your room as usual and prepare for the night, but when you come along to the shower make sure you leave your door and the balcony shutter ajar. I will be outside my room having my box checked, I'll annoy the guard or something to spin it out. I'll persuade you into my room, be as hesitant as you like but come, and have some trousers with you.'

It seemed stupidly reckless to discuss plans openly, yet there was so much she couldn't ask: if they should get clear away then this night's tape would come under minute scrutiny for clues to what they intended. She touched the shape under his shirt and lifted her eyebrows interrogatively. Unless he could somehow rid himself of the bleeper any attempt was doomed. 'I hope so,' he said obliquely, shaking his head. He slowed his pace and slid his arm around her, shoulder-blade fitting easily to his hand. 'And now we need to give some colour to our pleasures together in my room tonight. My guards have been fairly crude over the way I've failed to make the most of my opportunities so far.'

Taken by surprise, Anne felt a moment of recoil. So much of her was tuned to Millosh that even the touch of someone as familiar as Stephen seemed a betrayal. He sensed it too and instinctively relaxed his hold, face tight. Then his hand slid from her shoulder to her waist and he pulled her to him, lips just brushing hers. Neither spoke. If they had been strangers who cared nothing for each other, then Kaderi's presence between them would not have been so intolerable.

They lingered up the stairs, heads close together while their guards sniggered behind, and Anne gave Stephen her most enticing smile when she left him for her own room.

Once inside she undressed hastily, refusing to think beyond the moment. She had no idea how Stephen thought they might get out of the hotel when each of them had a guard outside their door, who looked in whenever he felt like it. She went out on the balcony and stared down into darkness. It must be fifty feet to the ground, and their rooms were separated by the one used by off-duty Sigurimi, who also kept a receiver tuned to the impulses from Stephen's bleeper; there had been a fuss one night when some fault had developed in it. Kaderi had also ordered barbed wire strung on a projecting barrier from the balconies below and either side of their rooms, quite rightly he considered it a more effective obstacle when kept out of their reach.

Anne shivered; she had a reasonable head for heights but had never dreamed that Stephen would try to run from here, where guards were piled a dozen deep, and since climbing the mine-shaft she wasn't sure how much nerve for climbing she retained. He must be crazy, a quick bolt in the streets surely would be easier.

She banged on the door for the guard to let her out, turned off the light and left her latch unsnapped, the man unsuspicious since she was not inside. The next part was surprisingly easy. Their guards had obviously been speculating on the likely outcome of the night; hers laughed knowingly when they turned the passage corner to find Stephen chatting with the sergeant outside his door.

He turned and smiled as they approached, eyes warm. Anne did not think his expression entirely a sham and felt bitterly regretful, how foolish and ungovernable were emotions which responded to Kaderi instead of Stephen, who was certainly the better man. 'You look very beautiful,' he said now.

'Considering I'm in Albanian state issue nightwear, I take that as a compliment worth having,' she retorted lightly.

'It's truth, no compliment. You'd add distinction to canvas.'

His eyes dropped to her body and she blushed furiously; guards and sergeant were staring too in open lust. 'I—I'll say good night then. I'm just going to the shower.' She made as if to push past.

'That seems a waste, let me come and share it with you.' He held her arm and forced her to face him. There was a vertical line between his eyes which she had seen before when he was angry. He jerked her to him. 'Or better still, come and join me inside.'

They were speaking English but a child could have understood the offer, the reluctance with which she allowed herself to be persuaded.

At last they were inside his room, door shut behind them, Stephen's back against it. He wiped his face. 'Thank God. Unwilling women are the devil.' He wasn't smiling, though. He turned and set a chair under the door handle. 'With luck no one will be surprised when they can't get in or see through the keyhole.'

'What now?'

'We'll have to wait but not for long, I hope. It's already very late. Find yourself a shirt and get dressed while I listen on the balcony to what's going on next door.'

She scrambled into trousers and shirt, heart hammering. Her watch had not survived the Dakota's crash but she judged it to be nearly one in the morning and there were few sounds from the guards next door, only the occasional shuffle of feet and mumbled conversation from the two on duty in the passage outside. They at least were pleased to have each other's company instead of being set at different doors around a corner of corridor.

Stephen came in, closing the balcony door. 'Turn on the light, will you? Are they both outside?'

She nodded. 'Down by the bathroom, I think, where they can smoke without the sergeant smelling anything.'

'Good, the further away the better. The sergeant's snoring already. I'm sorry to have been so arbitrary about this but discussion was too dangerous until we were ready to go, and this is the only way I've been able to work out which might give us the start we've simply got to have.'

He hauled Twodex on to the bed and swiftly began unscrewing panels. 'We'll talk in a minute if all goes well, but here's the first gamble we must take. Hold this, will you?'

Anne held the edge of some kind of plate and pulled gently when he told her, worried that he should waste time now with his blasted machine.

'Careful,' he warned. 'It's heavy.'

It was, and must make up a great deal of Twodex's weight, a black panel about an inch thick made of some immensely dense material. 'What is it?

'The screening which protects Twodex's computer from damage by ultrasonics. A major improvement to Threedex will be something much lighter.' He stripped off his shirt, chains across his chest gleaming where friction had rubbed them smooth. 'Listen, Kaderi doesn't realize it, but the kind of ultrasonic shock Twodex can deliver will certainly knock out a pipsqueak transmitter like this bleeper. The problem is not to collapse my own lungs doing it, and somehow we've got to get that protective screening under my harness. I've taken out seven-eighths of Twodex's power so then it should be safe enough, but we'll only find out by doing it.'

'Steve, for God's sake, what if you're wrong?'

'Then it will kill me a few days before Kaderi planned to do it. I don't think it will though, and I'm very familiar with Twodex after all.'

'You've never calculated safety factors for using it against yourself. And what if the sergeant wakes and notices the signal on his receiver's dead?'

'We'll just have to hope he won't. It would take too long to try it any other way; I'd hoped the swine would grow tired of checking the fastenings but they haven't; too pleasant stripping me five times a day, I suppose.' He had hidden it well, but his tone showed some of the rancour he felt against Albania and its works. He soaped his chest carefully and then stood against the foot of the bed, facing it, arms spread on the footboard, shoulders bent so the chain slackened slightly across his chest. 'Shove it under and work it across as best you can, and Anne – hurry.'

She bit her lip. The screening was heavy and rigid, his harness still tight in spite of the way privation had thinned him down. Soap helped but spread slipperiness everywhere, so she became worried that she would drop the plate and bring guards running. Stephen stood braced while she heaved and fumbled, trying to hunch more slack into the chain while still leaving space for the plate to fit between waist and shoulder.

'I can't do it!' she said despairingly, as it caught against the further cross-over, leaving part of a lung uncovered.

'You must. I'll hold it while you lever it up.' He shifted so the edge of screening was against the bed-board, nearly his full weight on it now. He closed his eyes; furrowed skin was preventing it sliding through and would tear when she added her strength to his. 'Go on.'

Blindly, she heaved as he ordered, the quicker the better if he was determined on this. He grunted once as it moved and then stood very awkwardly, blood bright at waist and shoulder.

He brushed her aside when she would have helped him and showed her the different firing sequences on Twodex now he had reduced its power. 'I'll lie on the bed with Twodex on top of me, sensors aligned on the box. Muffle it with everything you can find, but with only one system firing it should make more hiss than thud.' In the mountains Anne had been surprised by the relative silence of ultrasonics.

Rugs, bedding, clothing, she piled everything where he showed her: he looked white and strained now, knew better than she the nature of the chance he was taking. 'Be sure to get the firing sequence right or I'll have to set everything again.'

Anne fumbled, fingers trembling, then kissed him impulsively, meaning it this time, his sweat wet on her lips.

He smiled, Twodex a monster crouching over him. 'Leave well alone, my dear. Now, watch me. I'll breathe as much air out of my lungs as I can; when I have, fire at once.'

She watched as, helped by the weight of his machine he drove out air, then forced her mind into sequences of numbers, her fingers into precision.

There was a hissing thud of sound, and instantly Anne strained at Twodex, lifting it off him, bundling aside coverings. 'Steve?'

For a long moment he didn't answer, then he flopped over and vomited violently.

One of their guards thumped on the door. 'What's going on? Let me in! It is forbidden to lock the door.'

Anne's mind went utterly blank, mouth dry, words frozen

The handle rattled again. 'Let me in, or I break down the door.'

Somehow she took hold of skittering senses. 'Not at any price if I've a man worth having. Wait until morning, tonight is ours.'

Her voice jumped uncertainly and the guard laughed. 'So the Anglez has surprised you, has he? Me too, Sweetheart.'

'Go and screw yourselves, before I twist your equipment round your ears,' said Stephen, using an exceptionally coarse Albanian expression Anne had not heard before.

There was a startled silence and then the guards laughed, clattering slightly as they settled themselves again.

'Are you all right?' breathed Anne.

He lay with an arm across his eyes. 'Yes. Give me a minute and then we must get this screening out again.'

It was far more than a minute before he stirred again but she did not dare to hurry him, although haste was vital.

The screening came out easier than it went in, and she made him wait again while she patched torn skin as best she could. He was breathing in short hard gulps, face grey in unshaded electric light.

'Has that silenced the bleeper do you think?'

'God, yes. A dose of ultrasonics like that will have blown the transmitter. Tell me, now we can talk safely and before we are committed, have you thought of any plan you think has a chance?'

'The factory. I thought that at night it might be a possibility, sometimes there's a lorry locked into the yard ready for a morning run. I couldn't think how to slip bleeper and guards to get there though.'

'That's what I reckoned too. A consignment of talc from Tirana came down in sacks yesterday without the half-kilo containers to put it in. The driver is setting out before dawn to get them; I made such a damned fuss he promised to leave early so he'd be back within the day. Paperwork and everything is cleared ready for a quick journey.' He fumbled into shirt and sweater, his breathing still sounding bad. A lorry though, if they could make it then they would be able to drop over the tailgate on the journey and rest up until he recovered.

'How do you plan to reach the factory?' she asked, wondering whether he could stay on his feet for the hour or so which would certainly be necessary.

'Your room, if we can reach it across the balconies. Both guards are outside this door. You left yours open?' She nodded. 'It's around a corner of corridor. We can get down to the first floor from there and climb out of a window when we reach it, and so avoid the guard on the main doors.'

Anne thought about it, confidence suddenly growing; there were guards next door and in the passage, more in the main hall and hotel entry, but the rest of the building was empty. If only they could reach her room undetected, they could be away from the hotel before dawn broke—since this one night the routine of checking them several times while they slept was relaxed.

She turned off the light and opened the shutters carefully. Outside it was completely dark, wind brisk and noisy off the sea. 'I'll go first,' she whispered. Stephen needed every minute they could gain to recover, and waiting was worse anyway.

'Take it carefully, it's about a four-foot stretch.'

She certainly would, the drop to the ground yawned in her memory. After Bulqize shaft she had not intended ever to climb again.

Stephen stood close to the rail so she could use his shoulder to help balance, but there was nothing to hold to once she had to straighten, hands flat against concrete, feet on an inch-wide rail. Then she must step across four feet of space, making no sound as bare toes reached for the rail of the next-door balcony. And once straddled across space with a foot on each rail she was stuck, concrete rough under face and hands. There was nothing to hold, no projection to help ease her weight from one leg to the other. If silence had not been so vital she could have done it easily, launched herself sideways to land in a heap on the further balcony, but the clatter of her arrival would certainly have aroused their off-duty guards.

When she realized what she must do she felt the palms of her hands grow wet but there wasn't time to think. One hand away from the wall, the other dropped low, only her own balance held her now, legs quivering with strain. High and to her left was the metal strut which supported an awning in the summer. She must estimate where it was and reach both hands for it in a movement which would swing her body too. If she missed she would fall and the guards would wake; if her judgement was correct then her grip on the strut would arrest her movement and allow her to drop the short distance to the balcony without sound.

Twice she was ready and could not force herself to move, Stephen whispering something she couldn't catch, no one and nothing in all the world but herself and the drop behind her back. Then somehow it was done, not quite knowing how.

She pivoted and swung, a blow on her wrist instead of her grasping palms as she misjudged distance, a scrabble and then she was swinging from the strut, dropped the short distance to the balcony floor.

In a flash she turned, not thinking of it now. Not daring to think of it, because almost at once she must do the same again to her own balcony. Stephen. Exactly what could and couldn't he do?

In fact his height and length of leg probably blinded him to the difficulties she encountered. His breathing sounded dangerously loud but otherwise he managed quite easily. As they crouched on the balcony together they could hear snores through closed shutters. Unless one of the guards lay awake they should be safe enough. Very carefully, they edged past the window and Anne groped for the far rail, chill metal driving home fear. Stephen steadied her as she climbed again, God how she hated heights. Everything seemed worse this time. She could not stop thinking of the barbed wire barrier she would strike first if she fell, and suddenly was paralysed, forced to wait until the attack passed. Then she launched herself blindly, knowing that if she hesitated she was lost. One hand struck metal and slipped, the other gripped for an instant and slipped too. Feet and knees hit concrete and she landed sprawling.

20

Stephen moved instantly, speed more vital than any slight sound he might make. A moment later Anne was on her feet and they were inside her room, every sense stretched to catch stirrings from next door. If anyone woke and saw the dead needle on the dial which recorded Stephen's bleeper, then they were lost, and a check was probably routine whenever someone roused.

A minute passed, another. Nothing. No sound, no stir or raised voices.

'It probably didn't sound so loud through closed windows and a shutter,' said Stephen softly. 'Teach them to sleep without fresh air at night. Put on the heaviest clothes you possess and carry boots until we're out; make up anything useful you've scrounged into a pack. We'll sort it out later.' He had some kind of bundle on his back and untied boots from his belt while he waited.

Then, very gently, he edged open her door, listening. A mumble of voices as their guards whiled away time just around the corner, dim bulbs glowing on the staircase, a movement from below although it was impossible to guess where. They were a long way yet from being out.

Anne touched him. 'Ready.'

The hotel passages were wide and echoing, stairs yawning blackness, empty rooms locked off until the summer when workers who exceeded production targets came here free. Stephen hesitated, then shrugged. There was no possible concealment, they must simply walk down six flights of stairs and hope that no one was coming up, time only wasted by the instinct which urged them into caution.

At the head of the last flight of stairs a rat was sitting, delicately washing its whiskers. It stared at them, eyes glinting red, teeth showing in surprise, before scuttering off outraged by trespassers.

Anne grasped Stephen's arm and framed the words: 'Follow it.' They hadn't found a single unlocked door where they might get into a bedroom and let themselves down outside, the possibility of having to find a way out under the eye of more guards in the main hall coming disagreeably close.

Stephen lifted eyebrows interrogatively and then motioned for her to lead. While most of his faculties were concentrated on keeping upright Anne must think for both of them. Rats meant food, and food probably meant kitchens and back entrances.

This first floor corridor was wider than the others, dust-sheet shrouded chairs piled into corners, and for a moment Anne considered hiding amongst them for a day while Stephen recovered and the search passed them by. But unless his breathing steadied anyone coming close must hear him, and anyway, after so long as a prisoner, every instinct screamed for the open, for fields and forests away from eyes and ears tuned to their every movement.

The rat had disappeared, but they came to a bar, more piled chairs and a swing-door: through the door it was completely dark and smelled of damp concrete.

Anne went first, feeling each step, surface gritty beneath her stockinged feet. Another flight of stairs, unsurfaced and winding steeply downward. Socialism did not seem to have made much impact on the working conditions of Albanian hotel staff. Anne counted the treads, trying to judge how many would bring them to street level, it would be disastrous to pass some unseen entry and end up floundering through cellars.

Stephen's hand tightened on her shoulder and she stopped, listening, then realized what he had felt not heard. Air was blowing in her face.

Relief was so great that she wanted to laugh aloud, abandon caution and run alone under the night sky. She was shaking when tension ebbed, tripped over something before she gripped herself again. More passages, smelling of rubbish and full of what felt like ancient bedsprings, which twanged to an unwary touch.

The door at the end of the passage was bolted but by keeping their faces turned to the night breeze they found a window opening into backyards, the rear of the hotel far less modern than its façade. Then they were out in a street, where wind rubbed through palm leaves and lifted dust in starlit corners.

No movement anywhere but certainly there would be patrols on the main streets. They couldn't afford much caution though, their guards might rouse at any moment, the sergeant demand to see inside Stephen's room or notice the dead bleeper.

'Left,' said Stephen softly. 'We must stay in the side-streets as long as we can but keep parallel with the main avenue.'

They would have to cross the Avenue Hoxha though, the factory lay beyond it, in a raggle-taggle of streets skirting the port. Several times they heard boots and swerved into darker alleys, once a man called after them and Stephen swore at him until he gave a grunting laugh and slammed back into his yard.

'You seem to have made imaginative use of your chances to learn Albanian,' whispered Anne, the deceptive sense of freedom making her feel light-headed.

'There's nothing like obscenity for silencing suspicion. It must be left again at the end here and then the avenue should be ahead.' The plan of Durres was not complicated.

Anne shivered as they crouched listening in a doorway; at midday the sun was already hot down here on the coast but in this time before dawn it was easy to remember that snow would still lie thickly in the mountains.

The avenue was immediately ahead, a soldier standing with a slung rifle beneath the trees, a group of them talking just beyond, turning to welcome a patrol as it arrived then lighting cigarettes together. An occasional early worker straggled into sight, the whole business of escape and Twodex must have taken longer than she had thought. Even after six months in Albania Anne knew that she and Stephen would not pass the most casual of scrutinies, local clothes or not. Their difference from Albanians was indefinable, but unmistakable all the same; and guards, part-time militia, group leaders, or just plain busybodies asked for papers all the time.

They turned away from the soldiers and kept under the trees hoping to cross the street further away, it was infuriating to be walking back towards the hotel but their chances in open spaces were too slim for the risk of crossing near patrols to be worthwhile.

'Have you a light?' Without warning an elderly man accosted them, cigarette in hand.

Stephen fumbled in his pocket, but when he found and struck a match the head broke off, as frequently happened. 'One day they'll make them so they don't do that.'

'All matches do it,' said the man aggressively. 'Albanian matches are the best.'

'Yes, I suppose so.' Anne could tell from Stephen's voice that he found it hard to lie on a point of abstract fact, where he took pleasure in deceiving the apparatus of state.

The fourth match flared and caught, the Albanian looking at them curiously in its light. 'You don't come from these parts.'

'From the south, not far from Gjirokaster. We came up as a welding team to work in the port.' His voice roughened awkwardly as his breath caught.

God, thought Anne. What has that damned Twodex done to him, surely he should be better by now? He must have been crazy to try it. All the same she knew there had been no other way in the time.

The Albanian hesitated, eyes flicking from her to Stephen. He didn't believe them, but wasn't quite quick enough. Before he could call out Stephen fastened one hand on his throat and hit him on the point of the jaw with the other. 'Quick. Cloth or something to tie and gag him. An hour, half an hour perhaps, could see us clear.'

Anne dragged open her bundle, she had brought so little that even in such an emergency she felt a pang at sacrificing anything. She tore a shirt into strips and they left him unconscious, behind some stacked bricks; at least when he was questioned he would say that they had been heading back towards the hotel, which should puzzle Kaderi.

The maze of streets behind the port was unfamiliar when

tackled from a different starting point, and for five dreadful minutes they were lost. Then Anne recognized a bakery which meant that they were only a couple of alleys from the fig-factory where the truck should be waiting to depart at first light.

When they rounded the last corner they saw the factory gate was open, the truck already in the street, sidelights on, engine ticking over while the driver climbed down to check out with the guard.

Anne felt Stephen's hand tighten on her arm, urging her to run, but it was no good, they would be seen. Almost instantly he changed his mind, bundling her back around the corner and seizing a plank from a pile by a half-finished building. 'Quick, into the road with them!'

No time for questions. Anne strained at splintered wood, heard something heavy roll off the pile as she helped heave planks into the narrow road. The truck came round the corner fast, to find tumbled timber blocking the way. For a moment Anne thought the driver was going to chance it, the few baulks they had had time to shift forming only a flimsy barrier; then brakes squealed and he climbed out, swearing at the children of Durres who plagued truck-drivers' lives and sabotaged the revolution.

By the time he had climbed back in his cab, Anne and Stephen were crouched between the crates of figs he was taking to Tirana so as not to waste a journey.

Any time now their disappearance must be noticed but at least they were ahead of the chase, the ghost of a chance won if only their luck held. The chance to break for the open and give the Sigurimi a run they would not forget; probably death waited at the end of it but at least it would be in light and air instead of in some foul camp or cell.

The truck was hideously uncomfortable, crates sharp-edged and shifting at every swerve. The exhaust leaked diesel fumes and the driver seemed determined to cover the distance to Tirana in record time. He was stopped several times at check-points out of Durres, normal procedure and not necessarily a sign that the hunt for them had started, then the truck gained speed out of the city, gears grinding as bends steepened once the coastal plain was left behind.

'How long?' Anne had to shout to make herself heard, but they were insulated from the driver in his separate cab.

'To Tirana? An hour and a half, two hours, I suppose.'

'I meant, how long should we stay with the truck? Try and leave at the next block or go all the way?'

'At this rate we'll have to take the first chance offered, it'll probably be the only one. I shouldn't like to end up in a warehouse in Tirana.'

It would be disastrous, Anne realized. At the end of his journey the driver would probably pull into some loading bay where there would be too many people about for them to slip out unseen. And the streets of Tirana were closely patrolled, they would not survive more than a couple of blocks without being asked for papers. By now, Kaderi surely must be informed of their escape.

The sky over the mountains was a clear yellow, sun striking the higher peaks perhaps forty miles away. Anne sighed. 'You rest while you can, I'll warn you if there seems a chance for us to drop off.'

She lay between crates, attempting to see the lie of the road and anticipate any stop through a split in the tarpaulin cover. The bends were getting steeper all the time but their driver threw his truck at them with cheerful abandon, the road so empty that recklessness went unpunished. The occasional tractor and a few other trucks were on the road but only once was there the snarl of an oncoming car and as it passed in a blare of horns Anne had a clear view of its driver, although he did not look aside. An image of sculpted fury was printed on her mind as Kaderi went past like a squall and plunged on towards Durres.

21

They were much closer to Tirana than was safe before they were able to leave the truck, but Stephen was sleeping and Anne spent the time trying to put herself into Kaderi's thoughts. She was aware that she had seen the best of him but whatever the adage said, love is seldom blind and she thought she understood him very well. He was the man they had to fear, the directing mind and swift intelligence which would track them down, where they might possibly slip through the fingers of mere brute force. He would not forgive their defiance and their recapture would become a matter on which his prestige was staked.

He was also sufficiently astute to do what she was doing, to look into their minds and consider what chances they might have seen. He would order a blanket search, but himself cover the parts of Durres familiar to them: certainly he would discover that a truck had left the fig-factory early and instinct would make him suspect it, though nothing connected them with its departure. The question was, how long would it take him to strip down the situation he found in Durres to its essentials and take counter-measures, of which stopping this truck would be one?

Anne's thoughts were interrupted when they drew up in a village and their driver went into a cottage: an illicit stop with friends presumably. Anne hesitated, then thought of Kaderi again and let Stephen sleep on. This escape was like blindfold chess with a firing squad instead of checkmate for the loser. Only cool nerve and calculated gambling might keep them a move ahead of the hunt: once Kaderi wondered whether they might have jumped this truck, then he would check on where it had stopped and their driver would not succeed in hiding an illicit drink from him. So far, this village represented their only chance of leaving safely and Kaderi would search it first.

Soon after, the driver climbed back in his cab and they set off again. Anne shook Stephen awake almost at once, they must be ready to take the next chance which offered.

He seemed better and agreed with her reasoning when she explained it. 'The thinnest chance will be the best, a moment the driver simply won't recall under interrogation. We mustn't leave any trace we've been here either, so Kaderi will never be certain of it and have plenty of other possibilities to check out. A pity, figs would make good iron rations in the mountains.'

'I've brought some I took each day from the factory and hid in my room, thinking they might come in useful.'

'So have I. Not many, though, when they searched me to the skin at the slightest opportunity.' He heaved at crates so the space where they had lain was lost, while she ran her fingers around each sharp-edged corner for any fragment of cloth or hair which might betray their presence.

Then they lay and waited, minutes ticking away, Kaderi's hand perhaps already on the telephone to order this truck stopped. The Durres-Tirana road would already be closed behind them, but until he investigated closely Kaderi would not expect them to have gone so far in the time.

The road between Durres and Tirana was narrow, the bends like pleats set in the landscape, but as they came closer to Tirana hills gave way to rock-strewn slopes and eventually to a fertile upland plain. Their driver's foot pressed harder on the accelerator and Anne began to regret that she had not taken the chance to leave when it was offered. Scattered buildings punctuated the road; if they could have looked ahead then certainly Tirana must be in sight. Soon, city streets would make leaving the truck impossible.

Drainpipes beside the road, loose chippings, some children singing in a red-scarved pioneer group.

'We'll be there in a minute!' said Anne despairingly. Then, without warning their chance came. The truck slowed for some obstacle they couldn't see, stopped, jerked, and pulled away again in a flurry of stones: they watched it go from behind piled pipes before pushing their way into bamboo thicket which lined the road.

'He'll know,' Anne spoke almost to herself. 'When Kaderi finds nothing at the village he'll guess the driver must have had to slow for the construction work here.'

Stephen looked at her oddly. 'He's not God you know, and has a great many other possibilities to check.'

Anne shrugged, it wasn't worth arguing and they needed all their senses tuned to what they were doing.

The bamboo was only a weed-like straggle edging the road, and gave way almost at once to an open rocky slope. Morning mist helped conceal their movements and the country seemed deserted despite its nearness to Tirana, though that could be illusion and mist burn up in the sun to leave them exposed in straggling suburbs.

'A village,' said Stephen, as shapes hardened out of greyness. 'Whatever time it costs us we must stay up the slope and not blunder closer to where there may be houses.' Albanian villages were full of chained and noisy dogs, suspicion a habit of mind.

They worked their way higher, until the ground steepened so sharply that they were forced to climb down into a ravine as cultivated fields trapped them against a maze of rougher ground. A few dark cypresses dripping with condensation clung to bare rock, roots a welcome handhold as they went down, boots slipping on stringy grass growing out of crevices.

'The mist is clearing,' said Anne suddenly, not sure whether to be pleased or sorry. On the far side of this miniature gorge where they were wasting time another village had surfaced out of fog, sun gleaming on white concrete, the whole region apparently a mixture of wilderness and new development.

Stephen grunted. 'I can hear water at the bottom here. Once we're across we'll hide through the day somewhere with a good view of the country, and spy out a route for tonight.'

It was certainly too dangerous to move far by day in such a populous area, on the other hand this infernal gorge confined them dangerously close to the road; they needed to cross it quickly and unseen. When they reached the bottom they found some ancient trees, black, wet and very dense. At their foot a torrent flowed, breaking over rocks with the cold and deadly force of melting snows in distant mountains.

'If we can cross here, then Kaderi will surely think his guessing must be wrong and look elsewhere for a while,' Anne regarded the broken water with a mixture of misgiving and calculation.

'We can't,' said Stephen. 'It's no good outwitting your pet demon only to break a leg in a third-rate torrent. We'll have to work our way further upstream, the trees give good cover.'

He was right of course, infuriating though it was to be forced into wasting hard-gained time while the chase closed up behind. Even so, to walk for the first time in six months without any guard, without watching words or having to endure gibes at whatever they did, was a reward in itself.

Anne tried the water once, wanting to tell Stephen that he was too cautious and did not understand the nature of the man he must outwit, but it was icy and moved with such deadly force that she scrambled back up the bank without speaking.

'Satisfied?'

She nodded. 'He'll look too and know we couldn't cross. We must get over somehow, though; by tonight he'll have every bolthole stopped and this will be one of them.'

'Kaderi is a man to be feared, but you mustn't let him suck out your mind,' Stephen said gently. 'The rabbit and the stoat. That's often how he and his kind choose to kill, by letting a victim's fear work for them.'

They walked another half mile before Anne spoke again. 'It's easy for you. Deep inside you don't believe you will be beaten. I come from a different tradition, where police with guns and truncheons always win in the end.'

He slipped his hand under her arm. 'Not this time, God willing. Of your own choice you left that heritage behind ten years ago, and by your own wish you're with me, not Kaderi, today. Let's keep it that way, shall we?'

His voice was impersonal though, and for the first time Anne wondered whether he quite simply considered her relationship with Kaderi as high treason, the kind you were shot for in the Tower of London, and laughed aloud at the absurdity of it. What she had seen as resentful jealousy perhaps was simply part of an ancient heritage which she and her kind found difficult to grasp any longer: however far he wandered Stephen Astell was part of the warp and weft of his country in a way she could never be, since her inheritance had forced her to reject it.

He looked at her curiously. 'One day I'd like to ask you why you laughed.'

'Why not now?' she replied lightly, to stop him asking.

'Because given time, your answer may not be quite what you think it is at the moment.'

'Do you always talk in riddles?' Suddenly, she liked him enormously.

He grinned. 'Bloody intellectual snobs, that's what Cambridge breeds. If you don't mind wet and cold, I think we might get across here.'

Anne regarded the torrent with dislike. It was flowing as swiftly as before but a fallen branch had wedged across the rocks; it looked insecure but the best chance they had seen.

Stephen exclaimed aloud as he let himself into the water. 'There's a hell of a current. Watch your footing, for God's sake.' He was bent by the force of it as he worked his way along the branch, sometimes needing the full strength of his arms to make any progress.

He stopped at the first boulder to stand clear of water, legs braced. 'Come now.' He needed to shout to make himself heard above the roar of water, without his help she would certainly lack the physical power to keep herself from being swept under the branch and held there until she drowned. The water was colder even than she had imagined, chilling into bone within moments of wading from the bank; she stepped out cautiously, feeling her way and clinging to timber. Two, three steps through a tearing helter-skelter of water; she had almost reached Stephen's outstretched hand when her feet were swept from under her, mud on her tongue and icewater in her lungs. She emerged before shock released her mind to thought, instinct making her grab for trailing branches as the current swept her under again. She could feel Stephen heaving on her arm but her legs were under the branch and however frantically she thrashed the race of water was too powerful for her to regain her footing.

All around was only coldness, her grazed and battered body, darkness as her head went under; sharp pain when her hand tore on bark. But she was damned if she was going to be held under an Albanian branch until she drowned, like a puppy in a bucket. She hauled desperately again, felt Stephen heave too, and somehow her head was above water, her breath crackling in frozen lungs. Haul again, drive legs downward: nothing. The force of the water was too great, her weight too light. Again. She must try again, her mind growing sluggish now. This time she felt something, probably a branch projecting under water. Her strength was ebbing fast, the monstrous mass of water sweeping past beyond endurance.

'Now!' shouted Stephen, and she dredged out strength for one last effort, hands clawing at rough bark until there was solidity again at breast and stomach, water holding her against rock where it had been her enemy before. She retched, spread-eagled over stone.

Stephen shook her roughly, shouting at her, forcing her to move on deadened legs from boulder to boulder, hands leaving blood on each as she passed. He had to prise her grip loose before she could take the last few steps to the bank, make the unimaginable effort of dragging herself up slicked earth and on to grass again.

She was only dimly aware of him levering the branch loose from its hold: the deadly game they played meant that surviving such a crossing was only part of what they must do. When he came this way looking for them, Kaderi must be denied any clue as to how, or if, they had crossed.

Anne stumbled to her feet when Stephen touched her, knowing this was no safe place to rest. The far side of the ravine was steep and slippery, but the need to climb set blood flowing again; feet and hands harnessed to the simple purpose of not curling up on the first flat ledge she reached and refusing to move again. It was difficult to realize that they were only a few miles from Tirana, their journey just begun.

They broke into sun without warning and lay looking out over flat country patched with trees. In the distance mountains were hazed against the sky, close at hand ramshackle farm buildings were surrounded by the inevitable barbed wire fence; fresh green grass and blue sky dazzling to the eye, the nearer landscape disconcertingly featureless.

Anne recollected only fleeting impressions of the next couple of hours. Light splintered through delicate birch tracery as they kept to such cover as there was, stumbling over rocks tussocked with grass. The pair of them crouching in a ditch when some dogs roused while they were still half a mile away, a cacophony of barking sufficient to make any Albanian reach for his rifle. So they must trek further than they intended, and she next remembered loud fretful argument with Stephen when he urged her across pasture and up a slope which seemed hideously exposed. It was absurd to attempt crossing open land in daylight, but she felt too tired to defy him. Too tired to do anything except go forward blindly. All that mattered was to put one foot before the other, hoping it soon would end.

Then at last she heard Stephen say, 'Now you can sleep, my love,' and she knew nothing more at all.

When Anne woke, at first she thought she was back in Haibuk, curled gratefully into warmth. Then she remembered how Haibuk was another lifetime and filled with a different pack of faces howling for her destruction, and came fully awake.

Her body was sore and sluggish, her head ached and her eyes felt gummy. Somewhere a bird was singing though, soft sweet notes poured out of a flawless sky. She stared stupidly around the little dell where she lay in full sun, brambles enclosing a secret circle of turf. Beside her Stephen slept, face flushed from the sun and lined with fatigue. He was frowning, moving and muttering restlessly.

Anne slept again and could tell from the slack-limbed feel of her when she woke that a long time had passed. It was a good feeling and her headache had gone.

She lay quietly, thinking. There were no sounds of pursuit, only stillness and an edge returned to the air which told of evening. Kaderi sought them elsewhere for the moment.

When she moved, the feeling of comfort vanished. She was

horribly stiff, sensation sharpening into pain at hands and legs.

'How d'you feel?' Stephen was sitting a little apart, back propped against an earth bank. She remembered clearly how he had called her his love in the haze before she slept.

'Not too bad.'

His smile deepened. 'If you must tell a lie, let it be a good one. I was worried whether I ought to let you sleep longer, or rouse you once it chilled. I don't know how the hell you made it so far as this in the state you were in, but if it's any consolation I felt a bastard driving you.'

'How safe are we here?'

'Safe enough for the moment. Goats are grazing not too far off but they were milked two hours ago. Otherwise there's nothing except a series of shacks which I imagine is a collective farm about a mile away.'

'Not up to Exmoor standards?' Anne couldn't resist a dig at his censorious tone.

'Ah well, Balkans will be Balkans,' he observed blandly.

She laughed and stood, every muscle protesting. Through bramble she could see a few distant lights in the dusk, and pools of shadow which told of undulating land under a setting sun. She shivered, suddenly it was cold again but there was no question of lighting a fire. Thank heaven, at least her clothes had dried.

She was ravenously hungry though. 'What food have we got?'

'Figs, of course. Some dried maize the factory people gave me; they chew it like gum but I think they knew it might come in handy. Hoped it would perhaps, we being the first foreigners they'd actually met and found not to be ogres. A little sugar and some very stale bread. That's all, I'm afraid.'

Food in Albania was scanty anyway, and their guards under orders to keep any surplus from them. 'I've quite a few figs, and some olive oil they left on the table one night, if the bottle hasn't broken. A little cheese. The bread I had will be pulp I'm afraid.'

It was, but they scraped the mess off her spare shirt and ate it, licked a little sugar and dulled the rest of their hunger with figs; the sticky heaviness was nauseating but pumped fresh energy into drained bodies. When they counted up they had sixty-eight figs between them, a comforting reserve however unpalatable.

They induced fierce thirst though, until Anne longed for full darkness so they could move again and find water.

'Your breathing, it's not right, is it?' she asked suddenly. Ravine, torrent and the journey half-supporting her was enough to aggravate any weakness.

'It's better than it was. For a moment my lungs felt as if they'd been electrocuted while the rest of me went on without them, most odd. We're returning to each other's acquaintance now, and if Kaderi leaves us alone for the next couple of days I'll be all right.'

'He's missed us with his first cast,' said Anne slowly. 'He must have done. I thought he'd see the fig-truck as a probability at once, but perhaps there were other chances which looked more likely. Or if he did see it, then he missed that stretch of construction as a place where we might drop off.'

'One thing's certain though, he's not short of manpower.'

No, he wasn't short of men, when Albania swarmed with uniformed young. He would be back, covering every possibility, sniffing along their trail until they made a mistake; probably they had already made one. Then he would loose a pack after them which would be too large to outflank or avoid.

Unless they could reach the mountains before he headed them off, and disappear into wilderness where numbers lost their impact.

'We really ought to double back and go south, where we've never been and he won't expect us,' said Anne reluctantly. She hated the thought of a long detour.

'Yes, I thought that, too. But they had to let me work on maps when I was plotting my survey, and I studied the road network very carefully. If we go south then we must cross two main valleys, each with a road up it. Tirana-Bulqize and Tirana-Elbasan-Korce. Not to mention a railway unless we go into the mountains beyond its terminus. Kaderi will have those roads staked out every few yards just to make sure he keeps us cornered in this section while he sweeps it. At least here we're in open country right to the mountains, with only tracks to cross until we reach the Drin.'

The Drin valley.

Anne remembered it with a sinking heart. Steep-sided and slashed by a wide, fast-flowing river whose few bridges would certainly be guarded: it was a natural trap. Leaping waterfalls and brawling currents guarded the river's upper reaches, and along the lower it was too cold and wide to swim at this time of year.

And the Drin barred the way to the Yugoslav frontier unless they went south and crossed the roads Kaderi would have sealed off, or into the far north and back towards Durres again.

Kaderi could afford to wait, and watch, and feel his way towards them, when there were so few directions in which they could run.

22

Eventually darkness came and they were able to set out again, stiffness and chill dispersed by movement. No disturbances or alarms, everything immensely peaceful under a dull sky before the moon rose, then too much brightness for safety but easier travelling as it sailed across the horizon.

They seldom spoke, crouching and watching from each lift of ground, caution instinctive at the first suggestion of a trodden path or an outbuilding which might contain dogs.

The ground continued mostly open and cultivated, ploughland merging into pasture without the hedges and ditches which would have hindered progress cross-country in England. The lights of Tirana gradually disappeared behind them, the glow helping with direction for several hours; then the northern horizon became roughly black as if trees sloped down there from the hills. With luck, Kaderi might calculate that they would aim for cover there, and open ground be more lightly guarded.

Anne felt uneasy, though, peace was deceptive when all around them the country must be like a mown anthill; she was amused to find herself annoyed with Kaderi for proving her calculation of his actions wrong. He ought to have responded faster and with more imagination to their challenge. In her heart she knew that probably he had, only they couldn't see it, wouldn't see it until his trap snapped on their throats.

They did possess some small advantages: when Stephen had asked for a helicopter to help in his survey, he had been told there weren't any in the country. No tracker dogs either, he had commented caustically before they set out that night. Albanian dogs were like their masters, made aggressive and savagely suspicious through a lifetime of blows and threats, but lacking the years of training which added discipline to ferocity. 'In the West we're clear enough about the consequence of brutality to the victim,' he had observed. 'Few make the point that it must ruin a police force too. Why the hell bother to use your intelligence, sweat blood over evidence or patiently sift facts, when you can beat whatever you want out of the first person you see? Shove a knife in his belly when he says a mine is unsafe because he's a prisoner and must be wrong, and who the hell cares when a shaft collapses?'

Anne could see him now as he walked ahead of her, shoulders a little hunched, head turning as he tried to detect the first signs of danger in the dark. He was an unusual man, she reflected, as she had several times before. It seemed a long time since she had regarded Kaderi as an enigma and Stephen Astell uncomplicated by comparison, a series of compartments ready-made into which his personality should fit. Scholar, and a civilized sophisticate also, who had seized the chance of profit when it came without caring about cheated taxpayers, though with his research closed down she did not blame him. A man of peace, rooted in Cambridge quadrangles and Exmoor hills; skilled and scrupulous in his profession.

Then you discovered that the compartments did not fit as easily as you thought: he had killed Nako, and if she had not been there might easily have killed Kaderi too. He must have known the extent of the risk he ran when he directed Twodex on himself, still be enduring discomfort without complaint, as he had done earlier, stripped and handcuffed to freeze in the night. Yet only chance words revealed cold rage against his captors, the strength of which no one had suspected, and also a clinical insight into their weaknesses which they would do well to fear. His attitude towards her was contradictory too; she had thought that he either wouldn't know or wouldn't care about her relationship with Kaderi, she was certain now that he disliked it very much indeed.

She cannoned into him, attention distracted by her speculations. He brushed fingers against her lips enjoining silence, head tilted to sniff the air. Then Anne smelled it too: tobacco. Stephen jerked his head, hand urging her off the goat track they had been following. The grass either side was dew-soaked, they would need to make a wide detour if they were to pass a sentry undetected, since dawn could not be too far off. They left no print on a goat-track, but spilled dew-drops would show clearly at first light. They had made such good progress through the night that already the land was tilting into foothills: not steep enough to make a path essential but the ground sufficiently broken for paths to be the obvious thing to guard.

They crouched in undergrowth a long time, trying to decide whether the man ahead was alone or part of a cordon: if he was caught smoking, Kaderi would surely have him shot.

Anne saw a shift in the shadows as Stephen turned. 'Back, I think. We passed a fork in this track, we could try the other way and keep out of dew.'

She wanted to argue but it was too dangerous. He was wrong, all the same. If there was a line of guards then they needed to slip past in the dark. When dawn came, Kaderi surely would move his sweep inwards, a step and section at a time, missing nothing. Not too far away she heard the unexpected whine of an engine, there must be a dirt road the far side of the hill ahead, which he intended to use as the start-line for a search.

Silently, step by step, they withdrew. Once behind a knoll of grass, Anne grasped Stephen's arm. 'We haven't time! An hour to dawn perhaps, and then they'll move. We can't get back far enough to be out of the area they'll search today.'

'I know, that's why I want to try the next path down.' He set off briskly so she had no choice but to follow. Damn him, she thought resentfully, why must he always think he's right? Every second is irreplaceable now.

He turned, the moon was down but her eyes were so adjusted to the dark that she could see him smiling; she wanted to slap the stupid complacency of it. 'Wait here and meditate on my sins. I'll be back as quickly as I can.'

She lay full length on the path, fronded grass on either side trembling dew ready to be spilled and reveal any movement there. Throughout the night she had scarcely felt tired at all although they must have walked twenty miles, now she was aware of exhaustion and her stomach shivering from hunger, the throb of her torn hand. If they had to run from aroused sentries then she would soon be caught.

She drowsed, and would have cried out when Stephen touched her except his hand was across her mouth.

His grip shifted to her shoulders. 'Steady.'

'I'm all right,' she was annoyed by having slept only yards from Kaderi's guards.

'Listen. Not far along this path is another sentry, also smoking behind a rubble breastwork. It would appear that Kaderi is not so greatly feared as we supposed.'

Anne shrugged, unsure what he expected. Kaderi was feared, and rightly so.

Stephen nodded as if she confirmed something in his own mind. 'I don't believe it either, I'm damned if I'd smoke on Kaderi's guard duty. I think he's double-bluffing. He has every goat-track leading to this ridge staked out, the guard obvious so we go round. Then we fall into the real trap. Probably men just under the skyline, hidden this time. And once we leave these goat-walks our tracks could be followed by a simpleton until the dew burns off.'

Anne felt her pulse change beat, heavy hammer-strokes offering their own warning. Millosh had chosen the first rock barrier across their likely track and waited for them to walk into the trap he set. He had judged the time they would take correctly too, dawn dew no accidental ally, the open country they had crossed offering few hides against the next day's search. 'We must keep to the path and chance the sentry?'

'I think so, yes. Two can bluff and that's where he's not expecting us.'

Perhaps, she thought. At chess, triple bluffs were a master's gambit.

Their path was no more than an animal trail, loose stones rolling underfoot. There must be hundreds like it in foothills grazed by goats, surely it was impossible to guard them all? They had to move very carefully as the path twisted, the strengthening smell of tobacco their only warning of a sentry.

Anne could hear Stephen trying to control the rasp of his breathing, once the effort made him choke and he went on his knees, stifling sound with his teeth in turf. After that it was worse. If Kaderi leaves us alone two days, I shall be better he had said this afternoon; he had not left them alone, and the end of a long night made the strain more obvious.

Anne waited in an agony of suspense for him to recover, but soon his breath caught again and while he was forced to wait she walked on lightly down the path.

This she could do far better than he.

Bluff, Stephen had said. She was beginning to guess what he meant, and why he had wanted to try another path to confirm what must have seemed an unlikely hunch.

The smell of tobacco was overpowering now, a breeze from the hills bearing it towards her in thick wafts. Surely anyone who smoked like that must be kippered: Stephen had been quick to detect the bluff though.

All the same, she moved with finicking care. An unexpected twist in the path and then she saw it: a loose breastwork of stones and behind it an old can punched with holes, a handful of tobacco smouldering inside, rank from a night's accumulation of nicotine. Kaderi had not wasted men on criss-crossing trails, instead he intended them to be frightened into lying up in cover which could easily be searched, or forced into detours which dawn would instantly reveal. Then he could slaughter them in comfort.

Anne went back at once, time their enemy now. Even in darkness she could tell that Stephen was not in an amiable mood and had to suppress a chuckle. How stupid men could be, when he preferred to risk their lives rather than let her go forward first.

They knew now that it was safe to stay on this track, but somewhere ahead Kaderi's watchers must be waiting. Soon, they had to crouch and then crawl while grass trembling with water closed in on either side. To the left, smooth wet grass; to the right a curling slope ended in broken rocks stretching against the sky as far as the eye could see. An exposed strata weathered by time and less than a hundred feet high, but a good place for armed men to wait unseen. A thousand guards in undergrowth might possibly be outwitted, but along that ridge one every quarter mile would do, once they had been frightened off their goat-track.

Anne sensed that Stephen was branching upward, keeping to whatever trail offered, passing another smouldering tobacco can on the way. They needed height but must not leave the safety of a path until they reached rockier ground which would be free from betraying dew. And once there, they must slip past sentries somehow and lie up while the search moved away from them through the day. Surely they could not do it, when each yard of this ground must be watched from above.

Stones became rocks, and rocks outcroppings. They worked their way past an eroded shelf and saw a watcher immediately. He was leaning against rock, rifle in hand, cap pushed back on his head. He had not seen them but easily could if he turned.

Panic zig-zagged through Anne; at any moment he must turn.

She saw the blur which was Stephen's face, the sky still dark but less so than it was. He hesitated as if debating which way to go, then carefully came to his feet, gesturing for her to do the same. No time. No time to wait or detour. No time for anything except to walk away and pray the watcher would not turn.

Pray too there wasn't another behind the cover they must reach, for suddenly there were men everywhere. From a crest of rock they glimpsed the far side of the ridge where another grass slope led to a dirt road, trucks pulled up at intervals along its length.

Nowhere to hide there, and already it was too light to attempt crossing the road.

Stephen gestured. 'Up on one of these rocks, it's the only place.' He cupped his hands and after a struggle she was up, limestone harsh against her face, leaning down instantly to offer him some handhold. She thought he would never make it, the rock smooth and the need for silence as great as ever; in the end he had to use her body to give the grip he needed.

They weren't a moment too soon. Men were being mustered along the road ready for a dawn sweep, the silence broken by barked commands.

The ridge surfaced around them out of mist and morning shadows. It curved like a chipped edge of saucer, never high but always the same formation so far as the eye could see. In places sections lay shattered by the elements, elsewhere the tilted edge formed a vertical barrier ideal for Kaderi's purpose. And along its whole length it overlooked a sea of grass, where a single unwary footprint would show. Once light strengthened they dared not lift their heads, but from where they lay on the summit of the ridge men and trucks in the valley behind were also in clear sight – and just beyond them, the first mountain-slopes folded into alpine pastures; further again, and snow-capped peaks, plumed waterfalls and soaring rock were etched against the sky.

The massive boulder on which they lay was scattered with loose stones, the top of it about twelve feet by eight, a jagged spike thrusting up at one end. Very carefully, lying prone, they began clearing rubble from the centre towards the edge, hoping to gain depth in case they were visible from below. But the gain was minimal, the only benefit slight dampness where night chill had condensed. Anne was famished but eating soon produced thirst, and the sun rose in a dazzle of gold which promised a shadeless day to come.

Water had been plentiful on the journey and neither of them had given it a thought, nor did they possess a container to carry it in if they had. Before the day was out they would be thinking of nothing else.

23

Anne slept through most of the morning and woke to hot rock and a blazing sun; it lacked the power of summer but already her head ached and her tongue stuck to her mouth. She lay watching the single strip of shadow from the rock spike as it crept across her legs, and willed it to move faster.

She shifted restlessly on sharp stones, biting her lips as punished muscles protested. Her hand hurt too and it was impossible not to wonder whether she had been a fool; remember her wish to stay with Kaderi and how she had never quite believed that he could not change. She moved again and saw that Stephen was awake too, head on one arm, sweat streaking stone-dust on his face. 'The search has moved away,' he said softly. 'They fired at something a while ago. Rabbit for the pot perhaps.'

Anne licked dry lips, it didn't help. 'They'll be back tonight.'

They had not passed anywhere on their journey so well suited to watching and waiting. Kaderi would not be alarmed when his sweep caught nothing today, they could easily take another night to reach as far as this from Durres. Stephen shrugged. 'The longer he waits here the better. Did you say you had some oil in your pack?'

She nodded and fumbled with tied cloth; he was welcome to it, the thought of oil nauseating when she was so dry.

But when she handed it to him he poured a little on her cut hand, massaging so she had to clench her jaw to prevent herself from crying out. Afterwards, the throb eased slightly. 'Very biblical,' he whispered, and grinned. 'Wine and oil were the chief cures there if I remember rightly, and some of the prophets lived to a hell of an age.'

'We can't afford to waste it,' she protested, when he did the same later.

'You can't afford a poisoned arm, or keep going long once you must use a puffed hand in the mountains.' He stiffened, listening. 'Aircraft.'

The beat of engines grew rapidly, and a moment later they identified the source as two spotter planes sweeping slowly from the hills to some point out in the plain. They were flying low and very methodically, at the end of each sweep passing low across their ridge.

They would be overhead inside half an hour.

'They're using the ridge as a checkpoint but not really looking here,' said Stephen, watching. 'We can't go down, there's too many troops about. We'll have to lie still and break up our outline as best we can.'

They had to lie on their backs so they could use their arms to balance stones and rubble on legs and bodies, it would have seemed safer if they could have buried their faces away from those inexorably closing aircraft. A third had joined them now, circling in no particular pattern over the plain.

'Kaderi,' said Anne, lying rigid, stone on her throat and another ready to balance on her face. He would be leaning forward, face expressionless, eyes darting as he directed the hunt below. She looked away from the aircraft's glinting wings, as if the fine-tuning of her thoughts might attract him to them here.

Then they had to lie utterly still while sound became a shattering roar, passed overhead; through more crawling seconds while the plane banked and came again, this time further away but all the more dangerous for it, since an observer would have a clearer view.

Then it was gone while they lay limp, thirst back in the forefront of their minds.

So great a thirst that to swallow was sharply painful and skin felt like leather, brain swooping dizzily each time they moved in an attempt to ease their position. And failed, since there was no ease anywhere on that rock.

Imperceptibly, the sun dropped towards the horizon and

disappeared behind storm-cloud, blurring outlines sufficiently for Stephen to risk a watch on the road; he looked as ghastly as Anne felt. Tonight they must attempt only an easy stage or they would never last through the mountains. But first they must slip through the hive of activity below and gain safer, more broken country beyond.

If only they could steal a truck, drive through the flimsy barriers they could see and be twenty miles into the mountains before anyone dared tell Kaderi. But Stephen shook his head when Anne suggested it. 'Even if we succeeded, Kaderi would know then precisely where we are. At present we could be anywhere in northern Albania. Keeping it that way is the best chance we have.'

'Instinct brought him within sight of us in that aircraft.' She shivered. 'He ought not to know we're here, but he does. Or somewhere very close. When we don't walk into his line tonight, he'll guess we're through.'

Stephen rasped hands over his face, eyes on the road. 'Perhaps. You're guessing too, though.'

Anne felt helpless; as if she had been in that aircraft she knew Millosh had been there, felt him very close now. There was even a treacherous corner of her mind which did not want him to fail, wanted to see him again. If she won through to the frontier then she would never know whether if she'd stayed they might not have found something together.

She drowsed, exhausted.

They set off as soon as it was dark, making a good deal of noise as they half-fell from rock. A sentry called out further along the ridge and another answered; they froze, frightened into alertness again, then fiercely impatient as they had to wait out a desultory search. It died down at last and they were able to make their way down towards the road, the sentry uncertain what he had heard and probably reckoning it to be one of his fellows.

The grass was wet and they licked thirstily at dripping stems, a fine rain falling now the torment of the day was over. At least it meant they need not worry about tracks in grass.

There were men camped along the road, their fires illuminating rutted mud, but it was surprisingly easy to cross amongst so many in thickening cloud and rain, when no one expected them there.

They drank and drank again, from pools and puddles and waterlogged leaves, tilting their heads to the rain as they walked. Anne could feel herself unfolding, and sheer physical relief carried her through the first part of the night; they were climbing steadily but not steeply, trees reaching down rocky gullies towards them. Care was still necessary though, houses and barns guarded, dogs rattling chains if they ventured across open pastures.

Once someone called out and fired a shotgun, sound shattering although pellets splattered harmlessly into bushes.

Anne heard Stephen swear. That shot would be reported, anyone in these hills questioned as to whether their dogs had barked in the night. There must be sentries here too, Kaderi would never rely on his own expectation of catching them before they reached so far. There would be similar reports to sift from all over Albania, but Anne realized now that Stephen's scepticism was for her benefit: he too thought that Kaderi would pick the clues which mattered from a mass of irrelevance.

'How do you feel?' he asked abruptly.

'All right so long as I don't think about it.' She was thinking about it now, weighed down by weariness, legs trembling, chilled where she had been unbearably hot only hours earlier.

'I think we should turn directly north into the parallel valley. Can you make it, do you think?'

'Oh God. Why?'

'We can't outdistance pursuit, it will probably be closed in on us from ahead as well anyway. On Exmoor—' he paused and she guessed he was smiling. 'We have one of the few staghunts left in England. I'm not fond of hunting, and less so now, but watching a wily old stag throw off pursuit is an extraordinary experience. I've seen one leap fifteen feet directly to one side when it comes close to a deer-run and then reverse track. The hounds over-run the break in scent and before they can turn for a cast they pick up a mass of scents from other deer. So the stag lies quiet a few yards off while the pack chases its tail in confusion. I can hear a river, I think we should turn there and make Kaderi think we've used it to gain the pass leading out of this valley towards the Drin. Instead we'll go straight over the shoulder of mountain into the next valley north.'

'I'll make it,' she said briefly.

She did, quite how she never knew. The steep-sided cleft they had been climbing hid the nature of the country from them though Stephen had the lie of it from the maps he had seen; the ridge separating them from the next valley must have been nearly three thousand feet above, wet snow lying at the top. Then they must slip and slide down the far side until descent seemed worse than the climb had been. And all the time it rained or sleeted, deadening sound and making vigilance impossible. The valley they were entering would have men and dogs in it too; and the next one and the one after.

Anne never remembered the end of that journey, only woke much later to find herself in near-darkness, tightly held and warm. She stirred, too tired for curiosity. Something hard was digging into her and she wriggled, seeking comfort; she realized then that Stephen was sleeping against her, his coat wrapped round them both so the box chained to his chest stuck into her ribs. He did not wake when she moved, unshaven face rough against hers, arms slack but his body giving warmth. Fully awake now she stared around and finally grasped that she was lying on leaves with her back to a fallen tree-trunk, some kind of cloth stretched just over her head: she touched it experimentally, twigs and more leaves piled on that. In their minute scrap of space they were surprisingly snug, Stephen's back the only part of them exposed, and cautiously she tried to scuffle more leaves against him. She couldn't reach and was afraid of waking him so lay back again, but this time sleep refused to come at once. She could remember eating figs during the night but was hollow-hungry, wished Stephen would wake so she could reach her pack. She put aside temptation to reach it anyway and chance disturbing him; she had a hazy recollection of him urging and half-carrying her as they came down the slope. He must be, and looked, in desperate need of rest.

She considered the face so closely against hers; the sharp edge of jaw, the way his lips quirked close to a smile, the height of skull and fine scrollwork of ear. Laughter lines at eye and mouth, deeply vertical lines between his eyes and either side of his nose. More contradictions. A severely disciplined and formidably intelligent face, yet peaceful even in complete exhaustion, lacking harshness and . . . she fumbled, wondering at herself. Lacking also the ultimate dedication which makes it impossible for a man to set his purposes in their due proportion.

Unlike Millosh, where almost everything which might have challenged single-minded purpose was consumed long before she met him, the destruction of what remained easily completed once she was gone.

Whichever way she turned the same landslide of loss lay across her path.

24

Anne slept and woke throughout the day, hearing nothing except the drip of trees, no pursuit, no sentries calling, nothing. Stephen scarcely stirred, muttering and holding her more tightly once, face moving against hers. She did not mind, aware of him as she had never been before and a prey to very bitter thought. In the end, she was so grindingly hungry that she could not stay still any longer.

He woke as she moved and she felt him tense against her, the instinctive reaction of a male who wakes to find a woman in his arms. Then the muscles of his face tightened while the rest of him relaxed and he kissed her with disconcerting courtesy before rolling free: the kind of kiss a man offers when trapped in a situation where shaking hands is insufficient. 'I meant to wake before you did.'

'For God's sake, why? From the look of your housekeeping you were awake quite a while after me this morning.' She crawled out and stood stiffly on piled leaves, a minute slit all that showed of their hideout. The cover off his bed at Durres had secured the roll of possessions across his back, and he had stretched it from a fallen tree-trunk to driven pieces of branch and piled leaves over. A search would have needed to come very close to spot them.

He shrugged and bent over a hollow of bark where he had put dried maize and stale bread to soften in the damp. 'You'll find the sugar with the rest of my things under the cover. I don't know about you, but my stomach won't accept figs much longer.' He stirred the soggy mess and added a few drops of oil.

Anne burrowed back into leaves and darkness, he had

192

wrapped the contents of his pack in a shirt and used it to pad her back against the tree. She unwrapped it carefully, every item they carried was precious, a single lost maize husk irreplaceable when there was virtually no chance of stealing food from dog-infested farms. The bundle was heavy and she soon saw why: it contained two oblong black panels etched with a tracery of circuits and indented to accept rank upon rank of microchips. 'I thought you were surprisingly unworried by leaving Twodex behind,' she observed, fingering them. 'What are they, the computer memory?'

'Yes. The sugar, please Anne.'

She found it knotted in a piece of cloth, and then sat on the tree-trunk, thinking. Stephen could easily have reached for the sugar himself, and had woken to full intelligence within seconds. 'You wanted me to see them, didn't you?'

'I thought the time had come for a little reinsurance. If anything happens to me, I should like you to save those if you can. Send Kaderi a transcript of the results later if you like, and the authorities will let you. I agree with him on this at least, crises are less likely when they can be anticipated.' He divided the cold mush meticulously and handed her half.

Anne was too ravenous to talk until she had finished, forcing herself to eat slowly and swallow carefully: the taste was disagreeable but after two days of little except figs the stodge was what they needed.

She looked up when she had finished. 'Have you any idea what your survey will show? I know you need time and computers to be sure, but I watched you sometimes when we were firing and wondered whether you could tell anything from your headphones, from feel and instinct as it were.'

'Instinct can be wrong, and experience in mining isn't particularly useful when trying for a profile of strata twelve thousand feet down.'

'But?'

He smiled. 'Too much persistence can be a dangerous fault. Let us say that I shall be surprised if nothing shows up at all. When Hoxha dies, I think we should all be prepared for trouble. Remember, though, we've less than half the country recorded on those panels, and only random lines at that.'

'You chose the lines you wanted. I think you've much of what you need, for the north at least.' She felt immensely better for the food. 'I'd like to think about it. Is there a stream nearby where I could wash?'

He showed her a pool fed by a trickling melt-stream; her reflection was disconcerting: hair wild and eyes dark in a pinched, exhausted face. She stripped without allowing time for thought, the water shudderingly cold but her self-confidence restored as familiarity surfaced out of squalor. She had brought a comb and jerked out tangles until her eyes watered, changed into such spare clothes as she possessed, the respite of normality exactly what she needed. She heard air-craft engines in the distance once, otherwise they seemed free of pursuit, Stephen's Exmoor stags leaving Sigurimi rootling disconsolately elsewhere for the moment. But they must cross the Drin and lacking food it must be soon, as Kaderi certainly knew.

She gathered beechnuts while she waited for Stephen to show up, this high forest was deciduous and there were also a few chestnuts. She had gathered quite a pile before he appeared, clean-shaven and looking as if the effort had helped him too.

Anne smiled. 'You found the right voltage for your razor, I hope.'

'The Albanian grid leaves a great deal to the imagination, as such things often do in places where I work. I've used my grandfather's cut-throat for years, although I prefer soap and hot water.' He joined her gathering nuts, discussing what they should do next and showing no impatience for her reply over Twodex.

'I think the answer is no,' she said abruptly at last. 'If anything happened to you . . . if you were killed and could not control this information, then it's probably best to die with you. I'm sorry, Steve.'

'Suppressing scientific fact is always unsuccessful in the long run, and it can choose an inconvenient moment to hit back at you.' As always, his reaction was difficult to judge.

'Yes, but . . . if there was nothing of great importance there, just enough minerals perhaps to help Albania reward its

194

people with more than a carton of talc, then I might risk something for it. But you think there's more than that. It's like the sorcerer's apprentice, I wouldn't know the significance of facts I was so carelessly releasing, and nor would you, not really. I wish you hadn't brought that memory. Why did you?'

'For profit, why else? I run my own company now, or had you forgotten? All I possess is tied up in the kind of information Twodex can give and God knows what kind of a mess my affairs are in with me fooling around for six months in Albania. If we make it, I couldn't have a better advertisement than information Western governments and the CIA would give blood for. Twodex is lost but I'd have no difficulty then in raising the capital I need to develop Threedex. Fourdex too, for surveying the sea-bed where most of the world's remaining minerals are.'

'I don't believe you,' said Anne flatly. 'He may have been lying and was certainly concealing ambition, but if Kaderi could visualize Albania's minerals as a threat to peace and not simply as a vehicle for his own power, then you surely would not think of profit first and damn the consequences.'

He gave her a long, considering look. 'Do you know, you have surprised me? Like everyone else I suppose my motives are mixed; if I can make a profit I will, but I also happen to believe that accurate knowledge will help defuse a crisis which in some form or another is going to blow up anyway when Hoxha dies.'

'There speaks a scientist surely, not the world's politicians. and why should you be surprised if I refuse to accept you as a wicked capitalist? Because I was born in a communist republic and nothing I've done or seen since will change prejudice?'

She spoke with unexpected bitterness, remembering how Kaderi also had taken it for granted that ten years in the West disqualified her from understanding the certainties which ruled his life. Yet she did understand only too well; life is harsh on those stranded beyond conventional tracks and patterns of thought, a prey for the hunting packs of other men's convictions.

Stephen put his arm round her shoulders, sitting beside her

on wet log in drizzle. 'No; because you compared me to Kaderi and I was not the loser. Or nearly not the loser, I haven't worked out exactly what you said yet.' He grinned. 'Just that I couldn't possibly accept lower standards than Kaderi, which in my reckoning isn't the highest praise.'

She laughed, also unwilling to study the tangle of her own emotions. 'You haven't changed my mind on Twodex though. I won't throw those panels down a gully while your back is turned, but I'm not making myself responsible for a third world war by becoming the heroine who risked all to smuggle them out to London.'

'It would be easier if we knew what we'd got first,' he admitted. 'I shall just have to make sure then that Kaderi doesn't succeed in the intentions he undoubtedly cherishes towards me.'

'You do that,' she said fervently. 'If he did, then I don't think I'd be worrying about Twodex anyway.'

He shot her another of those level, considering glances but apparently changed his mind about whatever he intended to say. Instead he began dismantling their shelter. 'We'll take it easier over the next stretch but so long as you feel fit enough I don't think we can afford to take a night off.'

She thought he also did not want to lie close enough to her to keep them warm without exhaustion to bludgeon his senses. 'Down to the Drin?'

'Soon, but I'd like to strike it further north. Over the next shoulder again tonight before turning east. If my reckoning is right then we should come out close to the area where we had to discontinue our survey. That valley where the blizzard struck, remember?'

'Where you said you saw a way to escape? I remember.'

'You haven't studied Albanian maps as Kaderi was forced to let me do. My God, even telephone directories are state secrets here. He wanted to put my brain through a combine harvester after each session in his map room.'

'You can see why,' she said pointedly.

'Oh, sure. Even though he intended to shoot me the moment I'd done what he wanted.'

'Steve . . . I can't argue with you because of course I know you're right. I also know that I would infinitely sooner be us, hunted to death through mountains, than Kaderi setting his hounds on our track with orders to kill. And so would he. Whatever else I gave him, I also brought him to a torment he will never outlive no matter what happens in the next few days.'

'And you?'

'I don't know,' she said helplessly. 'And now for God's sake let's get on. What was it you saw while surveying that valley?'

'You remember how it looked, about ten miles long and rising to a ridge and waterfall, without any crossing point at all?' She nodded, the Drin formed a deep and dangerous barrier there, and must be even more so as the snows melted. 'I don't think Kaderi will expect us there. He'll look first where we finished surveying and know the country well, concentrate also on keeping us from breaking south.'

'He'll have men along the Drin, however unlikely we are to succeed in crossing.'

'Watching every bridge and summer ford, anywhere we conceivably might try, yes, of course. Patrols along the banks and in the mountains beyond too, the Yugoslav frontier is about eight miles off once we've crossed. I don't think he'll have a special guard at the waterfall.'

Anne felt her blood chill. Even at the beginning of winter there had been a great deal of water coming over that waterfall and in spring . . . 'What makes you think we could cross there?'

'Geological maps are a damned nuisance when you're looking for tracks and passes, they have their uses in plotting rock faults. There's a cleft right across that valley filled with late shale, which crosses the Drin at the base of the waterfall as you'd expect, the rocks forming the fall oozed up through the cleft. I thought the force of water falling there might have had some effect and studied it as carefully as I could. I believe that centre leap of water is so striking because it falls deep into the cleft, the force of it scooping shale to form the rock sluice of the lower fall. In doing so it has cut lower and lower, shale washed into a bank either side. You can see flaked debris forming beaches beside the fall.'

'But—but the water must—that won't help us! The force of water scours on down the fall.'

'Yes, of course. No one could live there, even in summer. But right under the fall, the gravel must have been caught in backwash and compacted through a million years or more. I think there's a way through there. There damned well ought to be, or I'll take up fig processing for a career when I get home.'

'If there is such a way, wouldn't shepherds use it? It'd be known locally and one of the places watched.' She didn't want to fight her way through a cavern where cataracts of water formed roof and side.

'It may have been known when these hills were full of blood-feuds, but it certainly isn't used now. There's no sign of a track, probably because the far side is forbidden. Too near the frontier, you see. And you'd never drive sheep or goats through such a passage, they'd refuse to go anywhere near.'

'So would people with any sense,' said Anne with resignation.

They left immediately after, angling down through magnificent trees as soon as light was deceptive enough for an unexpected shot possibly to miss. For there would be no warning, just tearing impact, or if they were lucky a few more hours of life hiding in undergrowth while the beaters closed in. I bet the stags of Exmoor don't fool the hunt very often, Anne reflected wrily.

The trees conspired to drain the last glow from the sky, the valley narrow and devoid of cultivation. Kaderi probably had the obvious exits guarded but in such a confused pattern of hills there must be better places for him to post men in waiting. Then they climbed up the opposite side, an even steeper slope than their descent had been, beech left behind and stunted pines in their place, shapes spinning with each gasped breath.

After a while Stephen stripped off his coat so she could see the gleam of his shirt in the dark: soon it was all she could see. And hear him breathing again, after a day when he had seemed recovered. At last they came to a ridge and looked into a wider valley than the one they had left; a stream glinted in starlight far below, haphazardly strung with lights. There was no obvious village but scattered cultivators lived there, a brighter spark of light where a track crossed the water.

'Guards and plenty of them there,' said Anne when she recovered her breath sufficiently to speak. Stephen was slumped on rock and she squatted beside him in concern. 'Steve, couldn't we at least strip that chain and box off you? Your pack is heavy enough without those as well.' They constricted each breath and dragged at him unmercifully in such conditions.

He shook his head wearily. 'No, I've had a good look at them, you may be sure. Albanian blacksmiths believe that weight of iron makes up for shortcomings in craftsmanship. A powered, precision sheer would cut through easily, but nothing much less, and I'd need to be damned sure of the operator first. It's not a job for the first Yugoslav mechanic we meet.' He stood again, shivering in a shirt where he had been sweating moments before. 'I don't like the look of that valley, do you?'

Reluctantly, they decided to stay on the ridge and work their way east along the length of it. There were unlikely to be guards in so inaccessible a place, but the penalty was hours of exhausting scrambling for a handful of miles gained. Patches of slushy snow slowed them further but slaked their thirst, and a splendid sunrise confirmed their direction as correct.

'We may be able to stay on this ridge all the way to the Drin,' observed Stephen. 'Hard work and the hell of a climb down at the end of it, but safer and probably quicker in the long run.'

'We shall need to reach it in daylight, or we'll never know which descent to take for your waterfall. We can't wander about looking for it when there's bound to be soldiers everywhere.' The sun had revealed a wild confusion of mountains and ridges, sweeping up to snow-covered peaks ahead.

'We must push on as fast as we can. We've food of a sort for two more days and could possibly last another afterwards, but the mountains on the frontier are too high to cross without proper nourishment.'

'How high?'

'Seven-eight thousand feet. There are some passes as low as three thousand but they'll be guarded. God knows how high we'll have to go to slip past.'

They were sitting in a sheltered gulley just off the ridge, awake after the sleep of exhaustion, but sleep with a difference this time. Both had suffered stomach cramps and woken unrefreshed while the sun was still high; Anne had a nagging pain behind her eyes and from the look of him Stephen had too. The signs were clear: they could not last much longer before nature forced surrender, even if Kaderi did not find them.

They ate cold gruel and figs without appetite, and once heard the beat of engines again.

'South,' said Anne, glimpsing the flash of wings. 'They're searching where all those dogs barked and the pass beyond. Your Exmoor stags won this time.'

'It's going to be tight though. If Kaderi decides we were definitely there thirty-six hours ago, then he'll concentrate his search. There aren't too many places we can have gone in the time, but he won't be certain yet.'

Not certain, but confident enough to begin drawing his net tight.

During the afternoon they heard more engines, and dogs in the valley below.

25

When the next dawn came they were looking down on the Drin valley. Gorse and stunted pines far below, the river obviously in fast spate.

'The Black Drin,' said Stephen, and laughed. 'They call it that up here. It's going to be an awkward scramble down.'

That was a massive understatement. They could see perhaps twenty miles in either direction, the waterfall they wanted twelve hundred or more feet below and north of where they stood. Everything was ominously quiet; the silence of high mountains without their peace.

'Is that Yugoslavia?' Anne refused to look at the Drin; it was waiting for them, very soon.

'The next range. We must climb the far valley wall and cross the mountain beyond. The reverse slope is Yugoslavia.' They were lying on a thin covering of grit below the ridge, and he rolled over to face her. 'When we were surveying up north, one of my guards told me how the Yugoslavs sometimes handed back fugitives to the Albanian police, another reason why few people try escaping. You must say you are British, and the moment will be past for shifty deals across barbed wire long before the facts are sifted.'

'We have a valley, a river and a damned high mountain to cross first.'

'Some things are best not left to impulse in the aftermath of God knows what between now and then. Promise me this, and the devil take the consequences. England has offered a good few refuges over the centuries, it's yours to claim if you want it.'

Anne sat up abruptly, turning her back on snow-covered

peaks and black valley. 'Steve . . . what do you know that you haven't told me?'

'Nothing. But this place is a prison cell, and they've spent thirty-five years double-locking it; if anything goes wrong I'd like to feel I'd helped give you a future after a lifetime trapped by the past.'

'All right,' said Anne slowly. 'I promise, if you'll promise too. Promise not to believe that I'd find your gift worth much, with the giver shot in Albania.'

'I promise,' he said, and smiled. As if he had spoken she knew exactly what he thought: it would take his death to exorcise Kaderi from her mind. Until Millosh succeeded in his intent she would always cherish the hope that for her sake he could not, would not, commit this particular murder. As if it mattered, when one did not differ from another.

Then she would be freed from the past, but adrift in the future too.

'I wish you weren't so cold-blooded and intelligent about everything,' she said in goaded irritation.

'I'm not able to wish facts away, down mineshafts or with women. I'd have been dead long since if I was. Or the equivalent.' He touched her face, so fleetingly she wasn't sure what she'd felt. 'But I'm not cold-blooded, I assure you.'

This was his weakness. He saw problems too clearly to believe that mere physical power could solve her dilemma: he refused to seize her senses as Millosh had done and face the consequences after.

They began climbing down to the valley while it was still light. There was a risk that watchers below would see movement, but it was slight. The rock face was deeply fissured so they were able to keep in shadow for most of the distance, and such a climb would be impossible in the dark. Some of the rock-slides were poised on a single boulder, others safe provided their slope was gauged correctly. The cliff edging the valley was beyond their limited skill and exposed to observation; unless they wasted time in a detour back through guarded forest, these slides of shattered rock were their best chance. So daylight they must have.

Even so, it took longer than they expected and by the time

they reached the final rubble-slope, darkness had closed in and any reconnaissance to find where sentries had been placed was out of the question. Perhaps three-quarters of a mile separated them from the waterfall, all tussock-grass and scattered goats which must not be panicked into bleating.

From higher up the cliff they had seen smoke from a guard-hut down the valley, the flash of metal from where a drove-track forded the river in summer. With the Drin in spate nothing could cross there now, and it was alarming to find that even such unlikely places were watched. What they did not know was whether sentries were also posted along the river bank, regardless of the fact that here the river was impassable.

Except at the waterfall, if Stephen was right. If he wasn't then they were trapped in a sealed valley, lacking the food to retrace their steps and try elsewhere.

Once clear of rattling stones the first part of the valley was easy after hours of muscle-tearing effort over rocks. They went very slowly, for fear of goats as much as sentries; it was difficult to avoid the complacence of success. They had come so far that failure began to seem unthinkable, yet each step took them closer to unknown frontier defences.

The sound of water increased rapidly as they moved forward, a ripping express of noise, the fall was very different from the delicate tassel of spray Anne had seen here as the first blizzards of winter fell. Now a great bowl of peaks was shedding snow and much of it coming down the Black Drin.

'Wait here,' breathed Stephen. 'I'm going to collect some goats.'

He vanished, leaving her with an absurd desire to laugh. Absurd indeed when some nervous boy with his finger on the trigger might be standing within yards. The roar of water blotted out any warning her senses might have given. She jumped when a goat butted her unexpectedly, then scratched its ear and waited. It stank but was embarrassingly friendly in cold Albanian dark. Another blew on her legs and moved squelching in wetness to tear at grass by her feet, then Stephen reappeared leading another by its horns. It was licking him with comprehensive thoroughness and a kid followed behind.

'Make every move slowly so they don't panic off again,' he said in her ear. 'We'll move them down to the water with us and then if a sentry fires they'll scatter and make him think that's all he saw. First though, this creature's in milk, hold her for me will you?'

The kid snickered resentfully as he milked a teat at a time into their olive oil bottle. It was a messy, wasteful business but by the end of it both had swallowed several mouthfuls. Anne gagged at the taste but felt her stomach close gratefully on nourishment.

When they had driven the goats to within a hundred paces of the waterfall they refused to go further, quivering uneasily, beginning to bleat, more danger than protection now, so Stephen sent them trotting away down the bank while they stood tensely listening. Surely a lone sentry would be jumpy enough to shoot at shapes looming out of spray and darkness.

Nothing. No sound except the boom of water, ground shuddering from the shock of it, nor point in waiting any longer. The whole attempt became worse by the minute when faced by that monstrous fall, and a sentry couldn't stand there all night and be sane at the end of it.

Stephen climbed straight to where water drove into a foam-whipped basin before tumbling over a rock-chute and into the torrent below. Nothing could live there, nor in the force of water above; it wasn't guarded and no wonder. Waves from the basin thrashed on a gravel beach and Stephen picked his way carefully across, gesturing for Anne to cover any footprints they made. Directly under the fall the noise was overwhelming: Anne could feel her muscles cringe, inner ear vibrating from the force and pitch of it. She stepped blindly wherever Stephen went, her only contact with him one end of plaited bedcover. He had cut it into strips with his razor and plaited rope from the pieces: it wouldn't withstand strain but was a lifeline of sanity now.

The rocks were wet and frighteningly slippery, but spray ceased abruptly as they moved into blackness beyond the basin, pressure alone half-collapsing lungs as the fall plunged directly over their heads. The booming beat of it, the complete disappearance of hearing and sight, the merciless thrash of countless tons of water an arm's length from her face, all combined to rob Anne of will, the tug of sheet scarcely sufficient to force her into such a dreadful place. The gravel cresent edging the basin swept back under rock ledges and narrowed to a few footholds among a wilderness of debris. Once she fell and experienced such terror as eddies slammed her body against rock that she screamed – and could not hear it for the triumphant blare of water. Her balance was lost and but for Stephen's grip she wouldn't have known which way lay safety and which oblivion.

Then the forces she fought changed, the torrent no longer a single column but bruising, irrational hangmen leaping to tear loose her hold, sucking unexpectedly at legs, throwing derisive, icy fragments of water in her face. She was staggering as if drunk over shale and boulders, so void of strength that when she became aware of grass and stars, they lacked significance.

Blood flowed again as the sound of water faded behind them, she had not been so much physically exhausted as mentally bludgeoned. She touched Stephen in reassurance, words too dangerous now they were out in the silences of the Drin valley again. He took her arm and tucked it into the crook of his, holding tight; she could sense that he was smiling.

The emptiness this side was eerie, no stars, no animals, nothing; as if the curse of ideology blasted everything it touched. Soon they were climbing steeply again, stones rattling, the slope wickedly dangerous in the dark. They scarcely noticed. They must keep going, and effort absorbed every thought and sense.

26

Anne woke lying on thyme-scented turf, looking out over mountains. The sun had the clear burn of altitude, the scene bringing a fleeting illusion of hot baths and après-ski. Voices increased the sense of fantasy; loud, confident, masculine voices somewhere close.

Illusion faded and in its place was deadly danger, voices here meant Sigurimi. Anne moved convulsively as if to bolt into non-existent undergrowth, and felt herself held; there was nowhere to run, if searchers came into the dip where they lay then it was all over. Uniformed figures came into sight the next minute, three men with rifles slung across their backs, the leader using binoculars, the other two straining under the weight of a container painted with military symbols. They were swearing a good deal but did not seem to be doing anything in particular. Anne gathered that they thought their quarry still the far side of the Drin and the binoculars an entertaining novelty. Kaderi would probably have done better to rely on mountain-tuned senses, but in a country short of everything binoculars indicated the degree of vigilance he expected.

They did not stop and soon disappeared from sight.

'Wait.' A single word and Stephen was gone, after what madness she could not guess. Instead she lay and looked at the mountain they must cross: very lovely and without a scrap of cover. Snow reached down almost to the notch where a pass must be: a pass they must climb above. The mountain was certainly no ski-slope; no skier in his senses would have ventured on those unstable expanses, rock showing where the sun's heat reached, overhung with cornices where it didn't. In summer that mountain would offer an exhilarating climb, a child could see how many perils trapped it now.

Stephen slipped back beside her, the grass muffled movement and she had heard nothing. 'I wanted to see what was in that container they were carrying. Mines. They stopped lower down and set some under turf.'

Anne felt a fresh lurch of dread. 'They'll be doing the same all along the frontier.'

'Have done for years, I expect. This is just an extra effort for us; Kaderi operates on the overkill principle.'

Anne winced. 'We'll be safe if we keep to outcroppings and rockface.'

'And snow. They didn't look very sophisticated mines to me, a foot of snow would probably spread sufficient weight not to trigger those already there, and they can't bury more without making their efforts obvious. In daylight, that is.'

She bit her lip. They could not move on that slope in daylight. They lay looking at it trying to think of a way, Stephen holding her now as if he knew that the time for reserve was past, human contact the only comfort for worn-out body and baulking mind. They would try this last stage since no other choice existed, yet success seemed infinitely remote.

The slope where they lay was steep but presented no difficulties, lower down there were even a few scrubby trees. Then, stretching up to the snowline beyond, was the kind of stone-strewn waste which the very word Balkan conjures into many minds, a faint track just visible where melt-water lay in tyretracks, probably it was only used by frontier guards for all but two or three crossing-points out of Albania were permanently blocked. In a straight line they had perhaps four miles to go.

After careful consideration they ate everything they still carried except for five figs each, a last reserve although even in griping hunger their stomachs could scarcely accept more figs. Anne could feel her own weakness, the flabbiness of legs and back which came from more days than she could now calculate without adequate food. Stephen too, looked ill. His face was gaunt and breath uneven under strain; she ought not to be thinking of her appearance, but grimaced when she realized how she too must look.

They rested just long enough for the food to give them fragile strength, then went down towards the track, eyes anxiously sweeping turf for mines. They lay again when they came to the outer edge of trees, beyond was nothing but stones, tufted grass and emptiness.

Except for a patrol coming towards them down the track, and a glitter on the mountainside as if the sun caught a rifle-barrel or binocular.

'We'll have to wait for darkness,' said Anne. 'They're using the track, that must be clear of mines.'

Stephen nodded and did not need to say that because it was clear, the track was certain to be guarded.

Anne slept a little while they waited and thought Stephen did too, both waking as the sun set. He smiled and kissed her as she stirred, and for a moment a spark was struck which banished everything but itself. 'I wanted you to know,' he said softly. 'Too late perhaps and nothing will be this simple again if we live. I've loved you a long time now, tonight I need to say it.'

She held his face between her hands thinking, no, nothing ever is this simple. Love free from doubt, passion part of a whole, like an incoming tide without a rock in sight. But whatever was reality, this moment must be treasured, set out of destruction's reach. So she was unable to find the right words to answer him and after a moment he sighed and stood, hands tender although she did not deserve it. She kissed him fiercely then, clinging, holding her mind tight against the thought of Millosh where her lips belonged.

So the moment was spoiled, and she followed him down to the track, eyes blinded by tears, not thinking of mines at all.

The track was so faint they never noticed when they crossed it and only realized that they must be on the far side when the ground began to rise. They conferred in whispers and decided to chance a slow curve back to where the track must be. By do-ing so they would waste less distance and also reduce the time when they must expect patrols every step of the way. Unspoken was the thought that minefields could be anywhere, each jar of feet and shifting stone bringing its own terror. Only the fact they were so spent made it endurable.

They nearly missed the track again. Stephen was past when Anne saw a single tyre-track printed where a stone pressed into mud. Really, it was scarcely a track at all. They stood very still, gripped by reluctance to move, wind whining strongly, cold and wet in their faces. Both sensed that by taking this way they were entering a trap, and if they ever reached the end of it then the frontier would be blocked off with nowhere else to go.

Anne felt Stephen move, his hands on her shoulders. 'Go on?' he breathed.

She shrugged, then nodded. Better a trap than be blown to pieces on that bleak mountain, when he insisted on going first.

'Take off your boots then.'

Kaderi's one mistake, Stephen called their boots. He ought never to have left them with good mountain footwear once their survey was over for the winter, but had been lying hurt at Bulqize at the time.

Even through two pairs of socks the way was agonizingly rough, each step needing to be measured, progress crawlingly slow. But only two miles perhaps to the frontier now.

A slight sound followed by a snarled order less than thirty paces away. Anne froze, then realized Stephen was still edging forward. They had nowhere else to go, no trick or stratagem to use; men lying in wait here almost certainly meant a minefield everywhere else.

To crawl risked sound twice, from hands and body, while standing meant a silhouette against the sky, however dark and wet it was. They crouched instead, aching with strain, taking a quarter pace at a time, hearing voices mutter so close that surely they could have touched the watchers. A stone slid under Anne's fingers, a single scraping clink; she stopped, weight on leg and hand, blood pulsing.

No reaction, but her muscles began to crack, leg quivering so she had to lie full-stretch, head on her arm, the smell of unwashed Sigurimi blowing downwind. God, they must almost be beside her. She dared not lift her head, expecting a boot tramped on her face.

Stephen had stopped too; how long they lay on open stones Anne did not know. Once they had stopped the notion of moving again seemed beyond possibility. But after quite a while, half an hour at least, she thought, there was a rasp of boots from somewhere up ahead, subdued voices and a clink of weapons. Inspection or relief, some detail coming down from the pass or patrol moving between the two, they never discovered which, but heard movement all around as bored and frozen men took the excuse to stretch and whisper, urinate and curse. Anne felt Stephen's touch but was already on her feet, stealth vital but speed more important still. A flurry of imprecation as an unseen officer swore at his command, a ribald joke and snicker of laughter the response before men settled again. Just possibly settled to sleep, huddled against wet in felt and goatskin. These watchers weren't really alert when no traffic ever came this way, nor was there reason to believe that fugitives would either; even Kaderi must think them still trapped against the Drin.

Anne felt her fingers held and guided towards . . . wire. Steel spikes and wire set into concrete. Some blocks must be moveable if this track was used; she felt the opposite way from Stephen and came to three set slightly apart from each other. Without waiting, she wriggled between them: Stephen would come when he found nothing and every second was precious.

She heard him returning with a rush, her ears fine-tuned but the slight sounds he made an indication of haste. He was lightly built and bone-thin anyway, but chains and box and Twodex memory hampered him, and after a few moments Anne realized he was caught, wire hooked into his back, chest trapped on concrete edges.

She heard him grunt, the faint twang of wire, a rub of cloth as he attempted to free himself. Then silence.

In rain and darkness it wasn't easy to judge her distance back to the gap; Anne moved a couple of paces, felt cautiously, touched warmth. He was awkwardly pinned, unable to reach the wire at his back. She fumbled at unseen strands, fingers bleeding from rusty barbs, the weight of his body keeping wire solidly hooked. Then she thought of his razor and slid a hand into his pocket, feeling the beat of his heart before she found it. The blade was blunted from their efforts plaiting rope but still sharp enough; very gingerly she cut cloth to release him, holding wire with her other hand to let him wriggle clear.

Metal snicked not far away and someone called out.

'What is it?' Authority from further up the track.

'Thought I heard something.'

'Where?'

A muttered consultation: half-heard sounds through wind and rain were difficult to place, and shots loosed off haphazard would be lethal to other men lying in ambush.

Boots crunching and a shaded light swinging from side to side, someone coming down the track towards them. The desire to bolt was overwhelming, concrete blocks offering scarcely any cover at all. There was no other; solidly made barriers were double stacked across the track except in that single gap where the moveable blocks stood.

They crouched between the double row of them, heads and hands huddled to avoid betraying a paler gleam while the gabble of voices grew, the waiting men delighted by any break in monotony.

'What did you hear and where?' demanded the man behind the torch.

A rattle of stones as someone stood. 'Beyond the track and further down.'

'No, this way, up towards Tomas.' Half a dozen voices joined the argument.

'Silence!' A harsh bellow from further up the track. 'What kind of piss-gutted squad is this, when you cannot keep silence a single night? Am I to inform Shok Kaderi that a nest of saboteurs is here at Stabljevo?'

'The men believe they heard something,' said the one with the light stubbornly, a sergeant presumably.

'Then send a patrol along the track and shoot anything that moves. Remember, cold meat in the morning is the only excuse Shok Kaderi will accept when he hears how you've all enjoyed a party here tonight.'

The sergeant swore under his breath, then curtly ordered a couple of men out of hiding and down the track, informing them that he would personally peg out their skins if they fired a shot unnecessarily. All the same, he was a typical sergeant; having reduced his squad to a state in which they were most unlikely to use any initiative, he used his own, poking about with the torch amongst rocks, kicking each man he passed to ensure maximum wakefulness, walking across to where the minefield began. Anne ventured a glance and saw the warning notices at the end of the barrier: elsewhere there would be no warning at all. She also saw a fragment of cloth hanging on a barb where Stephen had been caught; if the sergeant saw it . . . Her stomach swooped queasily; she was shivery-cold but her face burned as if every eye in Albania was focused on her, knees and legs so painful from crouching that to stay still was agony, to move soon would be impossible.

Still the sergeant stood, flicking his torch irresolutely in every direction. Then he cursed again and snapped it off, walked back the way he had come. The sudden release of tension was overwhelming, so great that it was easy to forget they were still crouched in the middle of a Sigurimi road-block. But they were Sigurimi who now would hesitate to raise the alarm unless certain of what they heard, and wind keening over rock made certainty difficult. When Stephen moved, at first Anne could not follow, had to lie biting her lips against cramp in her legs; then she went and untangled that scrap of cloth before she followed him. She couldn't tell whether they would reach Yugoslavia before daylight, if not then their only hope was the enemy's ignorance that they were close. Without realizing it, for the first time she consciously thought of all the trappings of a People's state as the enemy, without qualification.

Stephen's breathing was more obvious again. She would have missed him without it and felt a stab of anxiety absurd in such a place; she was not the only one who would not easily win clear of damage if somehow they reached safety tonight.

He was crouched over something, she wanted to shout at him to hurry, not wait for anything or their luck would never last. She heard a faint clink of metal but was unable even to whisper, impatience fanning anger where she had been concerned for him before. He stood at last, holding something she couldn't see, and they were able to lie and wait until the patrol they had heard arrive moved off again on its beat back to the pass. They followed it; military boots made a great deal of noise to ears attuned to stealth, although in fact the patrol moved cautiously and often stopped without warning, bringing panic every time.

One foot before the other, climbing steeply to a glow of light ahead. Not sunrise yet, surely. They were heading due east but the clouds were too thick for such brightness; it took Anne a while to realize that they were approaching a huddle of huts surrounded by arc-lights on stripped pine poles.

The frontier.

Stephen touched her arm but she needed no urging to turn aside; strange how easily they combined together in situations neither had faced nor dreamed of facing before. She watched the patrol smarten up before marching into light, challenge and reply alertly sharp. It was beginning to snow, thick flakes streaked between them and the lights, not fluttering as in the crisp falls of winter. Up here there would still be blizzards while fruit was flowering on the plain.

Anne could see scattered huts under the arc-lights, an old-fashioned half-tracked vehicle mounting some kind of gun, several loopholed emplacements surrounded by solidly tangled wire, the frontier here a stone wall ten feet high. Either side of the pass the hillside rose steeply, and the wall gave way to wire illuminated by more arc-lights. High on the slope above was another cluster of lights: patrols probably moved between fixed guardhouses on a single path free of mines.

'Not that way out, certainly,' whispered Stephen, studying huts and wall.

The relief of being able to talk again however softly, to reach through silence to another human being, was immense. It must be two or three in the morning but men were moving about amongst the huts, the lights bright: somewhere Anne could hear the thump of a generator, out of reach inside the compound. 'Full employment in Albania. In one unused mountain pass they must have fifty men.'

She sensed his surprise; exhausted though she was, this was the first time she had been flippant about the opposition. He made no comment though. 'Are you able to climb up to the snowline?'

Anything to be away from here. 'Yes, but . . . what about mines?'

'They've too many men around here not to mark the outer edge of the field. Even Sigurimi need to move about for training and to reach latrines. White pegs by the patrol path, stone cairns this side, see? They'll have pockets of mines away from the main field but I think we'll simply have to risk it and keep as close to the edge they've marked as possible.'

Anne nodded. 'Less risk than lights and a stone wall. But don't you think the wire will reach right up to the summit of the mountain, and the minefield too? And on such mushy snow—'

'And us without any climbing equipment, yes, I know we can't go high.' He didn't sound as if he'd be able to go high either, and she certainly wouldn't. 'We need to find a deep, well-packed drift to take us over the minefield, that's all.'

'And then?'

He put his hands on her shoulders, urging her off the path and up the slope beyond. 'I have an idea which might work for the wire, but let's get up there first. Make sure you step exactly where I do.'

She worried about his idea all the way up, thoughts floating in disconnected sequences. She nibbled a fig to steady herself and hunger suddenly kindled, where before she had noticed only weariness. She ate another greedily and her stomach cramped in anger, her system revolted by figs. They burned some fresh energy into her though, another hour, two perhaps, somehow she would keep going. And never eat a fig again. One left. She giggled aloud and then crushed her hand to her mouth, shock at the sound enough to send her senses sliding.

Stephen holding her was the next thing she knew, and for a while it was the only thing. She was finished with struggling over rock and burrowed into his warmth, away from death and near-starvation on a bleak hillside. He was murmuring words of endearment and she listened in sluggish content, feeling his lips on hers. How she longed for peace, of mind as well as body.

27

They reached the snowline at last, sleet falling heavily, ice-slicked rubble slipping underfoot. They both fell several times, twisting ankles, bruising elbows and knees; they were very nearly finished. They worked their way along a melting rim of snow until they found a stone cairn which they hoped marked the outer edge of the minefield, light from the wire barrier ahead a useful guide of direction. Perhaps five hundred feet above them were the pinpricks of light which they supposed to be the next guardhouse in a chain. They were about a thousand feet above the pass and had to flounder through hip-deep drifts, icily wet, until they reached a gulley where snow was sufficiently compacted for their purpose. Their tracks would be seen in daylight, sleet clearing now they needed it, there could be no going back.

'Stay where you are,' said Stephen at last. 'This should be safe, but wait until I come for you.'

'Not on your life,' said Anne. 'We can't afford the time, and I'm damned well not waiting here while you tramp a path over mines for me.'

He gave way when he realized that her mind was made up, progress painstakingly slow as he tested each step, sinking sometimes to his waist and warning her to transfer weight as delicately as she could. The arc-lights on the wire ahead gave them warning when a patrol approached up the path between minefield and wire, and they crouched in their drift to let it go by. Anne recklessly ate her last fig, the only defence she had against cold sinking into bone.

All at once she felt a bounding confidence; patrols moving between fixed points seemed simple to outwit compared to the other hazards they had faced. She chafed at inactivity, could scarcely wait until the patrol was past before setting off again. Then the diagnostician in her surfaced and she recognized the last reserves which excitement and anticipation had dredged out of near-collapse; when this was gone there would be nothing left.

Once the patrol had passed Stephen angled uphill to reach the path as far from a light as possible. Even so, when they emerged on the path their churned tracks looked as if a dinosaur had passed, the next patrol could not possibly miss them. From a distance the wire had looked formidable, but Anne had hoped that a closer inspection would show some weakness: when they examined it, she could see at once that without wire-cutters it was impossible to force a way through. A series of concrete posts held loose-coiled loops either side of strands strained closely together; burrowing into snow would not help when the posts must be set in rock, and the coils prevented climbing. The wire was rusty and thinly made but proof against bare hands.

'What's your idea?' she asked; it would need to be good. Half an hour perhaps before the next patrol came past.

'I brought some mines from the road block. There were containers of them there and I thought they might come in useful. Go back to the snowdrift and wait. Warn me the moment you see a patrol coming.'

'What are you going to do?' Her lips were stiff.

'Blow a gap through, with luck. I doubt if they'll make a clean break, but it's our only chance.' He thrust her back the way they had come. 'Don't argue for God's sake, I need to have my mind clear of worry for you. They're simple pressure mines and ought not to be difficult to set.'

She went. As he said, it was their only chance and she must not jolt his concentration. This was the end which had been waiting for them ever since they flew into an Albanian hillside, the spring of the trap which must be prised open if they were ever to be free. Or blown open with mines which Stephen could not know how to handle, when he lacked even a screwdriver to help him.

She watched him crouched over coiled wire, intent, never

216

looking up or allowing himself to be diverted by the fact that he was silhouetted against lights only twenty yards away. She could picture him exactly: eyes narrowed, lips tight, the full force of formidable mind and will concentrated on the delicate movement of his hands. The mines were flat and round; she wondered how many he had brought wrapped in his jacket, four or five, she thought. He was packing snow now, piling it against a post, fiddling with something on a mine: a loud click made her jump as if it was a shot. He stood and Anne felt her heart thump against her ribs, willing him to finish, but he crouched again, gently parting coils of wire.

She darted glances up and down the path, no sign of movement yet. How long had they been here, and how often did patrols pass? They had seen two in the time it took them to climb up to snow, but the intervals had seemed irregular.

Stephen stood again, doing something with their plaited rope, laying it along the ground, tying separate strands to wire. Hurry. Hurry. Hurry. His nerves must be screaming too, but his movements remained slow and deliberate. He looked up at last. 'No one in sight? Come over here then, will you?' He retreated towards her, laying out rope behind him: it was pitifully short. 'Have you still got my razor?'

She felt in her pockets, fingers fumbling before they closed around Victorian ivory haft. He snicked a couple of strands and knotted them, gaining extra length although strength was lost. 'Right. Dig yourself into snow. The moment the mines blow, run for the gap. I've set them so a single barb holds each pressure plate off the detonator, they're pretty primitive things. Once I slide out the clip a puff of wind should set them off so when I jerk the wire with this rope—'

Anne climbed back to the drift, legs trembling, while he added another length to the rope. She thought she could see movement against the lights of the guardhouse above and certainly the sky was paling: they hadn't long.

'What the hell—' said Stephen angrily when he saw she was trampling a barrier of snow by the rope's end. 'Stay in the drift.'

'No. And you can't argue, a patrol will be here within twenty minutes.'

He gave a gasp of laughter. 'Lie down then and wait for me to come.'

She lay, but watched as he moved soft-footed from mine to mine.

She thought she did not breathe the whole time he was gone. If she had understood him correctly then this time he must ease out some safety clip and rely on precarious poising to keep the mines from exploding. Each one he touched shuddered others already set. He eased upright once and flexed his back as if to unknot intolerable strain, otherwise he worked in smooth sequence, utterly intent.

He stood at last, and stared down frowning, as if uncertain whether it was done.

'Steve, for God's sake,' said Anne, quite loudly. Silence no longer seemed important.

He came over then and lay across her, she could feel him trembling deep into bone. His face was iced with sweat and he did not speak. An instant later there was a sharp explosion, followed by a massive roar as one mine triggered the rest, he had not even touched the rope. No debris fell as snow liquidized, just a suck of air and flash of explosion before all the lights along the wire went out.

They were up and running before the echoes died, a jungle of torn wire looking more formidable than before. The lack of light was dangerous now, the explosion of course had sheered the cable.

Anne's ears were still ringing, it was difficult for either to tell the other what they were trying to do. She realized that the posts were pitted but intact, lower strands of weather-weakened wire fragmented, coils spraying in every direction. Working at panic-speed they trampled broken ends flat, they would have to burst through what was left by force. Deep drifts of snow had piled against the wire barrier, and unseen barbs snagged at Anne's face and throat. She could feel blood wet on her skin but not much else through cold and fear, frantic to free herself and Stephen, crushing back coils for her and caught himself. She needed the razor again to cut him loose. She slashed blindly, felt him wince, stammered a crazy apology, and then they were running again, floundering in neck-deep drifts.

No time to wonder whether the Yugoslavs set their side of the border with mines too. The slope angled down but snow was still a trap from which they must drag themselves yard by yard, this east face of the mountain caught the full force of winter's blizzards.

There was no sign of life, no welcoming or suspicious guards the other side, only shots behind and the wail of a siren from the frontier post in the pass. Like sensible men the Yugoslavs watched their side of the border from the valley in winter, up here no one would know what the Albanians did until it was too late.

'They'll need time,' gasped Anne. 'Even Sigurimi must have to ask permission before they cross the border and risk a fuss. We have a start.'

'The Yugoslavs may hear the shooting too,' Stephen's voice sounded flat, as if he didn't believe the Albanians would wait before they came after them, their trail like a waterfall behind them, progress desperately slow. Ahead, the sun was just rising over the mountains.

They broke on to crisper snow and increased speed, although overhung cornices warned that avalanches waited to punish haste. They were traversing the lip of a giant bowl, a ridge curving above so the lip offered the only way off the upper slopes of the mountain. Fifteen hundred, two thousand feet perhaps below were snow-free pines where their tracks would be lost. Then they could go at their own pace to find soldiers who would not shoot on sight, and sleep for a week by a roaring fire.

A shot echoed harshly from the skyline above, where it went Anne did not know, the angle impossible and light deceptive for marksmanship. They had a start and must keep it, trust to luck and the outdated weaponry of Albania to protect them. No armalite rifles or high-velocity automatics here.

The next shot was shatteringly close, throwing a fistful of snow into Anne's face. She spluttered, too startled to realize how fearfully near to death she had come. It must have been chance though, ridges of snow reaching down and almost hiding them from sight, their pursuers floundering in the same drifts which had slowed them.

At last they gained iced rock and the promise of easier conditions to come; they were going to make it, Sigurimi setting off a series of miniature avalanches which panicked them into care. Stephen held her hand in his but had little strength to spare; he tripped and fell, dragging her down with him.

It was then that they heard aircraft engines. Kaderi must have had his spotters in the air before dawn, just in case first light brought a lucky sighting.

The machine came low over the ridge, shadow enormous in early sunlight; their tracks would stand out like a scar. For an instant Anne thought that their fall into a drift had saved them; the aircraft passed overhead, sound shattering back from rock, and dipped over the central bowl of the mountain. Then it banked and came back.

It was a single-engined flying club type of machine, manoeuvrable and light, the same one Anne had seen directing the search for them over the plain.

'It probably isn't armed with more than a machine-gun. We can't afford to let him pin us down until the Sigurimi come,' said Stephen. 'To hell with him anyway. The last lap, my love.'

He stood as soon as the plane passed overhead again, shielding her with his body and leaning over to help her up. She remembered the smile in his eyes, the only spark left in a worn, blood-smeared face.

Bullets came reaching for him in little puffs of snow, light flickering from the aircraft cabin. He grunted once, deep in his throat, and sprawled back in the drift.

'Steve!' Anne scrambled somehow to her feet, fell again beside him. Snow around his body reddened instantly, blood spreading theatrically through slush.

He did not move, a dead weight face down and suffocating in snow. She hauled at him, hands slippery, terrified of what extra damage she might do, but if he lived then he must breathe. She had forgotten everything except his life trampled scarlet underfoot, but turned to a screeching, ripping tear, and saw the aircraft landing, engine throttled back, wheels up, between her and the pines which only a moment before they had thought to reach for safety.

The plane hurled a storm of white into the air, slowed as if it had hit a wall and flipped on its back. No flames, no great sign of damage; Anne turned back to Stephen. Nothing else mattered now.

She found herself cursing the snow in a frantic undertone; it was everywhere, inside his shirt, over his face, the trampled hollow where he lay like a slaughterhouse.

'Is he dead?'

Kaderi was behind her, face remote as ever but grey from the shock of that landing, the arm he had broken at Bulqize hanging loose again, a gun in the other hand.

'Yes,' said Anne. 'Oh God, yes. I hope you are satisfied.'

'Nearly. He was carrying something I want.'

'Why bother?' she demanded bitterly. 'Without him you can't decode anything Twodex found.'

'So the next best thing for Albania is to make sure that no one else can either, since Astell thought he'd found a good deal of interest, didn't he? We'll have to cover the same ground again by slower and surer methods. Such knowledge as he gained is best to die with him.'

Anne laughed hysterically. 'So that's all you have to say to me, when I couldn't even return Stephen's kiss without you spoiling it.'

His face tightened, remoteness banished, as she had banished it before. 'How do you think I have felt this past week, giving orders for you to be shot on sight? You must have been mad to run like that, knowing what you'd forced me to do.'

Anne stared at her hands, where Stephen's blood was already drying black. 'I haven't forced you into anything. As you told me once, everyone has a choice, though some choices are more costly than others. Like my love for you. In the end you were not worth the price I began to pay the very first day I met you. You'll find it easier to shoot me now.'

He glanced at the gun in his hand. 'Yes, I suppose so.' His lips twisted. 'Your last gift to haunt me down the years. I've wondered . . . are you carrying my child?'

'I'm not sure.' She threw back her head then, and smiled, sun shining on her face. 'Yes, I think so.'

He shot her while she still smiled, and climbed to where

Sigurimi waited on the ridge above, black sections of Twodex in his hands. She had made it easier for him, since in the end he could not doubt that his suffering was infinitely worse than hers.

Anne was wrong, no price of love was too great if it must be borne, and his devotion was long since pledged.

He fingered his gun absently; there were bullets to spare but the cowardice of oblivion would turn him into the common murderer he was not.

As surely he was not? You will not live with what you do for ever, Anne had once said.

Kaderi wept as sun flooded light over the mountains.

Helen MacInnes

Born in Scotland, Helen MacInnes has lived in the United States since 1937. Her first book, *Above Suspicion*, was an immediate success and launched her on a spectacular writing career that has made her an international favourite.

'She is the queen of spy-writers.' *Sunday Express*

'She can hang up her cloak and dagger right there with Eric Ambler and Graham Greene.' *Newsweek*

FRIENDS AND LOVERS £1·50
AGENT IN PLACE £1·50
THE SNARE OF THE HUNTER £1·50
HORIZON £1·25
ABOVE SUSPICION £1·25
MESSAGE FROM MALAGA £1·50
REST AND BE THANKFUL £1·50
PRELUDE TO TERROR £1·50
NORTH FROM ROME £1·35
THE HIDDEN TARGET £1·75
I AND MY TRUE LOVE £1·50
THE VENETIAN AFFAIR £1·75

FONTANA PAPERBACKS

Fontana Paperbacks

Fontana is a leading paperback publisher of fiction and non-fiction, with authors ranging from Alistair MacLean, Agatha Christie and Desmond Bagley to Solzhenitsyn and Pasternak, from Gerald Durrell and Joy Adamson to the famous Modern Masters series.

In addition to a wide-ranging collection of internationally popular writers of fiction, Fontana also has an outstanding reputation for history, natural history, military history, psychology, psychiatry, politics, economics, religion and the social sciences.

All Fontana books are available at your bookshop or newsagent; or can be ordered direct. Just fill in the form and list the titles you want.

_____

FONTANA BOOKS, Cash Sales Department, G.P.O. Box 29, Douglas, Isle of Man, British Isles. Please send purchase price, plus 8p per book. Customers outside the U.K. send purchase price, plus 10p per book. Cheque, postal or money order. No currency.

NAME (Block letters)

_____

ADDRESS

_____

_____

_____

While every effort is made to keep prices low, it is sometimes necessary to increase prices on short notice. Fontana Books reserve the right to show new retail prices on covers which may differ from those previously advertised in the text or elsewhere.